COURAGE

dhtreichler

Dedication:

To all of the victims of civil violence and the peace officers who strive every day to approach each person as an individual who deserves respect, fairness, and objectivity.

1 – T.K. Jefferson

Deshaun has grown a set of wings.

I just can't keep up with him anymore. Who would have thought that skinny kid -- what was he? Maybe six when he appeared on the court for the first time -- that skinny kid who could barely see over a basketball -- would make it to the NCAA Sweet Sixteen in his junior year?

March madness they call the tournament. I nearly lost my mind watching him from the stands in Minneapolis, of all places. Never been so cold in my whole life.

Selfless player, Deshaun. Three seconds on the clock, down by two and he has a shot, but only a two pointer. Not good enough. He passes off to Reggie Black, the team's best three-point shooter, who is in the exact right place. Reggie takes the pass and loses the ball trying to bring it up for the shot when he bumps the player guarding him.

The clock ran out on their dream of moving on. But they'll be back next year. They're just too good not to.

Back in the present day...

I plant myself in the lane so Deshaun has to go around me. He just smiles, pulls back and lofts the ball over my head with a feather touch.

It seems like slow motion as I watch the ball sail over my head. I turn slightly as it drops through the hoop four feet above me. Nothing like that first time when he could barely get the ball up over his head.

Deshaun is all smiles as he high fives his teammates, all high school players. Two are younger brothers of his high school teammates. His team was good, but Deshaun grew into the star of the team by his senior year. He had the moves, he had the touch and he always knew where his teammates were.

When he first came out to play here, at the Fort Christian Boys Club, there was nothing special about him, other than a curiosity that remains with him to this day.

I was a volunteer coach then as I am today. My philosophy was and remains that anyone who wanted to play should be able to learn the game. I still spend time with anyone who will put in the hard work to improve.

Duke does too. Only he's been here longer than I have. In fact, I think Duke started the basketball program, if I remember correctly. In the many years I've been volunteering, I don't remember a day I've been here when Duke wasn't here too.

I don't know if we were as complementary as players when I first started. We've been doing this for so long now that we know each other's moves. We know how the other sees the game.

We love to mix it up with the kids. Show them a few things. Help them understand the importance of knowing your teammates and how to work with them in an anticipatory fashion.

Duke picks up the ball and passes it to me. I'm the better dribbler, so he usually wants me to bring it down. He makes his way under the basket and sets up to touch it in if the kids will give him the space.

As a police sergeant, Duke's not afraid to make contact. Bumping is just part of the game. We both know from experience that if these kids are going to play after high school they are going to need to be tough. They need to be willing to give as good as they get, on the court, and in life.

Deshaun is a great example of that. In his freshman year at Baylor he sat on the bench a lot. He was fast, he was accurate, but he let the other team's players take him out of his game.

He wasn't used to the other team putting their hands on him, stepping in front of him to trip him if possible. He pulled back rather than charge the basket, which is just what the other teams wanted him to do.

That Christmas he came home. Duke went to see him and asked him to come down to the Boys Club. The guys wanted him to play with them so they could get better for the second half of their season. At least that was what Duke told him. Deshaun was in a funk because he wasn't playing much.

When we got him out on the court, he didn't have much energy. He seemed tentative, second-guessing himself. Duke came up behind him, stole the ball and dunked it right over him.

Deshaun looked bewildered. I can still see that expression. The next possession I guarded him so closely I could feel his breath on my face. No space, no space.

"What are you going to do? Let me win?" I still remember yelling at him from three inches away.

I saw the determination return to him. Saw the fire light up his eyes. He gritted his teeth, spun around and moved past me before I could adjust. He sailed up to the basket and dunked it over me.

I grabbed the ball and tore down the court as fast as my aging legs would carry me. Deshaun saw what I was doing and caught me half way down. When he tried to cut in front of me, I was the one who spun around him and kept on trucking.

I could hear Duke coming along behind me so I dribbled left, bringing Deshaun with me and backhand passed to Duke who came up on the other side of me and lifted the ball in.

Now it was Deshaun's turn to grab the ball and hightail it for the hoop at the other end. Duke saw what I did. We converged on him from both sides, colliding with him, expecting the ball to come loose. Somehow he held on.

In just another moment he was under the basket for an easy layup.

Duke and I worked Deshaun hard every day that Christmas break. We must have played six hours a day every day except Christmas.

We toughened him up. Played a lot of two-on-one and three-on-two to help him focus. Helped him regain his confidence. Showed him he still loved to play and that he could play with anyone.

Deshaun went back to Baylor fired up and ready for anything, except the one thing that greeted him.

He sat on the bench for a solid month. Zero playing minutes. But he didn't give up. He worked even harder in practice because those were his only touches. He ran the legs off his teammates.

When his chance finally came at the end of a game they were losing and had no hope of winning, Deshaun took the team on his shoulders and turned it around.

In the final ten minutes he scored twenty points, picked up seven rebounds, had six assists, and stole the ball four times.

He's started every game at Baylor since. I don't know if it was the Christmas workouts or the subsequent month on the bench that fanned his competitive flame, but I'm so very pleased he found his inner strength and made things happen for himself and his team.

Back in the present day, Deshaun must think we're wasting his time. He sends one of his teammates off to the other end, lofts a full court pass and hits his teammate perfectly for an easy layup.

I trot down to get the ball as none of us followed the pass. Deshaun is waiting for me as I bring the ball up. I see Duke has slipped in behind Deshaun, so I send a bounce pass to Deshaun's weak side, or so I think.

He lunges forward and intercepts the ball in full stride, racing past me before I can move to head him off. I manage to trip him, but he recovers and continues down for an easy dunk.

He turns to laugh at me as he recovers the ball and passes it to me so I only have a half court to traverse to get to my basket.

As he trots by me I say, "Thanks for taking it easy on me."

"You got nothin'," Deshaun chides me, knowing I'll remember how many times I said that to him when he was still learning the game. I said it to goad him to work harder, but in this case he's right about me.

I got nothin'.

So I pass off to Duke and now I'm the one to post up. Duke doesn't like to pass off. He'd rather take it in himself, but in this case Deshaun has parked himself between Duke and me to steal another if Duke is as willing to give it away as I was.

Duke passes off to Will Bates, who sends it along to 'Shorty' Tallman, who is our nominal center, who passes out to Randy Sloan at the three-point line. He receives it and lofts a perfect shot.

Deshaun remarks, "Teamwork beats talent every day, all day long." Another phrase he heard from me many times.

Deshaun looks at the clock.

"Oh man, my girl's waiting on me. Sorry, guys, I gotta go meet her. Now."

Duke says, "You know how to score on the court, but how are you doing with the ladies?"

Deshaun starts looking through his backpack, pulls out a towel, ignoring the remark. He looks further. "Oh man, I forgot my house key. Must have left it at the dorm."

"You need a lift?" I ask.

"No. It's just that my parents are away until tomorrow and I forgot my key to their house. No problem. I'll figure it out. Shelly's waiting, so gotta go."

"She the one you were with in high school?" Duke asks.

"You got a good memory for an old guy," Deshaun says with a wide grin. "I'll be back tomorrow if you can keep up." Deshaun bumps knuckles with his teammates as he heads out the door.

2 – THOMASINA "SINA" JEFFERSON

T.K. needs a shower.

He usually takes a quick one at the Boy's Club, but for some reason he didn't tonight. When he misses that shower, the car smells for a few days.

At least I don't have to drive his car. Let him smell himself if he wants to on his way into work. I'm not going to be forced to do that.

He comes by for a quick kiss, but I turn up my nose so he knows I'm not about to kiss that sweat-sweet face.

He smiles at me, like he always does when he knows I want him to do something. He pretends he doesn't get my message.

But he does.

And I know he will shower. Because if he doesn't, I won't put any food on the table.

He goes to the microwave, peers into the glass window to see what I've queued up, but I haven't started heating yet.

I see an eyebrow rise, as I've pulled out of the freezer some of the leftover chicken parmesan from Sunday. That's one of his favorites. I know he will be in a good mood after dinner if we have that tonight.

It doesn't take long for him to disappear into the shower. I hear the water running and see a self-satisfied grin appear in my reflection on the microwave door window.

I generally don't look for my image in mirrors or reflective surfaces, but I was curious whether I'd put a paper towel over the chicken to keep it from splattering as the microwave heats it up and my reflection caught my eye.

Thank heaven the reflection isn't very good as I really don't want to see how badly I look after a full day at the school library. I'm sure I look tired, because that's how I feel after another frustrating day trying to convince high schoolers to read something. They just want to comment on the latest Instagram picture of a friend or someone they follow.

It doesn't take long for T.K. to emerge from the bedroom, clean clothes, wet hair and smelling soapy.

I reward him by letting him kiss me, which I know he's been wanting to do ever since he walked in the door. I don't think it's a ritual, so much as he's just wanting me to know he missed me today.

And I miss him and his ability to simply explain complex concepts. That would certainly help when I'm trying to explain why a student should take the time to read something I've suggested.

T.K. is better at motivating people than I am. Maybe it's that he's more patient than I am. He won't give up on someone until he's sure they understand what he wants them to know. I'll make an effort, but if the lightbulb doesn't come on quickly, I figure they're the poorer for not wanting to know something I think is important.

"Smells good." T.K. gives me a hug. I've been waiting for that, too.

I load up our plates with the aromatic chicken, cheese and ragu, a few vegetables, and we're good.

"Deshaun came home for the holidays," T.K. announces, which surprises me. Generally when Deshaun comes home, T. K. stays later at the Boy's Club, either talking with his favorite college ball player, or helping him work on some technique Deshaun wants to improve before going back to Baylor.

"It must be good to see him." I never know what T.K. wants to talk about and what he thinks will just bore me.

"I can't believe how much he seems to improve every time I play with him at the Boy's Club," T.K. muses. "It's like he becomes more instinctive about how to play the ball and where the other players are going to move in space. He seems to have this God's eye view of the court, just looking down, and everything makes sense to him."

"What makes Deshaun so special?" I have to ask.

T.K. leans back to consider my question.

"I think basketball is the embodiment of who he is as a person," T.K. begins to answer my question. I know there's more to come. "No question he has honed his physical attributes. Quick as lightning, strong – I mean I've seen him wrestle the ball away from players much bigger than him – and it's like he sees everything."

"You should have been a coach after college," I respond to the thorough analysis he just gave me. It must mean a lot to him, but I have no idea, never having played the game.

T.K. gives me that would-a, could-a, should-a shake of his head. He always does that when we talk about missed opportunities. "If I'd coached I never could have afforded you," he responds, as he leans over for another kiss.

"So I was worth giving up what you really loved."

"Every second we have been together has been the best second of my life." He looks directly at me, to make sure I know exactly what he's saying. And I do. He misses the game. It was a big part of who he was, both growing up and in college.

But he made a choice and I've been so happy every day since.

"I saw Flo today," I say. "She stopped by to have me help her research sources of comparative data on municipal salaries. The city has been trying to figure out why so many young people are leaving.

"Flo was considering introducing an ordinance that would provide scholarships for students who would agree to come and work for the city for a certain number of years."

"Like they do in private industry," T.K. responds.

"Except we couldn't find examples. Apparently civil service laws don't explicitly provide for that, so it appears Flo would have to lobby the state legislature to pass enabling legislation.

"Given our every other year abbreviated sessions, it's just not likely that it would get through any time soon. It would probably require most of the mayors to lobby for it, in a concerted effort. And it's just not high enough on their priorities list."

"The Texas Legislature is where good ideas go to die." T.K. repeats back to me something I've said to him every time someone brings up a change that is needed. "So what's Flo's backup plan?"

"She doesn't have one, but she asked me to talk to you about it. She said you always have ideas about how to get things done."

"What is the specific problem Flo is trying to solve?"

I guess the chicken parmesan is working.

"That the city wants to hire people and can't find qualified candidates? That the city wants to create jobs so kids will have a summer job to come home to that might lead to permanent employment when they graduate?

"Or is it that the city needs to encourage private developers to build apartments and condos adjacent to an entertainment district where kids can meet others their own age? I need to know the real problem before I can recommend a real solution."

I think about his question and the hour or so Flo and I looked in vain for a way to offer scholarships. "I think she was actually thinking all three need to be addressed. Do you think only one would actually make much difference?"

T.K. considers my question.

"I think that none would make much difference alone. If you find qualified candidates, but they have a job offer from a company in the city where they went away to college, it's not likely they will come home.

"If local companies offer summer jobs and they come back and take them, but have alternatives where there are more people their own age, or friends from college, that's still probably not enough of a draw.

"Now, if the city encouraged developers to build apartments and condos in areas where there is entertainment, restaurants and bars… that changes things, if the others are also in place."

"I knew you'd have some ideas I can give her. Maybe she'll ask you to come talk with the Economic Development Advisory Committee."

"Are you trying to get me on one of those again?" T.K. pushes back. I did that once before. He was appointed to the Zoning Board of Adjustments. He stayed on for the year, but didn't seek reappointment. He didn't see the value in putting in his time to decide if people could build in non-conforming ways on their property.

"No." I don't want to sound guilty, but I probably am. "I think Flo is thinking you might come and talk about your ideas of what needs to be done. She was just out of ideas and inspiration when there didn't seem to be a way around the civil service laws."

"The city has a lot of things it probably could do."

"Would you go and make your suggestions? People listen to you because they know you have good ideas."

T.K. looks at me like he's trying to figure out what I'm doing. "I take it you're trying to get me to spend less time at the Boy's Club, by giving me other things to do."

3 – ZANA GONZALEZ – EDITOR, FORT CHRISTIAN STANDARD

'Tex' Anthony is my city beat reporter.

I asked him to cover the city when Regina Blackwell was elected mayor. I assigned him to the city, because he had been the political reporter until then.

He covered the election campaigns and brought insights to his reporting that I thought made the nature of the choice clear to our readers.

That is a rare talent in these days of obfuscation politics.

Tex was the nickname he was blessed with, because he wears a cowboy hat everywhere he goes, even though he was born in Boston.

Tex went to school at Yale. So he's no dummy. Why he chose journalism and why he chose Fort Christian I have no idea. However, I am most pleased he did.

"The Reverend Lindo led a discussion at the Second Baptist Church tonight," Tex informs me as we sit in the large walnut paneled conference room just off my office.

"What was the topic?"

"Police harassment of black men, particularly young black men," Tex looks at his notes on his cell phone. He is probably the most tech-savvy of all of us.

"He brought this up in a sermon two weeks ago. I have not been able to determine what the inciting incident may have been. However, I have a few more sources I'm checking with. I expect at least one of them may be able to shed some light and provide background."

Tex talks like he writes. He is clear, concise and uses full sentences, something I rarely hear or read in Fort Christian.

"What is the Rev after?" I ask.

"The Reverend LeRoy Lindo has been a bit of an enigma since he arrived in Fort Christian from San Angelo about four years ago.

"The rumor at the time was that he was asked to leave San Angelo by city officials. Seems he tried to stir up his congregation to unseat those he disagreed with. The city fathers didn't much care for his rabble-rousing."

Tex has shifted into a quote, which I determine by his use of vernacular, which he seldom employs when he is talking. I wonder if that's a Yale tendency.

"The experience appears to have had an effect on him. His sermons have been well-researched, mostly focused on how to live a spiritual life in a temporal world of chaos and confusion.

"He has been a godsend to many families that have struggled with one personal tragedy or another, always reinforcing the need to put one's faith in God, and live the life He would want for us."

"Why is he reasserting himself now?" I finally insert myself into his narrative.

"If we can understand the inciting incident, I think we will have the answer to your question."

"Tell me about the meeting."

Tex consults his notes again. "I counted seventy-two noses, looked to be mostly his congregation."

"Meaning you were the only non-black person," I say.

"The Reverend Lindo was in rare form. He started out the meeting by asking those present if anyone had a child that had been stopped, or questioned, or searched by the police."

“Everyone did,” I guess.

“He then asked for volunteers who would like to recount what happened. His request elicited one story after another of white policemen roughing up their children for no apparent reason.”

“Did anyone tell a different story? Or were they all about harsh physical treatment?”

“There was one about a young boy who was on the street, apparently later than a policeman thought he should be. The policeman wasn’t rough with him, but he did put his hands on the boy’s shoulders as he talked with him.

“The discussion was that the streets could be dangerous at night. Someone as young as he is could easily find himself in a situation he would not want to be in. The parent remarked that the policeman put him in exactly that situation.

“‘Scared the shit out of the boy’, was the term he used.”

“How old was he?” I test a suspicion.

“About twelve, I believe.”

“So, seventy-two families came to the Rev’s discussion about negative encounters their children have had with the Fort Christian police. Do you think the Rev decided now was the time to do something about an issue that seems to have become a pattern?”

“I think, although I am seeking validation, that one of the Reverend’s donors flushed him out. He seems to have avoided inflammatory rhetoric, or taking on causes, in my estimation, probably because of what happened to him in San Angelo.”

“Your theory makes sense to me.” I know Tex is going to write a powerful story. It is going to be controversial because the Mayor and Council will need to respond.

These are charges that can’t simply be ignored. While Tex didn’t use the race card in his description, it's clear it is exactly where the Rev is going with his discussion.

While bringing this to the surface is likely long overdue, it won't be well received in most corners of the community.

"Just make sure you write for all of our audiences. That means you have to acknowledge all viewpoints."

Tex nods. He understands what I am saying.

"One more thing," I need to ask. "Is this for tomorrow or Sunday Opinion?" The Sunday Opinion section gives the reporter an opportunity to do a byline story where opinions can be expressed.

If this article is for the next day, it must be just the facts with no viewpoint.

In this instance I would prefer a weekday article of just the fact that the Rev held his discussion meeting. But I never prevent my reporters from writing an opinion piece.

I would like to violate my tradition in this case because I think it's too early for the newspaper to be expressing opinions, even if they are of the byline reporter and not the paper itself.

Tex looks at me as my mind churns through the pros and cons of an opinion piece, "I'll have it to you before I go home tonight."

That means it won't be an opinion piece. Tex knows me well enough to make a decision I will be happy with. He can sense the story is likely just developing. There will be more stories to follow.

The right time for an opinion piece or editorial is still down the road.

I nod in concurrence. "What else is being discussed in the halls of the city?"

"You didn't let me finish what happened at the discussion," Tex pivots me back.

I raise an eyebrow.

"The Reverend Lindo exercised his oratory. He was most eloquent in saying that the city government has been ignoring their grievances. It is not right, nor appropriate for people in this city to live in fear that their child may be mistreated by law enforcement because of racial profiling.

"He also said that those who chose to attend the discussion are just the tip of the iceberg. What they described goes on every single day.

"And then the Reverend Lindo exhorted the seventy-two noses to action. He confirmed that those in that room are powerful. If they work together, they can bring their grievance to City Hall.

"And if City Hall won't listen, then they take to the ballot box. Put those in power today into retirement. Put citizens on Council who will look out for black folk. Put citizens on the Council who will replace those white officers with powerful black men and women.

"Put citizens on the Council who will end racism in this city by taking over City Hall."

"Must have been some sermon. But was there an actual discussion?" I have to ask. "What you've described sounds more like the Rev asking for stories to justify his call to action. Were alternative viewpoints discussed?"

"No. The Reverend Lindo probably left the evening with the impression he has the full support of those who came to launch a full court press on elected officials.

"To take action against the police department for racially motivated profiling and discriminatory or at least selective enforcement of ordinances that impact young black men differently than young white men."

"Is that what you are going to say in your article?" I wonder aloud.

"I don't know yet," Tex admits.

"Depends on how you write the story."

"Do I want to tell them or lead them to draw their own conclusions?" He wonders aloud.

"Good question. Have they delivered your pizza yet?" I ask.

He has a different kind of pizza delivered every night about this time. Apparently it gives him nourishment, but also inspiration. Some of his best stories have been on nights he's had the 'everything' pizza on whole wheat crust.

"You want a slice, come help yourself."

4 – PATROLMAN RICHIE WEBSTER

I don't know why Duke has to bust my chops every time I do something. He may be the Sergeant, but that just means he's old.

He needs to understand there's technology now that makes our job easier. Not everything needs two guys in a squad car chasing down speeders on Seventh Street. Besides, these squad cars are old. The city needs to get with the times.

I could do my job so much better if they replaced these old junkers with Teslas.

Hey, no perp is gonna get away from me if I've got Ludicrous Speed available. Zero to sixty in less than three seconds? It wouldn't be a fair rundown.

I can totally see that.

Like why wouldn't the city want us to be able to arrest the bad guys? From what I've been reading the real action is on the cybercrime side anyway. Stealing millions without leaving their living room. That's just mind blowing.

Too bad I don't understand all that shit. I mean, a computer might as well be on the moon as far as I'm concerned. I can do Facetime, Facebook and Instagram. Does that make me a computer whiz?

I just catch a car that speeds by out of the corner of my eye. I'm looking at Instagram pictures Jose posted and didn't catch how fast. Can't write the ticket if I don't have some evidence of his speed.

Shit.

An alert on my phone indicates Jose just posted something. What?? The picture is of him and Denise. What's he trying to do? Put on a move on my girl?

Well, maybe she's not my girl. I've been trying to get her to spend more time with me, but working nights is just putting such a crimp in my party time.

Nobody wants to hang on Monday or Tuesday night, but since I'm low man on the totem pole, I'm Mister Weekend shift.

Really can't say anything to Denise about hanging with Jose when I'm not there to defend my turf.

Damn. Sometimes I wonder if it's even worth having a job.

I look up and see another car coming towards me that appears to be going too fast, so I train the radar on him. There. Got him. Forty-seven in a thirty-five zone. Absolutely ticket time.

I turn on my light and let him pass me. He appears to slow, probably hoping I caught someone else. I watch a moment longer. He doesn't pull over, so I pull out into the lane and follow with my light turning.

This guy just doesn't get it. A cop with a light on, following him and he's still doing forty-two in a thirty-five zone.

I accelerate. Certainly is no Tesla, and Ludicrous Speed? No chance. If this guy had just kept going… made a run for it… I'd probably not have been able to catch him.

Dumbass.

The driver sees me following him, light turning, but no siren. Duke's told us not to use the siren when it's late unless absolutely necessary. Don't want to disturb all the sleeping citizens who go to bed early.

Probably thinking of himself.

So Mister Speeder is pulling over. 'Bout time. I come up behind the older model muscle car. Looks to be a Dodge Charger. Black of course. Stealthy.

I input the license into the computer. It only takes a moment before Ricardo Hernandez smiles at me from his high school graduation picture. At least that looks to be the dude who owns those wheels.

I scan his record. A dozen speeding tickets, but nothing that makes him dangerous or wanted. I check his birthday. Shit, this guy has my birthday, only two years older. Does that mean I'm gonna get attitude that someone younger than him is about to write him up and make him pay a big fine?

Well, if he does, I'll just haul his ass in, fingerprint him and set his sorry ass in a cell for the night. See how you like that, Mr. Dodge Charger.

I'm fairly close behind so I get out of my cruiser, although that's not an appropriate name for this rust bucket. I shake my head as the door doesn't close and I have to step back to push it shut.

I'm already annoyed by the time I reach Ricardo Hernandez.

"License and insurance card, please."

I'm actually surprised when he hands me what I asked for, no questions asked. I check the documents, they match what came up on the computer. So I pull out my ticket book and start writing in the information.

"You going to tell me how fast I was going?" Ricardo Hernandez asks

"Forty-seven in a thirty-five. More than thirty percent over the limit."

"I can do the math," Ricardo responds.

When I finish writing the ticket, I tear out his copy and hold it out to him along with his license and insurance card.

"You can plead guilty and mail it in with the standard fine, or appear in court. Call the number on the back of the ticket and they'll schedule your hearing."

"Don't you want to know why?" Ricardo asks.

"Why what?" I respond.

"My wife is on her way to the hospital with our first."

"Congratulations. A ticket and a kid on the same night. Hope it takes after its mother."

I watch with satisfaction as Ricardo Hernandez says something under his breath that sounds something like 'asshole'. But he says it such-a-way I can't be sure. And I hear Duke saying, 'if you can't be sure, it didn't happen.'

So I stand there as Ricardo moves his car forward and rejoins the traffic.

I return to rust bucket and again have difficulty getting the door to close. Is this what Pederson deals with when we're patrolling together? Maybe I'll just let him continue to drive us.

I start the car and return to the blind where I'm watching traffic, but decide not to pull in. I keep on travelling down Seventh Street. The West Side is where most of the dispatch requests have been recently.

I hate Thursdays because there's just not much going on. Everyone tucks into bed early and I'm left to look at dark houses and those where the only glow you see is from the Netflix users who are watching horror.

It's almost midnight. This is where even the Netflix glow starts to disappear. I pull into a Seven-Eleven for a cup of cheap coffee. Can't afford a Starbucks because I'm still on recruit pay. Barely enough to pay rent. Don't know what I'd have to do if I had to buy my uniforms.

As I pour the coffee, I glance at the magazines. I've not seen some of these. I open one and glance at the pictures and wonder if I can find this one online somewhere. Don't want to spend money to buy it.

A little cream, stir, and I'm ready. No sugar. I've read it's bad for you, but what isn't? Sergeant Walters was the one who told me sitting around is just a killer on your fitness.

So skip the donuts, skip the sugar. Eat meat and vegetables. And never ever drink soda. That just stays with you forever.

I like Walters better than Duke. He seems to be more with it. I mean he even knows some of the bands I listen to. Says he doesn't listen to them like I do, but he knows some of their early work.

Duke probably hasn't listened to music since Hendrix or Janis Joplin. Why is it we all know their music, but they haven't taken the time to learn ours?

I go to the register to pay for the coffee, but the young Middle Eastern looking clerk doesn't take my money.

"Have a good night, officer."

I guess he like cops. I nod 'thanks' and head back out to the rust bucket. I hear a dispatch coming in.

"Possible burglary, 1723 Ashbrooke. Family's away but someone's in the back yard."

I respond, "Unit thirteen here. I'm about two blocks away. Should be there less than five."

"When you arrive, surveil, but wait for backup. They're probably fifteen minutes out."

"Ten-four," I reply as I start the car. A quick glance behind me and I accelerate out into the street, spilling the coffee, because I didn't get a top. This is where Ludicrous Speed would really help. I'll have to pass that along to Duke.

No, I'll pass it along to Walters. He would understand.

I approach the address in just about five minutes, slowing so I can see what's happening.

Small house. One of the older ones in this neighborhood. They've been rebuilding with bigger ones here, including the one next door. Probably called it in, since I see lights on there.

I pull to the curb in front of the house. Dispatch said to surveil. Didn't say anything about staying in the car.

So I get out and go to the front door. I look through the window. No lights, no movement that I can see inside. If it is a burglary, doesn't look like he made it inside yet, or has already gone.

I decide to move around to the back yard to see what I can find.

When I'm about halfway there, I hear a voice.

The back yard is open to the street. I slow my approach and try to understand what the person is saying. I only hear one voice, but I assume he must be talking with someone.

I draw my service revolver and double hand it, arms extended, so I can be sure of an accurate shot if needed. I feel my heart pounding and the blood welling up in my ears.

Dispatch said to surveil, but what if whoever is back here is armed? I can't just stand here and let someone shoot at me or get away, can I?

I'm sure to get promoted if I can show I can handle this one all by myself.

If Pederson were here, I'd still be back in the car. Him calling in sick may have been the best thing that could have happened. Now maybe Duke won't treat me like a baby.

I step around the corner of the house, very carefully. I'm trying to surprise whoever is here. Don't want him to escape. I'll catch him in the act. Open and shut case. This perp won't walk.

COURAGE

I keep moving slowly and silently along the street to see beyond the trees and bushes that obscure the back door. I can still hear that faint voice, talking with someone.

And then I make out the shadow.

Now it seems my heart's going to burst it's beating so fast. Whoever it is stands at the back door to the house. No lights.

The subject must sense my presence or something. He turns slightly, but I can barely make him out, other than he's wearing dark clothes and jeans, looks to be black and --

Oh, shit, he has a gun.

"Stay right there," I shout in my most authoritarian voice, although it sounds pretty shaky to me. I try to steady my weapon, but know it's shaking, too.

Whoever it is turns more towards me, and lowers the weapon like he's going to point it at me. No time to think. No time to wait for backup.

I squeeze the trigger three times, watch as the force of each bullet strikes him and carries him a little further backwards. The dark figure staggers for a moment and I'm about to squeeze off more shots if he points his weapon at me.

But instead the dark figure collapses to the ground. The weapon falls away from him.

I stand there with my service revolver still pointed at the downed suspect and just stare at him, heart beating furiously and the pressure still in my ears.

I watch to see if he really is down. Or do I need to do anything else?

Then I realize, I just shot someone.

Holy shit. What do I do now?

5 – T.K. JEFFERSON

The alarm's going off.

Is it time to get up already? Seems like I just got to sleep. No, that's not the alarm. It's the phone ringing.

What time is it? I finally open my eyes and turn around to look at the clock.

Who's calling me at 2:00 am? People only call at this time of the night when there's been an accident. Maybe I should ignore the call and get the bad news in the morning, when I'll be better able to deal with it.

No, that won't work. Sina will reach over me at some point and answer if I don't.

"Hello?"

"T.K., it's Duke."

Duke? Why would he be calling me? Particularly in the middle of the night?

"Yeah? What's up besides you and now me?"

"There was an officer-involved shooting tonight."

What does this have to do with me? "I'm sorry to hear that. What happened?"

"Deshaun… well, there's just no easy way to say this, Deshaun is dead."

Now I'm fully awake. "Deshaun? That's not possible."

Sina must be awake, reaches over to touch me, "What's happened to Deshaun?"

I reach back and squeeze her hand, but don't answer, waiting for Duke to say more.

"I know you were close to him," Duke continues. "We were both close to him. That's why I didn't want you to hear about it on the news."

"How is this possible?" My mind is still screaming at me that it's not.

"I don't know," Duke sounds as bewildered as I feel. "We're investigating now and will be back with Internal Affairs in the morning to finish when we can see more."

"Internal Affairs?" I'm still not understanding what Duke's saying to me.

"That's standard procedure when an officer is involved in a shooting."

"An officer shot Deshaun?"

"What?" Sina has overheard my end of the conversation. "A police officer shot him? Why? Deshaun would never do anything…"

"The officer involved has confirmed it," Duke responds, now sounding like the cop he is rather than the friend who wanted to break bad news to me.

"What else can you tell me?" I still haven't heard why and for whatever reason, and Duke isn't offering to tell me. I interpret his silence to mean he doesn't know either.

"We'll know more when we complete the investigation." Duke hesitates, apparently crossing back from cop to friend. "I'll tell you what I can when I see you at the Boy's Club. I'm sorry to call in the middle of the night like this, but I knew you'd want to know."

He apparently doesn't want to make any assumptions. That's probably the right thing for him to do. "Thanks, Duke. I appreciate the call."

"Night, T.K.," he says and is gone.

Sina sits up in bed now, and turns on the light. I have to close my eyes until they adjust to the brightness. "What happened?"

I pull myself up to sit up, too, and put my arm around her to reassure her. "I don't know. Duke said they're still investigating."

"But a policeman shot Deshaun. Killed him." Sina sounds like she can't believe it either.

"Apparently," is all I can say.

6 – ZANA GONZALEZ – EDITOR, THE FORT CHRISTIAN STANDARD

Tex called me from his car.

He heard the dispatch reports of an officer-involved shooting while he was still rewriting the article on the Rev's racial profiling discussion. He headed over to see what had happened.

He said the police department had portable spotlights set up at the scene and officers were looking for clues and evidence of what had occurred. The body was covered and being removed when he arrived. No one would give him any details other than to confirm that an officer was involved.

I called Regina Blackwell, Mayor of Fort Christian, who had been informed and planned to hold a press conference this morning once they had more information that could be discussed. Tex and I are at City Hall waiting for that conference to begin, along with television and radio reporters and crews.

Regina and Clyde Andrews, the Chief of Police, enter the conference room where we are waiting. "Thank you all for coming on such short notice," Regina begins.

"As you are aware, there was an officer-involved shooting early this morning. We are thankful such incidents are infrequent in our city. We take each and every one of them very seriously. We want to thoroughly investigate, make sure we completely understand the circumstances and the events, and ensure the actions taken were justified.

"While the investigations are still underway, I wanted to provide as much information to the public as we can release at this time. I'd like Chief Andrews to give you the facts that we have established so far.

Chief?"

Regina steps away from the podium and Chief Andrews takes her place.

"Morning, everyone. It's been a long night for a lot of folks. Some of us have yet to get any sleep, so I'm going to be brief.

"Our records show that at 12:07 am today, the department received a call from a neighboring homeowner that motion detectors on his property detected movement in the backyard of the home at 1723 Ashbrooke. The reporting homeowner speculated that someone might be trying to break into the neighboring house, since the parties residing there are away.

"Dispatch made a call at approximately 12:10 am. Units 13 and 21 both responded to dispatch. Unit 13 was the closest, but both were sent to the scene to investigate."

Tex raises his hand. "Just a point of clarification, Chief."

Chief Andrews stops and nods, with a look of annoyance. Apparently he would have preferred not to answer any questions yet.

"Both units 13 and 21 were sent to the location. Is that usual for such a vague report?"

The Chief considers how to respond for a long moment. That tells me he's uncomfortable about something.

"The dispatcher used her judgment as to what resources were needed. That is standard operating procedure." I detect a bit of annoyance in his voice, but he said up front he's not had any sleep.

"Could you tell us what indicated to the dispatcher that two units were needed?" Tex pursues the point.

"As I understand it, from only a brief discussion with the dispatcher," the Chief says, "Unit 13 was about five minutes away. Unit 21 was writing a traffic citation and would not be able to investigate for an estimated fifteen minutes. So the decision was made to have Unit 13 respond immediately. Unit 21 would provide backup as necessary."

Sounds logical, but why did the Chief question the dispatcher on this point? There must have been something he wanted to know. Tex's instincts appear to be on the money.

"I take it the officer involved in the shooting was with unit 13. Is that correct?" Tex pursues clarification the Chief hasn't provided as yet.

"It is, but if you will let me finish the briefing, maybe I'll be able to answer your questions." The Chief is uncomfortable and wants to tell his story first, which means it's probably a carefully assembled version.

Tex nods that he will hold his questions for now.

"Unit 13 arrived at the location at approximately 12:15 a.m. The officer surveilled the premises from his cruiser, did not detect anything out of the ordinary, and approached the front door.

"He looked inside through a window to determine whether there was someone inside. Seeing no one, he walked around to the back yard where the neighbor's motion detectors had indicated movement.

"The officer encountered the deceased, who was standing at the back door. The officer, according to his statement, believed the individual was holding a weapon.

"He verbally engaged the individual, who did not respond, but instead turned towards the officer and lowered what the officer thought was a weapon, as if to fire upon the officer.

"Fearing for his own life, the officer shot the individual as a means to disarm him. Unit 21 arrived at approximately 12:25 am, and began the investigation."

"Who is the deceased?" Tex asks, now that the Chief has his statement out there.

"Deshaun Bush," the Chief responds and it's like the air is sucked out of the room. Dead silence. No wonder they didn't release that information earlier.

"You may not be able to answer this question, but why would a college basketball star attempt to break into a house? It doesn't make any sense. I watched him play in the game against Oklahoma two nights ago," one of the television news reporters from the Fox affiliate asks.

"The premises where the shooting occurred was that of the deceased's parents."

Tex doesn't wait to be recognized, "Deshaun Bush was shot and killed by a Fort Christian police officer while standing at the back door to his parent's home. Is that correct?"

"Yes."

Chief Andrews quickly moves to the next question, also from the Fox affiliate reporter, "Chief Andrews, can you explain the events in more detail? There must be a reason the police officer shot and killed Deshaun."

"At this point we are still trying to determine whether anyone witnessed the events. So far we have not been able to identify anyone, which means all we have is the statement of the officer."

Tex is looking at his notes on his phone, "Chief Andrews, you said the officer thought Deshaun was holding a weapon. Did you find a weapon?"

Chief Andrews looks over at Regina before answering, "No."

"What was Deshaun holding, if anything?" Tex isn't going to let this part go.

"A cell phone," Chief Andrews reveals, clearly unhappy about it.

Tex repeats, "A cell phone. You said that Deshaun lowered the 'weapon' as if to fire upon the officer. Does that mean he was talking with someone when the shooting occurred?"

Chief Andrews really doesn't want to answer this part. "Yes."

"Who was Deshaun talking with when the shooting occurred?" Tex asks.

"His parents," Chief Andrews admits and tries to quickly move on. "Does someone else have a question?"

The Chief appears to be tired of answering Tex's questions. Probably because he must know they will lead to a whole lot of other questions.

The Fox affiliate reporter asks, "Who is the officer involved?"

"Patrolman Richard Webster."

Tex thinks for a minute, then raises his hand again, "Richard Webster. I don't recognize his name. Is he new?"

"Yes. Patrolman Webster joined the force in April upon the retirement of Sergeant Donald Thompson, who had been with the department for thirty-two years."

Clearly, Chief Andrews would rather talk about Sergeant Thompson than Patrolman Webster. I can see how this story is going to play out. A rookie cop shoots a rising sports star because he didn't take the time to understand the situation or who was involved.

The city fires Patrolman Webster, who is exonerated because of one technicality or another. Patrolman Webster ends up in a police department in South Dakota or Wyoming and nothing changes.

Unless the Rev stirs the pot and it sounds like he already has his stirring spoon poised after his discussion last night.

I decide to ask, "Chief Andrews, has Patrolman Webster been suspended or fired from the department as a result of his actions?"

"He has been suspended as per department procedures when there is an officer-involved shooting," says the Chief, apparently hoping he is near the end of his grilling by the media.

"Do you expect he will be fired by the city?"

Chief Andrews steps back from the podium as Regina says something to him I can't hear. She moves to the microphone.

"It's still too early in the investigation to know what actions may or may not be required. I know you all have many more questions about the events today. We do too. As we are able to validate and confirm aspects, we will release additional information.

"Whether there will be legal proceedings will be up to the district attorney, who will be provided a copy of the internal investigation reports.

"What has happened is indeed a tragedy, for the deceased's family, to whom our hearts go out, along with his many friends. Deshaun had a promising future that was cut short as a result of last night's events.

"As I said in the beginning, we are continuing to gather the facts that will establish the circumstances and the events of last night. Once we clearly understand both, then we will be able to respond appropriately.

"Thank you."

Regina isn't going to discuss it further at this time, despite the fact that several hands go up. She shakes her head as she and Chief Andrews leave the conference room.

"Tragedy isn't the right word for what's happened," Tex turns towards me. "Where did you run the story on Reverend Lindo's discussion?"

"Page two of the local section. Didn't want to give it too much prominence and now it probably should have been on page one," I shake my head.

"You can't second guess the future," Tex reminds me.

"Patrolman Webster," I say and don't have to say more.

"He's the story here, yeah, I see that. Someone must have insights they're willing to share. I'd like to profile him as part of the front page for tomorrow. Is that in line with your thinking?"

"Side-by-side profiles would make a compelling story," I confirm. "The rising basketball star, whose life and career was cut short by a young police recruit.

"What doesn't make sense to me is: why was a recruit in a position to do this? Where was his partner? There was no mention of that, and they said there were no witnesses.

"Does that mean he was out there alone? That just occurred to me. Follow up on that. It might be important."

Tex makes notes on his phone. I still can't get used to that, but it reminds me of something.

"And talk to Deshaun's parents, if they will see you. It must have been awful to have been on the phone with him, to hear their son shot by a police officer as it happened, and not be able to do anything about it."

7 – SERGEANT FRANCIS 'DUKE' MARION

As I look around the scene of last night's events, I think things always look different in the light of day. I can see what Richie did not last night.

See how things really were. But what Richie saw is all that really matters. He saw shadows. He saw movement. He didn't see Deshaun.

If those same events happened now, the outcome would be different. Richie would have immediately recognized Deshaun. He would have simply asked if Deshaun had locked himself out, or what.

But in the shadows of a dark night, with only a sliver of moon illuminating things, moving shadows become sinister.

Walter Johnston, the police officer union steward is standing beside me, just looking at the back door where Deshaun's life ended. I don't know what he's thinking, but I assume he's blaming Deshaun for making a mess for him to clean up.

That's how Walter thinks.

Never about the impact on others, just what it means for him.

"Pretty cut and dried," Walter remarks. I'm assuming he's talking to me, but maybe he's just summing up what he thinks for himself.

"Nothing is ever cut and dried, Walter," I respond.

"There's nothing here," Walter says. "Cop sees someone attempting to break into a house, thinks he's armed, thinks he's about to shoot, officer defends himself. Cut and dried."

"If you think that's how a court will look at it, you're living on another planet," I respond.

"This isn't going to court if you write up the investigation properly."

I don't like his inference about 'properly'.

"The investigation report will be factual and unbiased. I'm not about to insert anything that isn't supported by evidence or statements."

"Come on, Duke. As president of the union you have an obligation to your members. Richie Webster is one of your members. You have to do what you can to help him get past this."

I get right in Walter's face. "I have an obligation to find the truth and present that to Internal Affairs. Where it goes from there is up to them, not me."

"Truth?" Walter laughs at me. "The truth is you let him go out alone in violation of department procedures that night. You did so because the Chief wanted all patrols out to reduce gang violence and because the Mayor was all over him about it. Are you going to put that in your report?"

"It explains why Richie did what he did."

"Bullshit." Walter looks across the street towards a large home that had recently been built to replace a small house like this one.

"Look at this neighborhood. Families like the Bushes are being pushed out because people with more money want to live close in, and not have to drive so far to get to work. The people moving in? Do you think they give a rat's ass about the Bushes or the others that take their offer for a lot of money and move out? All so the people moving in can build a McMansion here?"

"What does that have to do with the investigation?"

"Nobody cares about the Bushes," Walter assures me. "Nobody should care about Deshaun. What's over is done. Move on. Forget about the fact that the Bushes lost their son. Nothing you can do in the report will make any difference.

"If we help him get past this incident, he'll be paying dues for a lot of years. That gives us a chance to do a lot of good for our members. Get them more money for their salaries, more money for retirement. Better healthcare, so their kids get the best treatment. Those are the things the union stands for. We don't get involved in trying to make things right. That's not who we are."

"That's where we differ." I step towards him to get his attention. "We have an obligation to gather and present the facts. Then we let the relevant authorities decide whether we share in the responsibility or not."

"Clearly you think you do." Walter shakes his head. "That's probably why you're such a failure as union president. You let other things get in the way of getting everything you can for your members. Other union presidents don't have that problem. Look at the big cities…"

"Like the cities that had to be bailed out by the state because the pension obligations were unaffordable?"

"We've had this discussion before." Walter doesn't want to acknowledge that he was involved in bankrupting a city in California that negotiated huge pensions based on actuarial assumptions that were unrealistic and never materialized. And now he's trying to push me to do what will make him look good, help him move on to a bigger bargaining unit where he can make more money, like he used to.

"We have. And if I'm such a failure why do you stay?" I know the answer. It's because no one wants him. He's like a lightning rod. After what happened in California no city wants to negotiate with him.

Walter changes the subject, "What are you going to say? In the report? That's why we're out here."

"I'm going to say what happened based on the evidence and testimony."

Walter thinks about that for a moment, "Evidence and testimony," he repeats.

"So here's what you report. Richie went out alone because the department is short-handed. Point out that a single officer calling in sick required dispatch to send out a young officer alone. Push it back on the city. State that they won't give us the additional positions we keep asking for. Point out that the city won't provide additional training dollars that may have permitted Richie to be better trained in how to deal with the kind of situation he encountered.

"Point out that if the city paid more, we could attract more experienced officers rather than always need to hire newbies. Maybe some good can come out of this, if we play it right."

"That's not the intent of the report," I respond.

"But you need to provide the evidence and testimony that shows Richie pulled that trigger because the city is too cheap to provide the best police force it can."

"The best police force the city can afford," I say.

"That's the problem with you." Walter continues to push me. "You try to negotiate for both sides. That weakens your position. So stop doing that. Let me worry about how to get what your members deserve. Just don't undercut me when I take a position.

"Look, I need you to do your part. Ensure the city's culpability is clear in your report. This should be the catalyst for the additional officers we are requesting. We add officers, and sending a new officer out by himself is a thing of the past."

Walter is hitting me in my own feelings of guilt. I could have stopped Richie that night. We talked about it. Sent him back to the barn. But I didn't. I went along.

I didn't stop a practice that proved to be deadly. And now I have to live with the fact that I'm as guilty of murdering Deshaun as Richie is, if only indirectly.

I decide I need to put that aside. Get back to the reason I'm out here, which is to walk through the events of last night and determine the evidence and whether the testimony Richie provided makes any sense, or is at least plausible.

I walk away from Walter, who instantly frowns at me. I walk back along the side of the Bush home to the front door. I look inside and see Mr. Bush, Deshaun's father, sitting at the kitchen table.

Richie said he did not see anyone, did not detect any movement. That would be consistent, since Mr. and Mrs. Bush were in Dallas, visiting his sister and her husband.

Mr. Bush is an auto mechanic and Mrs. Bush an accountant. People would describe them as being of modest means. Deshaun was attending Baylor on an athletic scholarship as they would have struggled to pay the tuition with their incomes.

Is this important in the investigation? I shake my head.

The facts, not an assumption. I have not spoken with the Bushes yet. They may be able to fill in the why as part of their testimony. But I don't want to bother them just yet. I need to give them a little more time to absorb what has happened. Let them come to terms with it, as I'm sure they will not be receptive to a policeman asking questions when it was a policeman who ended the life of their son.

Deshaun's choices and actions also had a part to play in what happened. He chose to come home early for Christmas. Did he know his parents weren't going to be home? Another thing I'll need to clarify with Mr. and Mrs. Bush.

Why was he out late that night? I know from being with him at the Boy's Club earlier that he went to see his girlfriend. But that doesn't go into the report. As the investigator I can't submit any testimony. That would not be proper.

Is it relevant? Do I need to get a statement from T.K. about what he heard Deshaun say when he was leaving the club? But T.K. was also there when Richie came to see me about going out alone. He may say that he observed the conversation between Richie and myself. Might put me in the position of reporting exactly what Walter wants me to.

People will be criticized. People, including me, could lose their jobs, and I have no idea how to do or be anything but be a cop. That's all I've known since I got my GED.

I stop thinking about what statements I need to get, or not get. I go back to just being what I am: a good cop, ascertaining the facts.

8 – REVEREND LEROY LINDO, PASTOR SECOND BAPTIST CHURCH FORT CHRISTIAN

Lord, give me the strength to do what I must to right this wrong, I pray and then open my eyes to see my congregation before me in the sanctuary of my church.

My sanctuary. My congregation. My church.

I begin. "I was sent here by God. Sent to Fort Christian, to be here, at this moment, with all of you. I was sent by God to lead this community in a response to the events of last night.

"We, all of us, have lost one of the brightest lights amongst us. A young man. Yes, I know many of you probably were still thinking Deshaun Bush was just a boy, but that's because he grew up before our eyes.

"We saw Deshaun Bush become a symbol for achievement. A symbol that a determined boy of any color could hone his talents and be more than anyone could have expected of him.

"Deshaun was a symbol of hope for so many of us. Hope that Baylor would return to play in a championship game this year, because of his leadership and ability. Hope that Deshaun would go on to play in the NBA. Hope that we would be fulfilled by watching him on one of the largest stages of all."

I stop to look about my congregation. Let my words sink in. I'm setting the stage and I must have them with me before I get to the end. Before I get to the rage and the resolution I want them to support.

"Let me just say it so we all know why we are here today. We live in a racist community. You may say, 'but we live in a racist world.'

"I would agree with you if you were to say that to me, but I can't change the world, we can't change the world. But you and I together… I believe that together we can change Fort Christian. And that is where we must start. That is where we must concentrate our energy, our collective presence, our collective rage, anger and demands for change."

Another pause, because everyone agrees with my opening statements, but now I'm transitioning and this is where I need to keep everyone in agreement or we have no leverage.

"We are angry that Deshaun Bush has been taken from us. I am filled with rage that a black boy could be killed by a police officer in his own backyard. This is a clear indication that no one is safe in this city.

"There is no bubble within which we can exist safe from prejudice and racism. Safe from those who are sworn to protect us. What kind of crazy society is it that we live in, afraid of our protectors? Something is fundamentally wrong.

"And what fills me with rage is that we permit this situation to continue, day-after-day, year-after-year. And the result is we lose the brightest stars amongst us. We lose precious friends, neighbors and colleagues. For no reason.

"This has to stop. This has to stop right now. Today.

"We must take a stand. We must go to City Hall. We must demand change. But we are past the point of asking people to change. We must demand a change that replaces the racists with people like us.

"People who have experienced persecution. People who have been stopped by a white policeman, pulled from our cars and told to 'spread 'em,' while a second white cop inspects the car for drugs, or weapons, or Bibles, because in so many instances that's all they find.

"Why is Whitey afraid of the Bible? Whitey is afraid of the Bible, because it tells him what he is doing to us is wrong. What Whitey is doing must end."

Drink of water time. I need to keep everyone focused on what we have to do together. What we have to do that they have never been willing to do before.

“Imagine with me, for a moment. Imagine a police force that is all black officers. Imagine black officers pulling over Whitey’s kids when they are doing nothing wrong.

“Imagine black officers, pulling Whitey’s kids out of their shiny new and expensive cars and telling them to ‘spread ‘em.’

“Imagine Whitey’s kids being told to look straight ahead as a black officer searches their cars and finds drugs. Imagine black officers arresting Whitey’s children, bringing them to jail and calling Whitey to come down and bail his child out and prepare for a drug trial.

“A trial where the sentencing guidelines Whitey established will ensure Whitey’s son or daughter will have a conviction, will have served time for being in possession of an ounce of weed.

“A sentencing guideline that will prevent Whitey’s son or daughter from getting into most colleges. A sentencing guideline that will ensure Whitey’s son or daughter won’t be hired by most white companies because of a bullshit conviction.

“Imagine a world where Whitey feels trapped by the system Whitey created. Imagine a world where justice for Whitey is the justice we experience every day.”

I see members of my congregation who have glazed eyes. They can’t imagine such a world, even though I’ve only reversed the roles.

“You may say, Rev Lindo, you don’t know what you’re asking for. You may say that. You may say we need to forgive and forget. Isn’t that what the Bible says?

“Forgive, yes. Forget? Never.

“And in the case of Deshaun Bush being executed by a racist white police officer, there is no forgiveness. Mr. and Mrs. Bush are with us today. Right here down front where they are every Sunday. Right here down front where they have been with Deshaun so many Sundays, worshipping with us. Seeking guidance and inspiration from our Lord.

"And as devout and good Christians as they are, today they are seeking understanding. They are seeking change in the community. They are seeking our support to make sure what has happened to them can never happen to any of the rest of us.

"Mr. and Mrs. Bush know they alone cannot change Fort Christian. But together we can. Together we can demand action. Together we can ensure that our demands are heard.

"Together we can fundamentally change how our community treats us and our children. Ensure that our children's children grow up in a community that respects everyone.

"We demand that every police officer be black."

Shaking heads in the audience tell me most of my congregation doesn't think my suggestion would happen. Got to change that perception.

"I see many of you think that's a bad idea. Particularly Roxanne Williams and Alvin Hill, sitting in the back where they always sit together.

"As most of you know, they are Council members. Black Council members. Our only black Council members.

"But let me point out, since I'm telling the truth here, they've both sold out to Whitey in order to get elected. And if you think that's not the case, I ask you, what did they do to change how the police force treats us? What did they do that would have prevented a racist white cop from assassinating our Deshaun Bush?"

Roxanne is the first to her feet as I expect. Alvin's always running for cover. I'm surprised he had the guts to show up here.

"Reverend Lindo has made many good points today," Roxanne begins her defense. "But bringing about change through racist tinged demands is not going to happen.

"He said Alvin and I sold out to white folks in order to get elected. What the Reverend has not pointed out to you is that he has not been elected to anything. He doesn't represent you. No one here listened to his campaign and voted for him to lead us.

"But here he is trying to herd you into a cauldron of controversy by making unrealistic demands." Roxanne looks about for a moment to gauge the congregation, most of whom know her well and voted for her.

She apparently makes a decision about their silence.

"I know everyone in this room is impatient for change; no one more so than Alvin and myself. We go to the meetings. We negotiate for things that are important to you and to all of us. That's what government is all about. Negotiating, not demanding unrealistic change.

"I am just horrified by what has happened. I can't fathom the loss Mr. and Mrs. Bush are feeling right now. And I know this won't be popular here, in this room full of enraged friends and neighbors of Deshaun and his parents, but we need to step back for a moment.

"We need to let the investigations proceed, that will tell us what happened and why. We need to listen to recommendations that may lead to changes to prevent anything like this from happening in the future.

"And if those recommendations aren't sufficient, everyone in this room and every other citizen of Fort Christian will have an opportunity to comment, suggest something else, something that may be more effective.

"And that's my ask of you. Give the Mayor and those of us on Council the time we need to go through the process. Give us the time we need to not rush to judgment, but make the right decisions for all of us."

Deshaun's father stands and looks at Roxanne.

"We've been friends for a long time. Your son and Deshaun played on recreational teams together. We'd sit in the stands and talk about families and friends.

"I was one of the first to encourage you when you said you'd like to run for Council. I thought you would fix some things we all saw were a problem for black folks in this city. I have to thank you for many of the things you've tried to do. But I also have to say I'm sorely disappointed in you and Alvin.

"All the good things you've done weren't able to prevent what happened to Deshaun." Mr. Bush sits back down.

"Mason, I can understand why you think that," Roxanne responds. "But let me assure you that Alvin and I have worked tirelessly to address the racism and stop the practices that have made us all cautious about letting our kids be out late at night.

"My son is about the same age as Deshaun. Not a night goes by that I'm not worried about where he is, whether he's safe and whether someone may overreact to something he says or does.

"I know that Alvin and I will be doing everything in our power to address what's happened. But I ask that you not storm City Hall with impossible demands that will make our objectives just that much harder to achieve."

She's had her say, now it's my turn.

"Has Roxanne convinced anyone that standing back and letting things follow the usual path will result in anything different than what's happened in the past? Which is nothing?

"Nothing has changed in how the police harass us and our children. Racism hasn't fled our unfair city. If anything, it's more entrenched than ever.

"Change must be led. Change only results when what worked in the past no longer does.

"And the status quo will only become unworkable when we all march on City Hall and make demands. Extreme demands, because the situation demands extreme action. Extreme change."

Roxanne shakes her head and finally sits down. She leans over and talks with Alvin as I continue:

"Tomorrow night Council is meeting in their regular work session. It's not an open meeting where they vote on resolutions, but I expect they will discuss Deshaun's death and I expect they will discuss the investigation that has commenced.

"I will lead any and all of you who will join me here at 6:45 p.m. in a march on City Hall. We should arrive there at 7:00, which is the beginning of their session. We will fill the chamber with our silent rage, for they will not recognize us.

"But we will let them know we are watching. We will speak at the next session when resolutions are entered for a vote. We will speak on every resolution, not about that resolution, but about the need for fundamental change.

"And I will lead any and all of you to march and sit in at every Council meeting until our demands are enacted.

"This is fair warning, Roxanne and Alvin. Fair warning that we are watching. We are expecting. And if you do not deliver, we will rise up and vote you out. We will recruit those amongst us who will stand up for us. We will send a majority of new elected officials who can and will take action."

I look around my congregation. Roxanne and Alvin are still talking quietly, but no one around them seems to be paying any attention. I see nodding heads. I see resolve. I see the support I need. Now if I can just not screw it up like in San Angelo…

9 – T.K. JEFFERSON

Brian and Sandi have lived next door since before we moved into our house.

Brian is a tall and athletic marketing executive who travels all the time. Sandi is at least a foot shorter and is a perpetual motion machine. She is the organizer of any event that occurs in our neighborhood or the local schools and actively supports the social causes we all tend to support passively.

Whether it's save the whales or the spotted red-tailed road runner, Sandi is in the middle of it and making the rest of us aware of the need to do something.

When she's not organizing, she paints some of the most incredible scenes, generally from pictures. With Brian travelling so much, she stays at home. The irony is that Brian has seen many of the places Sandi paints and she has not.

We try to get together for dinner when Brian is home, which isn't all that often. Generally once a month.

Tonight is one of those rare occasions when a spontaneous dinner is arranged by Sandi calling Sina and simply telling her Brian is home and looking forward to one of Sina's specialty dishes.

That is ultra-thin home-made pasta noodles with a Veneto region red-wine lamb bolognaise. Sina was able to reverse-engineer this dish from a favorite restaurant we discovered in Bologna, Italy.

Sina has a creative flair for cooking. I'm just the kitchen help who preps what he's told and cleans up afterwards. Sina gave me the prep instructions last night and let the ragu simmer overnight over very low heat. I think this is the secret of its flavor, although I could be wrong. Sina made the noodles just before I got home and they are paper thin.

We always gather in the kitchen so we can finish preparing the meal together. Sandi makes up a salad, Brian and I sample the appetizers and wine, while Sina cooks the noodles and takes warm bread out of the oven to cool. Sina tells everyone she likes to cook with wine, but she seldom drinks it until the meal is on the table.

"San Francisco is becoming one of my favorite cities," Brian is explaining his travels from the past week.

"Always thought it was cold there, and you know I love the Texas heat. But this past week I wasn't locked up in sales meetings all week. The meetings I had weren't right on top of each other as they usually are. So I had time to get out and look around. You know, there's a lot going on."

"Did you see anyone over thirty?" Sina asks. "Everything you read would make it seem everyone is young and working for one tech startup or another."

"A few, but you're right." Brian responds. "A very young city. Much more so than Fort Christian. Here you see people of all ages wherever you go. Not so much there."

"While Brian was trying to figure out how not to look old in a young city, what were you doing this week, Sandi?" Sina asks.

We all laugh at the way Sina described Brian's week.

"I'm working on a painting of Portillo, a place high up in the Andes Mountains, near the border with Argentina. International ski teams practice there in our summers, because it's winter there at that time."

"Must be beautiful," Sina responds. "Are you almost finished?"

"Just getting started," Sandi responds. "I'll let you know when it's ready for showing."

"It's always fun to see it while you're still painting it, see it as it develops," Sina informs us. "I like to see the potential that's not realized yet and then come back and look at the finished product."

"What are you organizing this week?" I ask of Sandi.

"Something unusual for me…" Sandi sounds like she almost doesn't want to tell us. "I'm helping organize a march on City Hall."

This catches me by surprise and a glance at Sina tells me she has been caught by surprise as well.

Sandi is not a political person. She organizes a lot of things, but she's never espoused a political position on anything I can recall.

"A march?" Sina asks, "About what?"

"You know Roxanne Williams," Sandi begins. We both nod.

"Roxanne called me this morning. She asked if I would do her a favor.

"It seems her congregation is going to march on City Hall. And while I don't go to her church, she thought I might be able to help organize things so the march will be peaceful and well-disciplined.

"She's afraid the Reverend Lindo might try to stir things up a bit more than would be good. So she hopes I can talk with folks and maybe help keep things calm."

"I'm surprised Roxanne would reach out to someone who is white to try to calm down a congregation that is predominantly black," Brian notes. Sounds like this is also the first he's heard of it.

"Roxanne was hoping that if I was helping, it would be seen as less of an 'us versus them' kind of thing," Sandi notes. "That the march won't be just a black protest, even though most of the folks will be black."

"I assume the march is over Deshaun?" Sina looks over at me.

"Yes." Sandi glances at Brian.

“Deshaun?” he asks.

I can’t talk about it, so Sina fills in the blanks. “Shot by a police officer investigating a reported burglary,” she says.

“You talking about Deshaun Bush?” Brian is the one who now sounds incredulous.

I nod.

“That’s crazy… what happened?”

Sandi attempts to fill him in. “The city is investigating, so there hasn’t been an official anything yet. That’s what Roxanne is concerned about. Wants the city to have time to complete the investigation before being forced to take actions they can’t defend when all the facts are known.”

“Deshaun.” Brian repeats. Then he seems to pick up on one of Sandi’s comments. “Reverend Lindo. You said something about Roxanne thinking he was going to stir things up? What does that mean? Could it turn violent? If it is, I don’t think you should get involved. Let the police handle it.”

“That’s exactly what Roxanne doesn’t want to happen,” Sandi explains.

“The police are the problem,” she says and the air goes thick. All conversation stops.

“I agree with Sandi,” I say. Everyone looks at me.

The thoughts I’ve been having since learning of Deshaun’s death finally are bubbling to the surface. Sina looks at me, but Brian is still looking at Sandi.

“You think the police are the problem?” Sina asks me. “Duke’s been as dedicated to those kids as you have. How can you say he’s the problem?”

“I didn’t say Duke. I said the police. I think there are many aspects to this that Rev Lindo isn't going to look at. Aspects the city's not going to look at. And aspects no one else will want to deal with."

Brian takes a sip of wine to consider my remarks, and then asks, "What are you thinking?"

"I've done a little research since this happened," I respond.

"There are nearly a thousand officer-involved shootings that lead to the death of the victim every year in our country, at least for the last several years.

"And while there's a whole lot of data about the victims, I don't find much about the officers who were involved."

I stop long enough to sip my wine and gather my thoughts.

"It seems to me that the officers who are involved in what would otherwise be non-violent situations tend to be younger officers, relatively new in their careers."

"Interesting," Brian says. "But what's the relevance?"

"I'm thinking police officers need to earn the right to carry a weapon, by showing they can enforce the laws, settle disputes and maintain order -- without a weapon."

Brian cuts me off. "That just doesn't work for me."

"What doesn't?" I ask.

"You're suggesting disarming the police. If they don't carry weapons, how are they going to stop crime, prevent bad guys from hurting Sandi or me or our families and friends?

"You take away the guns of the police and the whole society collapses because the bad guys have them and the cops don't."

"Hold on. There's more to the concept."

Brian shakes his head, letting me know he's simply not open to the idea, but I plunge on.

"I'm thinking police officers need to earn the right to carry a weapon, by showing they can enforce the laws, settle disputes and maintain order without one."

Sina looks suspicious, but at least she's listening.

Brian is not. He goes on the offensive. "Most police officers would never get the chance to carry one under your proposal, because they'd be shot and killed before they ever earned that right."

Sandi doesn't appear to be buying the idea either. "You would just throw police officers out there with no weapon? What criminal would take them seriously?"

Sina hasn't said anything yet. At least she's withholding her skepticism.

But then she asks a question that in time could drive a groundbreaking change in police procedure around the world.

"What else are you thinking?" she asks. "I know that isn't all of it."

10 – T.K. JEFFERSON

Duke passes the ball to me.

I watch the ball all the way into my hands as I always do. Just as my Dad taught me, so many years ago.

Now that I have control, I turn towards the basket, and there he is, at least I think it's Deshaun, studying me with that look of excitement at playing well. A look of wonder as he tries to predict whether I'm going to quickly pass it along to set someone up, take the shot from here, or drive to the basket myself.

I've seen that look so many times, in so many games, here at the Boy's Club. Suddenly I'm brought out of my reverie by Tony stripping the ball and loping off towards the other basket. Tony thinks he's the next Deshaun. Maybe he will be. Maybe even better.

I don't know and at this point neither does he.

"What the f…?" Duke calls out. "Get your head out! We got a game to play."

I've lost track of Deshaun, although I know he was not here. Just my mind trying to recreate what should be, but knowing deep down that he won't ever be here again.

That doesn't mean I can't encourage those who are still here to be better players like I did with Deshaun. There are always more kids coming up each and every year.

Duke's right. I need to get my head out of my ass and play the game or these kids won't think I can do it anymore. Most players my age have long since retired. But that's not my real age. I'm only as old as I feel and I feel as young as these kids.

It doesn't take long for me to trot down to recover the ball that

Tony dunked on us, and he's not even all that tall for a… what is he? Maybe a sixteen-year-old.

I need to do that. Focus on Tony and the others. Do what I can to help them find themselves, build confidence, skills and resilience.

Duke comes up to me. "What's the matter with you? I didn't know better I'd think you'd not played this game before."

"I keep seeing Deshaun." I confide. "He should be out here."

Duke looks at me as if I'd just caught leprosy or something. "You're seeing Deshaun?"

I nod.

Duke leans into me, gets right next to my ear. "Deshaun's not coming back. You need to accept what happened and move on. Help these kids, not cling to a dream that's gone."

I can't believe what I'm hearing. "Are you thinking I got something out of Deshaun's success?"

Duke leans even closer. "We all did. If he was a success it was because we enabled it. We taught him how to be successful. We were there when he had doubts about himself. We pushed him over the top."

"You're wrong, Duke." I pull back. "Deshaun did it all by himself. You and I could have done exactly what we did for another player and it wouldn't have worked.

"It was Deshaun. It was all him."

11 – THOMASINA 'SINA' JEFFERSON

Flo Lopez comes into the library at the Fort Christian Senior High School where we both teach.

She is my best friend. We've known each other since I joined the faculty here six years ago. At that time she was the president of the teacher's union and all about contract negotiations. But she soon tired of the constant wear and tear, having to babysit several thousand teachers who all thought their grievances, comfort, and underpaid status needed her constant attention.

I can understand. But what I didn't see coming was her decision to run for City Council. Of course I helped out, becoming her campaign manager.

And to the amazement of both of us, she won.

"Hey there," comes her usual greeting. "How are you today?"

A quick hug and, then I say, "This a school visit or something else?"

"I'm trying to figure out how these things are supposed to end," she says.

"I need a little more from you to give you a relevant answer."

Flo considers my response and nods. "Guess what I'm trying to understand is why we have all this violence in our cities. And sometimes someone who's totally innocent of anything wrong… dies. Bad karma, some say.

I reach out and squeeze her hand, but I can't think of anything to say.

"So how are we supposed to end the senseless violence? How do we get to a place where we can just live our lives without constant fear of…"

"Being in the wrong place at the wrong time?"

"But we're not in the wrong place," she says, now rubbing one hand against the other -- a nervous tell, of which she is not conscious. But, as her best friend, I am. I reach for her again, but she walks away, growing still more agitated.

"This is our home," she says emphatically. "And home should be safe. A sanctuary of sorts." A pause, then she begins to declaim again, this time softly.

"I've been doing a bunch of reading lately. No one seems to have an answer that resonates for me. You know what I'm saying? You've got the folks who say, 'Nothing you can do about it. People have rights. So just live with it'. But that's not how it should be.

"And then you have the other extreme, which is 'Take away their guns and nobody gets killed.' But that's not a solution we can get to easily, either."

She stands perfectly still.

"So here I am. Confused and depressed that I went to all that trouble to get elected to Council and yet I have no answers to a huge problem we're facing."

"You're looking for affirmation," I say. "That somehow there can be a happy ending."

"I want to believe that people can rise above the bigotry, racial hatred and fear of the other that just seems to pervade our society more than a hundred and fifty years after we fought a civil war to end all that."

I reach out for her again, offering a smile.

"I'll bet you said to yourself, 'Sina will know the right book -- the one with The Answer. After all, she's a librarian'. Is that what you decided?" I laugh, knowing something like that is exactly what happened.

Flo shrugs with a coy smile.

I nod and start back into the stacks, "I do have a book for you, but I'm not sure it's The Book." I make air quotes with both hands. "It's something you may have already read, but even if you haven't, it sends the right message, I think."

Flo follows me back to fiction and alphabetically by author. When we get to the L's I stop and scan the shelves. Finding it, I pull the book and hold it up for Flo to see the title.

"*To Kill a Mockingbird.* Harper Lee," I say, handing it to her. Flo nods and takes the book from me.

"I read it, but you're right, it was a long time ago," she says. "I could use a refresh on Atticus Finch. Give me some hope there are still people in this world who will do what's right, regardless of the consequences."

"Is that what you're thinking? It's you against everyone else and you have to change their minds about racism?"

"Actually I've been thinking almost the opposite," she says. "Finishing up the *Autobiography of Malcolm X.*"

"Definitely a different view of the world," I confirm. "What do you think about his approach?"

"I can see how he would arrive at those conclusions given the life he led. But that's what's so hard about the whole problem. Everyone's life experiences are different. And how do you make things better for some, without making things worse for others?"

"The nature of politics," I observe. "Decisions should be about the greater good, not what's good for just some folks."

"I can't reconcile how we all live together when the person next door hates your guts just because you happen to have a different skin color or practice a different religion or speak a language they don't understand."

"The Malcolm X world view," I summarize. "Live segregated lives where everyone is like you, which is pretty much how we used to decide where to live.

"And that was fine until incomes rose, and all of a sudden more people who historically couldn't afford those middle-class neighborhoods suddenly could."

Flo nods. "Only Malcolm X thinks we should be the ones who decide to live together in black middle-class neighborhoods and keep all the rest of you out. After the events of this week I can't help but think maybe there's something to his ideas."

"How would that work?" I can't help questioning an idea I don't agree with.

Flo shakes her head, "I'm not saying I think that's what we need to do, and even if it were, it's not something Council would even get involved with."

She stops her declamation long enough to draw a long breath.

"It might be as easy as a tweet going out that we're going to all go buy homes on the south side or the north side. We're going to make that our part of the city. We're going to make those our schools and bring in our churches.

"Maybe it's as simple as that. Then all the racists can go live together and think what they want so long as they don't affect what we're doing."

Another pause, and I sense she's winding down a bit.

"I wonder if it's possible to put up firewalls on Twitter? Make sure we only see tweets from folks who are like us and they only see tweets from folks like them? We already got segregated news channels."

"Does segregation lead to freedom?" I pose as a thought for her to consider.

Flo has to think about that for a moment. "Freedom." She considers a bit longer. "I'm not sure if freedom is what I'm trying to get to here, unless you're thinking freedom from fear."

"Certainly part of it," I affirm. "A minute ago you were talking about choice, being able to live the life you choose. Isn't that wrapped into freedom? That you have the freedom to do those things? And does segregation give you freedoms you don't have today?"

"Why is it you always ask the hardest questions?" Flo complains, sort of, but with a knowing smile.

"Just trying to help by asking you the questions I'd ask myself," I tap *To Kill a Mockingbird.* "You might want to re-read this to see if you can gain some differing perspectives before you send out that tweet."

Flo starts to walk back up towards the checkout desk carrying the book, "I'm not sending out any tweets this week, so you don't have to worry about that. I'm just trying to decide how we get to answers that aren't 'let's just ignore the situation and hope it goes away.' It never does.

"At least it never has in my experience."

I decide to change the subject.

"You didn't go to the Reverend's discussion the other night. Why not?"

"The Rev and I seem to be on different wavelengths. He keeps wanting to take up social justice as a cause rather than spiritual health."

"And you get all the social justice you need in your city work," I surmise.

Flo nods. “He’s a spiritual guide. Someone who is supposed to help us live a moral, ethical, and Christian life. But he doesn’t spend much time on any of those things when he has his ‘discussions’. Did you ever look into why he left San Angelo?”

I shake my head. “Guess it was never something that mattered all that much to me since I don’t attend his services.”

“He was caught, bare-assed, in bed, with the Mayor’s wife.”

I’m speechless.

“Didn’t think you’d heard that one,” Flo says with a half-smile. “The Mayor could have shot him, since it was his bed they were in. But his wife told the Mayor it was all her idea. What could the Mayor do? It was consensual. So the Mayor got divorced, and so did the Rev.

“Then he left town.

“Since the Mayor didn’t want it getting out, no one knew about it here when the Rev was interviewed. He had glowing recommendations for his ability to grow a congregation.

“Which he did. Just no one ever figured out if the attraction was his sermons, his ministry to his congregation or his sexual prowess that packed them in on Sundays.”

I’m stunned as I’d heard none of this and wonder, “How did you find out if the Mayor didn’t want it out?”

“My younger brother went out with the Rev’s ex-wife. She had no compunction about talking about it. His comment was, the more she drank that night, the more details she offered up.”

“Was it a one-time affair?” I wonder, not sure if I really want the answer to the question.

“According to the Rev’s wife, no.” Flo sets the book down for me to check it out, which I begin to do.

"It had apparently started shortly after the Rev and his family moved to San Angelo. So years. And the Rev's wife thought there were at least a half dozen others the Rev was attempting to satisfy on a regular basis."

"No rumors here?" I follow up with the next question that comes to mind.

"Since he's no longer married, he's free to sleep with anyone he wants who isn't married," Flo responds.

"It seems the lonely married ladies are the ones attracted to him, from what you've said."

Flo picks up *To Kill a Mockingbird*, "Tell you what I think after I finish this."

12 – T.K. JEFFERSON

T.K. breezes into the kitchen as I'm pulling the evening meal out of the microwave. "Smells good, what kind of fish is it?" He comes around behind me for a kiss. I oblige him with a hug to follow.

"Halibut was on special at Costco, so a fish special for my special guy."

T.K. looks over my shoulder to see how I've prepared the fish, smell the blended flavors. "Olive oil, a little dill weed, basil and let me guess… Italian spices?"

Another kiss is the reward for his correct guesses. "Help me carry the rest of this into the other room."

He does, and sits down, focused on his plate. "What's the occasion?"

"I had a conversation with Flo today. How was your day?"

"A conversation with Flo." T.K. looks up at me, but seems only semi-serious. "Does that mean the two of you have discovered a way of saving the world from famine and pestilence, but it will only cost a trillion dollars and you want to know if I can write a check?"

"I already wrote the check," I say with a straight face. He jerks his head up, eyebrows in a set of perfectly inverted V's.

"But what I need you to do is help me," I continue in a rush before I lose his attention. "Well, help *her* more exactly, understand what she should do."

"Who is 'her', if I may be so grammatically incorrect? And with what?"

"Violence in our cities."

I see a flicker in his eyes, as if he's trying to shut down something that has already led to sleepless nights.

"There's not much one person can do, even if she's a member of City Council," he finally responds and takes a bite to let me know that's all he intends to say about that question.

"Why?"

T.K. takes a couple bites of his fish before he answers. "Because there is no consensus on what needs to be done. I think there is general agreement that unnecessary deaths have to stop.

"But we have allowed the voting booth to weaponize the debate to the point there simply isn't a debate about it. Those who spend their time, money and effort to get elected know they will be punished by the gun lobby if they vote for any restrictions at all.

"So none are willing to even discuss it."

"But what if someone didn't care about any of that," I push on him, although I see he's really not in the mood for any of this discussion.

"What if someone were willing to stand up and lay out a way to end the unnecessary violence. You're the one who is always playing out the 'What if' scenarios."

"One person doesn't get you to a majority vote in either house." T.K. keeps trying to draw this to a close.

"It does if you aren't afraid. If you speak with facts. If you put it in moral terms, and appeal to our humanity."

T.K. smiles as he always does when I use his words in a subsequent discussion. "Is that what you told Flo?"

"No," I admit. "I didn't think of it then and I'm not sure she's in a place where she could pull it off."

"Then why are you asking me now?"

“Because this is what you do. You look at situations and come up with a solution no one else has thought of.”

T.K. shakes his head. “Think about it. In 1963 the President of the United States was shot to death riding in a car in the streets of a city not far from here. The killing of the president did not even come close to changing the debate.

“If you can shoot a president without triggering a discussion, what else is there that can change the fundamental dynamics in such a way that the entrenched forces can be overcome?”

“That’s what I’m asking you to discover,” I respond using that ‘you really want to help me’ voice I reserve for only the biggest asks.

T.K. takes another bite of fish to consider my request, and that’s the signal I need to change the subject “So how was the Boys’ Club?”

T.K. sits back in his chair, apparently not intending to finish his fish, which he always does, having grown up in a household where there was never enough to eat. “It was a struggle.”

“In what respect?”

“I just couldn’t get into the flow of the game.”

That’s never happened. He loves playing ball with the kids. “What’s on your mind?”

T.K. looks at me for a long moment. “I kept seeing Deshaun on the court, studying me the way he did. Trying to figure out what I was going to do next.”

“It’s only been a few days, His presence in the game is still fresh in your mind.”

“What are you trying to say? That if I give it time, I’ll forget him? I don’t want to forget him.”

“I’m not suggesting you forget him. I’m only saying that in time you’ll find a way to manage your feelings, put your memories into perspective so you can manage them as well. So they don't interrupt your concentration, your flow."

I pause to focus. "Where was Duke in all this?"

"He was there."

"Was he struggling?"

T.K. almost laughs, "Duke doesn't struggle. He was his usual self."

"What does that mean?"

"Duke played as if nothing had happened. Played the same way he always does. Intimidates. He's physical with the kids and tries to knock them off their game physically."

"You told me you thought that was essential for these kids to learn," I point out. "So why are you criticizing him for it now?"

T.K. looks down, shakes his head. "Duke could have prevented the whole thing."

"How?"

"That night, just after Deshaun left the club, the rookie cop came by to ask Duke to ride with him since his partner had called in sick. Duke didn't want to, so the kid went out alone. Duke could have sent him back in because rookies aren't supposed to ride alone. He didn't."

"So you blame Duke for Deshaun's death."

"Not just Duke," T.K. reflects. "From what I can tell there were a whole series of choices that were made that night. Any one of them made differently and Deshaun would still be alive. So, no, I don't blame Duke, but I can't accept the fact that he, and I, since I was there but said nothing, could have prevented it."

"What are you going to do with these feelings? You see Duke every day after work. He's been your teammate there longer than any of the others. He's probably one of your best friends, although you've never treated him that way. Never even invited him over for dinner. Have you said anything to him about your feelings?"

"I don't know what to do about that."

"You know I've never been a fan."

"What?" T.K. seems surprised or confused, I can't tell which.

"Of Duke. I've never been a fan. Although I don't think I've ever even had a conversation with the man. But from everything you've said, it's always been his way or the highway.

"He uses his physical size to intimidate, he always has to play the offense. He's never one to support the rest of the team. He's there to be the leading scorer, or the one who knocks down a player who's becoming too good or too aggressive or whatever."

I see T.K. thinking about my description. "That's not entirely accurate."

"Well, if I'm wrong, tell me what I'm missing."

T.K. thinks a minute. Then I see him looking at Duke with his mind's eye. "He's always there for the kids and that's huge. Most of these kids haven't had a consistent male figure in their lives, and to have someone who is always there, always ready to play, always trying to help them better understand the game… well, that's probably the most important thing he could do."

"You're only looking at him from the kid's perspective," I point out.

"That's the perspective that talks to the future. He's trying to help them be better ball players and, through that, better people. He's trying to help them understand that someone who isn't like them can still be supportive, want to help them succeed, share with them life lessons that will help them on their journey."

“But he’s a bully.” I return to my earlier characterization of him.

“I look beyond what he says, look even beyond the exterior he puts up. I see who he is, and care only about what he does.”

“If he’s such a good person, why does he act that way?”

T.K. looks directly at me for the first time since we started this part of the discussion.

“I can’t tell you the answer to that because he’s never given me enough insight into what’s happened to him along the way to know. None of us have had it easy getting to where we are.

“I would assume his life’s journey has been no picnic either. For that reason I’m perfectly willing to give him the benefit of the doubt.”

“But he wasn’t supportive of your struggles today.”

“No, but I wasn’t expecting him to nor did I ask for his help.”

“Because you still haven’t figured out how to deal with his culpability in Deshaun’s death.”

T.K. shakes his head, “Because I haven’t figured out how to deal with my own culpability in Deshaun’s death.”

13 – REGINA BLACKWELL – MAYOR, CITY OF FORT CHRISTIAN

I'm watching as Council chambers begins to fill up. This is our regularly scheduled meeting and the first since the death of Deshaun Bush.

We knew there would be a big turnout and I put the matter on the agenda knowing it would be hopeless to try to transact any business before the inevitable discussion, so why bother?

Hopefully we can have the discussion, refer it to committee and then return to our regular business meeting.

Reverend Lindo comes in and sits directly across from me. I guess I knew he would likely do that, but hadn't been thinking about it until just now. He won't look at me, which tells me he is intending to unload on me personally and is working himself up to be able to say those things.

Another fun evening in store.

It appears that the Reverend Lindo has brought his entire congregation with him as every seat is filled, people are standing along the wall, and there are more out in the hallway who haven't been able to get in.

I wait until the scheduled time for the meeting to begin, but Flo Lopez hasn't arrived. That's unusual since she confirmed she will be here.

We have a quorum without her so better start.

"I'd like to call this meeting of the City of Fort Christian City Council to order. Madam Secretary do we have a quorum present?"

"We do," Barbara Pena, the City Secretary responds.

"With a quorum present I will move down on the agenda the approval of the minutes of our last meeting in recognition of the large number of residents who have appeared for another agenda item.

"So with concurrence of those Council members present we will go to agenda item one: discussion of the officer-involved shooting.

"I would like to make a statement prior to recognizing those in the audience who wish to speak on this matter.

"First of all, every member of Council has expressed to me their regret for what happened and sympathy for the family of Deshaun Bush. Nothing we can do at this point will bring Deshaun back to us, but Council is dedicated to completing the investigation of the events that led up to his untimely death and taking the necessary actions to ensure nothing like it can ever occur again in this city.

"Does any other member of Council wish to make an opening statement?"

I look to the other members. One after the other they shake their head. "Seeing no member wishing to make an opening comment, I will now recognize those in attendance who wish to speak to this matter."

Reverend Lindo rises and glances around the chambers before proceeding to the microphone just a few feet from his seat. "Mayor Blackwell, Council members Williams, Cochrane, Hill and…"

Flo Lopez enters the chambers from the side entrance and finds her seat. "…Lopez. Thank you for joining us this evening.

"We are here not to mourn Deshaun Bush, for we have all been doing that since we learned of the news. We will continue to mourn him. However, that is not the reason we have chosen to address Council this evening.

"We mourn the loss of a city police department that once enforced laws to keep us safe, and now has become the chief threat to our safety.

How could this happen in a city like Fort Christian? We are at a total loss for an explanation.

"And maybe no explanation is necessary since we all…" The Reverend Lindo looks around to a sea of nodding heads. "…we all expect Council will take all necessary actions to change that situation.

"The police must keep us safe, as we have no other hope of safety without them. And the police must take a deep look at themselves, a deep look at how they could become the source of our insecurity."

Having heard the Reverend's earlier comments I'm surprised at how reasonable he is being.

"The important point I would like to make is that we are watching to see what actions this Council and Mayor take. What changes result in the police department?

"How you reestablish credibility, because at the moment you have none.

"Now what does that all mean? That you have no credibility? That means you need to find something deep inside each of you. A willingness and plan that changes everything.

"And the failure to change everything will result in a change of every one of you who sits in those chairs. Each member of the police department who had any involvement in the events that led to Deshaun being needlessly murdered in his own backyard.

"If an armed black cop came into your backyard, I'm sure the cop would be the one we would be mourning tonight as each of you would shoot the cop for trespassing.

"Nothing would happen to any of you for killing a black man who happens to be a cop. So what chance do we have if your white policemen and policewomen can come into our backyards and shoot us? "

The Reverend pauses for effect. "This city has done an excellent job of hiding its racism. We've always known it was there. Too many things we have seen have been intended to keep us in our place.

"Any time we need something from this city, it never comes. Any time city services fail, our neighborhoods are the last to be serviced. And that says nothing about all the times police officers stop our young men, often for no reason other than racial profiling.

"If your children were stopped and questioned by a police officer as often as our children are, you would be in these chambers demanding change. We are here now for that very reason, to demand change. And it's a change that each of you sitting up there must endorse.

"We are all citizens of Fort Christian. There are no lesser citizens of this city. We all have one vote. And we will exercise that vote in the next election. We will be united in our vote if there is no action. We will be united in our vote if whatever action you take is ineffective.

"We are here to demand change. What you've always done is not acceptable. What you will do is what you should have been doing all along: ensure the safety of all citizens.

"Treat all citizens equally. Respond to all of us the same. Respect us the same as you would your own family. What you will do is end racism in this city, not because it's the right thing to do, but because we all know you're all racist and only your actions can save you from yourselves."

The Reverend looks at each of us now.

"I've known each of you since I moved to this unfair city several years ago. I came here because I knew this is a city that wants to be Christian in how it treats its citizens.

"It hasn't succeeded in being what it can be. But that ends now or we will elect your replacements with the same mandate, the same watchfulness from those who entrust the governance of us all to you.

"None of you owns this city. We all do, together. And we will truly make this city live up to its name, together."

Reverend Lindo smiles and turns a 360-degree circle before continuing.

"I know my friends in the audience here are all wondering where is the Reverend Lindo they know who is so articulate and passionate about what has occurred? The fighter for social justice, for equal treatment under the law.

"Where is that Reverend Lindo tonight? The answer is, my friends and neighbors deserve an opportunity to express their feelings about Deshaun's murder. They deserve an opportunity to tell you about their expectations of each of you.

"These are the people who gave you this job. These are the people you represent in that job. These are the people you must answer to because of your dereliction of duty, because of your inability to execute the office you hold in the interests of all of your constituents including Deshaun Bush." The Reverend Lindo leaves the microphone and returns to his seat.

I can't tell if the Reverend Lindo orchestrated this whole thing, but as the evening wears on it appears that the list of speakers grows. Most have reiterated one point or another made by the Reverend. But all end with the same phrase, "We are holding you accountable. Now, or at the polls we will make a change."

That part has clearly been rehearsed. I am becoming numb since there is little new being offered. I hear Jasper, our city attorney, approach me and lean over my shoulder with his cellphone. "Take a look."

I read the headline and realize someone has already posted the speech the Reverend Lindo gave this evening. He didn't read it, which means he must have memorized it and given it from memory. With the Reverend, I'm never quite sure as most of his talks seem spontaneous. I hand the phone back to Jasper and nod to him that I understand what he just showed me.

What seems like hours later, as the next speaker makes her way to the microphone I look up at the clock and realize we went into session at 6:30 and it is now past midnight with no end in sight as to the number of speakers who wish to be heard.

When council meetings go this long they tend to provide diminishing returns as we're all too tired to listen or care.

"Council members, my name is Rebekah Winston, I live at 1433 Live Oak. That's in your district, Roxanne, just so you know who's speaking to you. Anyway, you've heard what everyone's had to say.

"We're all pretty much saying the same thing to you, so you know this isn't some form letter sent to you by a bunch of people you don't know. We're not some special interest group that wants you to put into place some program for a small number of people who need help and can't afford to get one kind of service or another unless the city steps up.

"We're here because what happened woke us up. Everyone in this chamber tonight knew Deshaun Bush personally. He touched each of us in one way or another. In my case he used to carry in bags of groceries for me when I was just home from the hospital with my youngest son.

"No one sent him over to do that for me. He just happened to be walking by the first day I was home and saw me carrying the baby. He stopped by to take a peek at him and realized I had a car full of groceries.

"I didn't ask, he didn't offer, he just did it. He came by every Saturday for a month to help carry them in. You've heard a few stories about Deshaun tonight, but each of us have one. Each of us will miss him in our own way.

"What it all comes down to is that you are the only ones who can change things for us. Ensure Fort Christian is a safe city for everyone.

"And I know you think the only way you can do that is to keep tabs on the gangs, make sure they are kept under control. You think you have to harass them to keep them in line.

"Not all young black men in our city belong to gangs, but you wouldn't know it by watching what happens to all our kids. I think what I'm saying is there's got to be a better way of keeping the gangs under control. A better way to make sure we are all safe.

"Now the Rev, he tells us he thinks we ought to demand that you fire all your officers and patrolmen. Fire the detectives and Chief. The Rev, he told us the only way to end racism in this city is to have the entire police force be black men and women.

"Now I don't know anything about policing things, but I look around me and this city isn't all black, it isn't all white, we got lots of Hispanics and Asians and Muslims. We got people from all kinds of countries living here.

"So an all-black police would probably have as much trouble enforcing the law as an all-white police, at least as far as I'm concerned. But I do think it should be less white. More representative, just like you all. That's about all I got to say.

"Thank you for listening. But one more thing, we are holding you accountable. Now, or at the polls we will make a change, but I'd like to add we should make a change together if at all possible."

As Mrs. Winston leaves the microphone the next person comes forward, but I interject before she can start, "Thank your Mrs. Winston. We do appreciate you all coming out tonight and sharing your thoughts with us.

"The hour is getting late. As Mrs. Winston has stated, we know this isn't some form letter campaign. We know how upset everyone is at what happened.

"So I think I'd like to propose that those of you who have not yet had an opportunity to speak tonight, if you would send us an email, with your name and address and any comments you'd like to make, I will make sure all members of Council receive that correspondence.

"You can send it to my email if you'd like, it's up on the screen behind me now. I know many or most of you have to go to work tomorrow just as all of us on Council do.

"We don't want to deprive anyone of an opportunity to communicate your thoughts, so I'll let one more person speak. I'll also place this subject on the agenda for the next Council meeting so anyone who wants to appear can present their thoughts at that time."

The woman at the microphone looks at Reverend Lindo, who rises and comes to take her place.

"Thank you, Mayor Blackwell and Council members. I believe you have had an opportunity to hear just a small number of your constituents who have deep feelings about the murder of Deshaun Bush at the hands of one of your own.

"I think those who are with you tonight have done an excellent job of expressing the need for change and the determination that we all have in seeing that change occur.

"It can either be something we bring about cooperatively or we will be forced to remove you from office by voting you out. I have to believe that none of you wanted something like the events of last week to happen. But we have to look at the opportunity this affords us.

"Change is essential. Yes, as Rebekah mentioned, I personally believe every police officer in this city should be fired for what happened. Yes, I personally believe an all-black police force would be the best thing for this city.

"But I'm not the one with the power to make that change. You are, and we are holding you accountable. Now, or at the polls we will make a change. Thank you."

14 – T.K. JEFFERSON

Sina and I call on the Bushes at their home.

I didn't realize how small their house was until we pull up in front and see the McMansion next door. Guess I'd not paid any attention to the gentrification that's going on in this part of town.

I see the neighbor drive into his driveway. A white family in a big house in a predominantly black neighborhood. Pushing aside people like the Bushes so executives like me who are living on the outskirts of the city don't have to drive so far to get to work downtown.

Another source of the friction between blacks and whites. Why is it blacks are always being marginalized by whites? But then I realize, it's not just the blacks who are being marginalized. It's anyone else.

Money talks and the white people in town have the money. That permits them to do pretty much what they want to without worrying about anyone else.

We walk up to the front door and ring the bell. Since we'd called ahead, Mr. Bush answers the door promptly.

"Mr. and Mrs. Jefferson. Thank you for calling on us. Come in, please."

I shake his hand and Sina hands him a coffee cake she had made for them.

"Thank you for this, smells good. Lots of cinnamon, just the way I like it."

Mrs. Bush comes into the hallway and gestures for us to follow her into the tiny living room. "Would you like something to drink? Coffee or tea maybe?"

"No thanks," I begin. "We don't want to take up too much of your time, but just wanted to come by and say how sorry we are about Deshaun. You raised a fine son who made all of us who knew him proud to be his friends."

"Please sit down," Mrs. Bush insists. "You were special to Deshaun. He loved to play ball with you because you helped him to be better in so many ways."

"I wanted to share with you this memory I have of him," I begin as we sit. "Deshaun couldn't have been more than six or seven when he came down to the Boy's Club the first time I remember him.

"He went right to the closet where we kept the balls. He came out carrying a basketball that must have been nearly as big as he was then. I'm not sure he could see over it when he was carrying it around. But he was a natural, teaching himself how to dribble better than anyone, even the boys who were much older.

"He was determined, even on that first day. He was determined that he was going to learn to play that game and he wasn't going to be satisfied until he'd mastered it. Until he could play with anyone. That was Deshaun. The Deshaun who grew into quite a ball player and quite a special person."

"Wouldn't have happened if you'd not taken a liking to him, helped him," Mr. Bush responds.

"Deshaun was motivated to be successful, regardless of who helped him. I was just privileged to be there when he came in looking for someone to explain how to play the game."

"We never properly thanked you," Mrs. Bush remembers.

"For what? It's the duty of everyone to help bright young minds like Deshaun any way we can."

"For the scholarship your company gave him," Mrs. Bush clarifies. "It made all the difference in him getting accepted at Baylor. We knew you did that for him. No one else ever did anything like that.

I've wanted to thank you since he was accepted for making it possible for him to go to college."

"Deshaun embodied the qualities that scholarship was designed for. All I did was recommend him and he did all the rest."

I'm thinking it's time to leave and start to get up, but Mr. Bush motions for us to stay a bit longer,

"I've been wanting to ask you a question. I know you travel all over the world. You've been a lot of places I can't even begin to imagine. But it seems to me that the police in different parts of the world don't carry guns. Is that true?"

I settle back down. "Yes."

"Is it common? Like, are there more places where police don't carry them than carry them?" Mr. Bush seems to be focused on understanding why his son was shot to death and whether that's something particular to Fort Christian.

"I haven't researched that question so I can't really answer it for you. But I can affirm that I've been in many places where not all of the police are armed. You know the whole image of the Wild West was the peculiarity that everyone wore guns here in the latter part of the 19th Century.

"The truth is that only ranchers carried guns, and that was mostly to deal with predators killing their cattle. Gun fights occurred, but not nearly as often as depicted."

"Then why do the police need to carry weapons?" Mr. Bush is still looking for the answer to the question of why Deshaun was killed by a police officer when he was doing nothing wrong.

"I don't know, but you can be sure I will look into that question after this conversation."

"I would so appreciate understanding why. It just seems to me it's asking for bad things to happen. Now I know some police got to have access to weapons for those instances where crazy people go about shooting up things, killing people for no reason.

"Yeah, in those instances a policeman probably has to have a weapon to respond. But leave the weapon in the trunk unless someone's gonna die if the policeman can't stop a bad situation. Can't bring a shooter down without it.

"You know the first time someone used the phrase 'suicide by cop' I had absolutely no idea what the person was saying. But someone explained to me that someone who wants to die deliberately goes about shooting things up because they know the cop will have to shoot him or her to restore order.

"But if most cops don't have weapons, that won't happen, either. No more suicide by cop. Don't you see what I'm saying?"

"I do, Mr. Bush," I respond. "I see you've been giving this a lot of thought. I just wish you never had to. Now I need to do the same so at some point you and I can have another conversation where maybe I can give you answers to your questions.

"Where you and I can have a conversation about what might be the answer to prevent anything like what happened from ever occurring in Fort Christian again," I try to conclude.

"I see they had a meeting at City Hall to talk about what to do. But it appears that all that happened is a whole lot of folks came by to say something needs to change.

"Don't know what the city fathers will do with that information. They've known for a long time that things weren't quite right.

"Did you know that Duke Marion stopped Deshaun once when he was still in high school? Duke had been playing ball with Deshaun for more than a decade when this happened. He'd taught Deshaun to be tough, like him.

"Something Deshaun needed to understand to be more confident. Duke gave him a ticket. Wrote him up for failure to signal or some bullshit charge. Deshaun had to pay fifty dollars for his fine. For Deshaun that was a lot of money back then."

"You made him pay for it out of his own money," I seek to confirm.

"I didn't have it to pay for him," Mr. Bush shakes his head. "Besides, that would have sent the wrong message. He got the ticket, he has to pay it. Simple. It's what he would have to do when he's out on his own."

"You think if it was some white kid that Duke Marion stopped, he wouldn't have given him the ticket?"

"If it was a failure to signal? Not likely from what I've heard or seen. But that's what I'm saying. The police got this notion in their head that they got to keep order by continually touching the kids, letting them know they're being watched, that the police are just looking for a reason to bring them in, put them in jail, send them off to prison. That's just not right."

"What do you think the police need to do differently?" I decide to ask since Mr. Bush seems to want to talk further about the situation even though it won't help his son now.

"Learn how to talk to people would be a good start. I mean now it's all about fear. A policeman comes up to you, nothing good is going to result. That's for most everyone.

"If you're a black kid, you can be sure you're going to be roughed up. Told to spread 'em while the officer checks you over for drugs or weapons."

"That ever happen to Deshaun?"

"The only time he was pulled over and not told to spread 'em was when Duke Marion stopped him."

"So Duke did treat him differently than the other cops." I'm still trying to confirm, still trying to get over my surprise that Duke would treat Deshaun the way Mr. Bush described.

"Still wasn't right what he did. I know Duke Marion was out there playing ball and showing kids like Deshaun how to get better. But I don't get how he's able to switch on and off a relationship he has with someone. Maybe that's why he never got married, 'I love ya hunny, but I gotta take ya in because you're a litterer.' or some such bullshit."

A second negative opinion of Duke. I need to reconsider, try to understand why people are cautious about him. Especially Sina. "Were there any other negative experiences with Duke and Deshaun?"

"None he ever mentioned, but you know Deshaun. He didn't spend two seconds on any of that. He didn't have time to dwell on negativity. He was only focused on how to get better and how to make his teammates better out on the court.

"If Duke Marion had done stuff, I don't think I would have ever known about it. Only reason I knew about the ticket is he asked to borrow the money to pay it, and of course I had to ask how he got it."

"Let me ask another question." I get back to his earlier point. "If police officers weren't allowed to carry guns except in the trunk of their car, how are they supposed to enforce the laws?"

"How many people are there in this city?" Mr. Bush gets excited now, "Over a million. How many times does a cop need a weapon to enforce a law? Not very damn often.

"If cops were experts in de-escalation of situations. If they were taught how to negotiate resolutions, to have to convince people to do what they already know is right, maybe we can make a start.

"All I know for sure is if that Patrolman Webster hadn't had a gun in his hand that night, Deshaun would be sitting where you are right this minute."

"It seems to me that it takes a certain kind of mindset to want to be a policeman< I think through aloud. "And that mindset is all around 'enforcement' rather than de-escalating hostile situations. I don't know many people who enjoy cooling down verbal or physical fights or disagreements.

"And to go into them unarmed? I'm sure we are where we are because policemen found it easier to get to a resolution if they are armed.

"But as I think about it, it must be less likely that someone will take them on, because in the days of body cameras anyone taking on a cop is going to jail. That's an interesting question. How much has technology changed the nature of police actions? The body camera is there to protect both the person involved and the policeman. I'm going to have to think more about this."

Mr. Bush has been watching me talk my way through this conundrum.

"You almost sound like you really want to find a solution to the problem. You may be the only person I've met who seems to be taking it seriously. Like thinking it through rather than just saying there's nothing you can do about it.

"With the police unions and the businessmen wanting to deal with the gang violence and the fact that the city government is mostly white. A white mayor, white police chief. They care about their own, they don't care about anyone who's not one of them. Even the black members of council got there because they sucked up to the white folks. They didn't talk about black issues."

"Flo did," Sina interjects. "I was her campaign manager. She talked about all the issues, black, white, Hispanic, Asian, Muslim… inequality, lack of opportunity for certain folks and how to make the playing field equal."

"You just proved my point," Mr. Bush points out. "She needed a white woman running her campaign so all the white folks would say she's okay to get her elected."

15 – T.K. JEFFERSON

Brad Jones is a big guy, not only because he's a Vice President of my company, but he's also six foot six in his bare feet and well over two-fifty. He's built solid and as a tight end in college, he loved to run over defenders.

Kind of reminds me of Duke sometimes, although Duke would never be able to stand up to Brad in a clash of the titans, if you will. The reason I'm thinking about Brad is because he's standing in my doorway looking at me and waiting for me to finish the call I'm on.

"That's correct, Mustapha. We need to gather all the cost information before we make a recommendation on the next phase. Yes, I know the costs have been unusually high, but we have to take the data we have on the reservoir size and determine if we can recapture the overruns in phase two."

Brad doesn't indicate a reaction to my discussion, which is probably good, unless he's so focused on the message he intends to deliver next that this discussion with Mustapha is not important in comparison.

"That's right," I move to conclude the call. "When you have all the cost data send it over and we'll sit down and walk through it. I know we have the reservoir estimates, so I'll make sure we have them when you come by. That's great. Chat soon."

And I hang up. I look to the door to let Brad know I'm finished, but he has already started into my office, closing the door behind him. Never a good sign because it means he's here on a personnel issue. I wonder who.

"I'm sorry about Deshaun," he begins, which catches me off guard. We rarely talk about much other than work. Brad's personable and very knowledgeable of our business, but he just never seemed to want to socialize with the help since he's married into the family that controls the business.

He's always looking up and not down. "I remembered you submitted the scholarship request for him."

I'm surprised he would remember. I suspect his administrative assistant may have said something about it. Her son played with Deshaun in middle school, but didn't make the high school team. She's worked hard to find a sport her son was good at. She was probably more surprised than anyone when it turned out he was really good at math.

That was a clear disappointment when her husband had played college ball. I nod and say "Thanks," almost so quietly that I'm not sure I heard me.

"You want to talk about it?"

This is totally unlike Brad. Must be someone in Human Resources told him he needed to come talk with me. This is even more surprising since Human Resources seems to only focus on pay and benefits.

When things get good on pricing they go into their hire mode and when the price drops, they lay people off. But other than that I never see them.

"It's not really a work situation, so probably more appropriate over a beer after work."

"I think not," he says. "You seem to be struggling… in your work. You're not as laser focused as usual. Like you're distracted or something. And since this is so unlike you, and has only been noticeable since the shooting… well, I have to assume that maybe the two are related somehow."

"No problem, I'll fix it," I respond immediately.

"No… I don't think you will. Have you ever lost someone who was important to you before?"

"My grandparents," I confirm. "Both of them."

"And people talked about how they were getting older… probably for years. Lots of discussion about how to help them as their health failed them. Did they end up in a nursing home?"

"For a short time," I remember and voice my remembrance.

"So you had a long time to prepare for their passing," Brad is setting up his point, which I can already guess.

"And I had no time with Deshaun, is that where you're going? That I'm struggling with his death because it was so sudden and unexpected and… needless."

Brad displays a crooked smile, as if he's pleased I could see his point but doesn't want to seem insensitive to feelings I obviously have about the death of Deshaun Bush.

"You've never had to cope with a sudden loss like this. Most people find it becomes a distraction for a while as they try to make sense of it. What I'm trying to do is help you through that distraction phase. Get you back in the saddle so your work doesn't suffer as you come to terms with events."

I can't believe his only thought is how to get me to instantly snap back and be the same person I was a week ago. I'm not. I have a scar that is only beginning to heal over the hole in me that represents the good feelings I had for Deshaun.

The memories of all the hours we spent together helping him become a better athlete, better ball player and a better person. The discussions we had about so many things that had absolutely nothing at all to do with what we were doing.

But they were discussions that naturally came about because of his curiosity and the occasional tidbits I would throw his way about faraway places I'd been to.

Deshaun had virtual wanderlust. He saw all these strange and exotic places in the media, he listened to me talk about being there and he decided early on that he wanted to visit them as well.

But the opportunity had never presented itself because his family was poor and just saving enough so he could go to college was a struggle. Still, Deshaun knew he would get there someday. Basketball would make that life possible. Maybe that's why he worked so hard to make sure it would pay-off.

"Do you need a day?" Brad asks. "Go home and talk with Sina about your feelings. Get them out. Look at them from all sides and decide how you're going to get on with life? If you need a day, just say so. I'm sure I can work with Mustapha to make sure he gets the analysis done by Friday. You don't need to worry about that."

"I'm not worried, Brad," I respond, trying to not sound upset by the way he's approached me. But maybe I'm sounding too cavalier about it. How in the world do I thread this needle?

"I don't need the time. I really appreciate your concern, but you won't see any difference in my focus from this point forward. I know my priorities and I know you count on me to deliver what I always have."

Brad looks at me as if he's trying to figure out what I'm really saying to him. Another first for a guy whose future is guaranteed. He really doesn't need to worry about me or his job either. Daddy will ensure he's well taken care of because that's the only way Daddy can ensure his daughter is properly taken care of.

I suppose if I'd married Leticia rather than Sina I'd behave much the same way he does. But Leticia always liked big guys. As a skinny basketball player, she wasn't interested in me. And as I think of it, I'm glad it worked out that way, because if it hadn't I'd never have had my life together with Sina. A life where we really had to pull together just to make it in those early years.

There was no extra money for even a movie once in a while. Guess I can't imagine what it would have been like to not have to worry about money. And that's fine because I have Sina.

Brad finishes looking at me. Apparently his curiosity only goes so far since it's not followed by a question. But then he pivots on me, "You still play ball, don't you?"

"I do."

"Not in a league or semi pro or anything?"

"I play with the kids at the Boys Club several times a week. They give me a run for my money."

Brad nods, "High school kids. I thought you were really good or something."

Another shot, is he telling me he'd rather get rid of me? How do I respond to this? Guess I just change the subject, "Looking for lessons for yourself or your son?"

"No, my kid's a quarterback, at least so far. You know how small Letica is. Well, Junior didn't get my size, so we're trying him out at the skill positions first. Might stand a better chance at a Division One school.

"No, there's this charity event where they decided to have a basketball tournament. Leticia is the chairperson. I tried to convince her she needed to do a flag football or seven on seven event, but she was outvoted.

"Apparently there's a few adult basketball leagues playing in town so it was easy to get companies to sponsor them because they have younger employees who play regularly.

"Well, as you know, we don't have a program like that for our employees and Leticia's making a deal out of us needing to have a team that can actually win this thing. The old man remembered you played and suggested I get you to captain the team. See if you can find some guys who can play."

This is quite a turn. Guess he grudgingly needs my help so that's why he was willing to come down and chat about Deshaun and offer to give me a day. Then I think about his request. He's right. I'm not aware of any employees who are playing in a league or something.

"I'll have to do some asking around to see if anyone is playing. So let me ask a question. Does this have to be a team of employees or can it be a team that has others on it but is sponsored by the company?"

"Does it matter?"

"Finding a group of athletes here that we could practice up as a team would take a while. But if it's a team that the company sponsors, I could probably convince my Boy's Club adult team to come play in the tournament."

"You have an adult team that plays with the kids?"

"They all played college ball, so they know each other and they play regularly. We could definitely do some damage against most adult league teams. We're used to the high school kids who aren't old and lame and needing rest.

"We run them and they run us. I would be willing to wager that we're in better shape and can anticipate each other better than most of the adult teams playing around town." Never thought about it in those terms, but at least it sounds logical.

"Anyone else on your team work here besides you?" Brad seems to be trying to figure this loophole out.

"Not at the moment, but I'm sure we could add a few and even if all they do is sit on the bench most of the time it may make it more legitimate if they were expecting them to be teams of employees."

"Seems to me we hired that kid out of UT who was on the varsity team. Didn't play all that much, but he made the team, so he must have some idea how to play."

I suddenly put a face with his description, "Alvarez. Yeah. He was their backup center. Tall kid, what is he? Maybe seven-foot-two?"

I see Brad has no idea. Apparently this was another idea someone had given him as he was trying to figure out how to make Leticia happy, a task I don't envy him.

"If you need to take the day off tomorrow to put this team together, just go ahead. As I said, I can work with Mustapha to make sure the business case is ready on Friday. You want to run practice late afternoons, we could probably arrange that, too."

"Why don't you join the team?" I decide to test just how much he wants to make his wife happy.

"Me?" Brad looks horrified. He's big and strong but fifteen years away from lifting weights and running regularly. "About all I'd be good for is sitting on the bench and handing out beers at half-time."

"I'm serious," I push him since the table has turned in my favor for at least the moment. "You know Shaq. He won a few NBA Finals even though he wasn't very mobile, particularly in his latter years.

"I could see posting you up under the basket on both ends and letting the other teams come at you. Be just like college football, only now you get to play the linebacker."

"You really think I could do that?" Brad considers himself without pads running around an indoor court. He must think of the cheerleaders or something because he smiles for just an instant, but then it disappears and he notes, "Leticia'd have to choose the uniforms."

16 – REGINA BLACKWELL – MAYOR, CITY OF FORT CHRISTIAN

This is a press conference I had hoped to delay.

We have the facts from the investigation, but I'm not comfortable with the conclusions. No one assumes responsibility and the report tries to make it sound like a series of bad choices, but doesn't recommend any further action on the part of the city.

I just don't think that's going to fly.

Chief Andrews is standing to my left and Melody Simmons, the young and fashionable blonde, (what else?) Communications Director for the city is on my right. Melody made the arrangements for this press conference and identified the topic to ensure we would have a good turnout. She was also a cheerleader for Texas A&M football and that comes through every time she talks with you. Mile-wide smile and oh so pleasant.

"Mayor Blackwell would like to make a few comments," Melody begins the conference. "Then Chief Andrews will fill you in on the details before we go to questions. Mayor Blackwell?"

"Thank you all for coming over this morning on relatively short notice. We received the report of the investigation into the officer-involved shooting of Deshaun Bush. We wanted to provide the high-level details of what we now know, and answer your questions at the end.

Council members all have had a chance to review the document, although we have not had a meeting to discuss the findings and conclusions. The report contains a series of recommendations that will be taken into account as we discuss further. Chief Andrews will provide the details."

I step aside as Chief Andrews comes to the microphone holding his marked-up copy of the report. Jasper informed me that one of the deputies had confided that Chief Andrews had a chance to comment on drafts of various sections before the report was finalized, even though it was supposed to be an independent investigation.

But when I learned that Duke and Walter had conducted the on-site investigation the next morning and had re-written the physical evidence section I knew this was going to be a problem.

"Good morning," The Chief begins, staring down at the report and not making eye contact. "A diverse team of investigators have gone over every available shred of evidence we could find, not only immediately after the incident, but in the cold light of day the next morning.

"From my reading, it is clear to me that the investigators went into this task with an open mind. They let the evidence lead them to conclusions, since there were no surviving witnesses who could either corroborate or refute any of the assumptions that had to be made.

"There were a number that were crucial to the conclusions, there were a number that were crucial to the recommendations."

Tex Anthony raises his hand, but the Chief continues. "In the first press conference, we went over the chronology of events. The report has confirmed those details."

"Chief!" Tex interrupts.

Chief Andrews looks up, displeased. "If you let me finish this can be quick."

"I don't want quick, Chief, I want accurate. I want insight as to why these recommendations were made."

"That should become evident to you when you've had a chance to read the report," The Chief is barely disguising his contempt for Tex. They've had a few run-ins in the past, usually because the Chief will admit to no problems with the department that he isn't aware of and working on fixing.

"Chief Andrews, in a single sentence what is the primary conclusion of the investigation?" Tex presses since this is an answer the Chief does not intend to give in his current summary.

"Mr. Anthony, there are a total of fifteen recommendations in the report. Frankly, I have not determined that any one of the recommendations would have altered the outcome of the encounter that night. Taken together there is a greater probability that…"

Tex isn't waiting, "Fifteen things all need to change to have any effect on a department that is in chaos."

"That's an inflammatory characterization that is totally and wholly inaccurate," Chief Andrews responds with more than annoyance in his tone of voice. If I didn't know better, I would characterize it as outright hostility. "If you print that I'll make sure the city attorney sues you for… slander and deliberate mischaracterization of a public institution."

"Is that a criminal offense, or just offensive to you?" Tex shoots back. If they were both armed and on the street it would be like the 1870s all over again.

"That would be for a court to decide," Chief Andrews retreats from his threat, probably recognizing that Jasper isn't a fan of his and might not be willing to take the case. "Let me finish and then you can ask questions."

Tex gestures for the Chief to continue, which he does, "Please hold your comments and questions to the end so we can get the basic facts to you. The five significant findings were, as a result of understaffing, which has been ongoing in the department for several years, on the night in question, Patrolman Webster was assigned to patrol alone, with instructions to see if he could find an off-duty officer to accompany him.

"Patrolman Webster had conversations with three off-duty officers, none of whom were available. As a result Patrolman Webster proceeded to traffic duty on Main Street, which was deemed by dispatch as the least problematic for a recruit to manage alone."

Chief Andrews glances back at me to see how big my frown is from this pseudo root cause they put into the report as a causative factor. He must be satisfied as he nods once before turning back.

"The second significant finding is that Patrolman Webster had left the duty assignment at approximately eleven-thirty to patrol a nearby neighborhood. He did not report this to dispatch.

"The third significant finding is that when the neighbor of the Bush family reported his alarm system being triggered by movement in the Bush family backyard, the dispatcher did not attempt to ascertain who or what might be present, choosing instead to make a report and have an officer investigate.

"At this same time, Patrolman Webster was closest to the Bush residence because he was not on traffic patrol on Main Street as instructed by dispatch."

I see Tex shaking his head. I'm assuming he's dissatisfied that the Chief is suggesting the neighbor should have investigated, putting some blame on someone other than the department. Chief Andrews continues.

"The fourth significant finding is that upon a visual surveillance of the premise, Patrolman Webster did not wait for backup, emerged from his cruiser and moved into position to confront the intruder in the backyard of the Bush residence.

"Patrolman Webster failed to identify himself as an armed policeman when he confronted the intruder.

"The final significant finding is that the victim in this case was holding a cellphone in such a manner that on a dark night, after midnight, Patrolman Webster mistook that cellphone for a weapon.

"That the victim, for whatever reason, decided to lower the cellphone in such a manner that Patrolman Webster mistook his action as a threatening move, which may have resulted in a weapon discharging towards Patrolman Webster."

I see Tex about to jump out of his chair, but Zana whispers something to him, apparently in an attempt to calm him down and keep him focused on the report.

Tex shakes his head and stands, "Chief Andrews. Of the five significant findings you blame one on the neighbor who did not investigate the detected movement in a neighbor's back yard and a second on the victim who was such a scofflaw that he was holding a cellphone, and as I remember, he was talking with his parents at the time of the events.

"Two of the findings were that a young recruit who, by your own admission, should not have been patrolling by himself, deliberately left his assigned post to cruise a neighborhood, which placed him closest to the Bush residence and once there, he deliberately proceeded to investigate even after being told to wait for backup.

"Your final significant finding is that the department is understaffed, a condition you allege has existed for many years and yet it has not previously led to this kind of massive breakdown in discipline and effective response.

"What is the culpability of the department in this report? You would have me believe it is none. That the department did exactly what it was supposed to do.

"The fault lies strictly and completely with City Council for not permitting you to hire more officers; a neighbor who used good judgment; a victim who used his cellphone, and a wildly undisciplined unsupervised recruit who made two bad choices. Does this sound anything like a thorough investigation?"

I can't let that characterization be printed and Chief Andrews is only digging a deeper hole, so I step up and push the Chief aside.

"Good morning, Tex, Zana. I know you haven't received copies of the report as yet, and I apologize for that. The copies are being made as we speak and should be here for you to take with you at the end of the session.

"Please read the report carefully. The characterization of the findings you just made does considerable injustice to the report's findings and recommendations.

"And while the report is far from perfect, we are faced with a situation where we have to make assumptions about many aspects of what happened that night. The only witness did not survive.

"That is a tragedy on many levels because, were he with us, he could clear up many aspects where the physical evidence did not corroborate the testimony of those in the department who were involved, which included not only Patrolman Webster, but the dispatcher and the backup team who arrived within minutes of the shooting.

"It involved the several officers Patrolman Webster sought to ride along with him that evening. It involved the training officers who instructed Patrolman Webster on correct procedure and tactics. So you see, there is much more in the report than what was discussed in this high-level summary."

Tex shakes his head, Zana says something to him I can't hear and again Tex shakes his head. Apparently Zana is not on the same page as Tex.

"Mayor Blackwell. Chief Andrews, who works for you…"

"He works for the city of Fort Christian, Mr. Anthony," I need to correct him.

"But you are the person who evaluates him and signs off on his fitness and performance reviews."

"I do, in cooperation with the members of Council, our Human Resources department and the community advisory board for police-community relations."

"This report allegedly throws you and Council under the bus. What do you have to say to that?"

"I would hope you will read the report and not just the findings and recommendations," I can't get into this since it is clearly an attempt to influence the outcome of police union contract negotiations currently underway.

"Let me just say that Council takes the matter of public safety and law enforcement very seriously. It's one of the most important functions of city government. We look at data. Lots of data, about the effectiveness of our department and benchmark it against other cities, not only those that are comparable in size, but those that are larger and those that are smaller.

"There's even a special group of Texas cities we look at to ensure we are not understaffing, and not spending taxpayer dollars on toys that don't materially add to public safety."

"Is that the nature of the dispute between you and your police department? Toys?"

"Who said there's a dispute?" I push back as I can see the story that's emerging in Tex's mind and that's probably why Zena is trying to temper him.

"The Chief threw you under the bus, the report points a finger at you and Council in its first finding, at least that was the first finding the Chief referred to. I'd say there's a dispute."

"Mr. Anthony, you've been around the city government for several years now," I begin to try to diffuse things.

"You've watched us transparently create a city budget each year that allocates resources to the competing departments of the city and other initiatives to make Fort Christian a better place to live.

"There is always a certain tension when different groups seek additional resources and the taxpayers insist on keeping the budget flat. That's not what I would depict as a dispute. It's the healthy tension that protects citizen interests."

"You're not going to see healthy tension resulting from these events, you're going to see pitched battles," Tex responds, "The sides are lining up. Weapons have been chosen, tactics are being planned. All I can tell you is the City of Fort Christian will never be the same."

17 – REVEREND LEROY LINDO, PASTOR SECOND BAPTIST CHURCH FORT CHRISTIAN

As I finish reading the front-page story entitled, 'Chaos at City Hall', I realize that being reasonable is not going to change a thing. Veiled threats apparently were not enough.

Over six hours of constituents making the same plea went unrecognized, unheard, or so it would seem. A report that blames the victim more than the department that fosters racism?

That's just not acceptable.

But before I organize a protest march, maybe I ought to read the report. That way I can be much more specific in my demands. But then again from the tone of this story, it sounds like the reporter who wrote the article did read it.

Dismissed most of it as a whitewash, and that's a literal term he used for a not so subtle condemnation of the department and the whole city government that supports it.

I call Kesha Foster, who is the chairperson of my Lay Counsel and the best organizer I've ever met. "Kesha, good morning to you. I hope I am not disturbing you so early in the day."

"You're not disturbing me, but from what I read I have just cause to be. I must assume that is the reason for your call?"

"How long will it take you to organize the biggest turnout this city has ever seen?"

"An hour, but I would prefer to do it after work tonight. That would maximize the numbers and set us up for the morning news. I want people to be hearing about this over their morning coffee and during their morning drive when they can't escape the news cycle.

Make people deal with it for the whole day afterwards."

"How would you stage it?"

"Same as last time. Start at the park and march to City Hall. Only this time, if I work things right, we will fill the street from the park to City Hall and when everyone arrives for your oration, you will have the largest audience anyone could want."

"The city fathers and mothers on that council will not be able to ignore us as they apparently did in that report. I think they deliberately wanted to insult me.

"Make me think we're the problem, not them. How could the city let them write a report like that? I must be missing something. Maybe that reporter got the whole thing right. There's chaos in City Hall and they just don't know how to manage the racists in their police department, even though we've been pointing to the problem for a decade or more."

"You have insights I do not." I decide the way to really fire her up is to make her think about how long the racism has been affecting people of color in Fort Christian. I've heard tales of events, but only anecdotal tales.

Kesha hesitates a moment and then is very quiet in remembrance, "My father told me of times when he was stopped and questioned about minor incidents.

"He was only a teenager, just walking to and from his afterschool job at the auto parts store over on Industrial Road. The cops who would stop him knew who he was. They knew he didn't have anything to do with whatever had happened.

"It was just one of their scare tactics. Shake him up. Make him think they were going to take him in and question him at police headquarters. Then all his friends would think he must know something about the events. That maybe he told the police something.

"They kept on picking him up. Then his friends would stay away for a week or more, until it became clear that whatever the police learned had come from someone else.

"He had to live with that public shaming of him. That's what the cops of this city were doing. Public shaming of him, just because of the color of his skin, not who he was or what he did."

I'd not heard that story before. "How did your father get them to stop harassing him?"

"He never really did." Kesha responds. "But when he graduated from high school and got a full-time job, one of the first things he did was buy a car so he didn't have to walk to and from work. He figured that if he wasn't out there walking, the cops would be less likely to single him out.

"They would still stop him from time-to-time. But not nearly as often and people apparently thought the police were harassing him for traffic violations because his friends were less likely to avoid him."

"It sounds like to me that the police of this city have had a serious psychological impact on your father. Does he still talk about it much?"

"They destroyed his confidence," she responds bitterly. "He is a very smart man, but he got the message early that he needed to stay in his place. You know what that does to a man?

"Do you have any idea what it's like to know you can do more, be more, contribute more, but you don't dare? You don't want to look out of the fox hole, because you're expecting the police are sitting there in their shiny patrol-cars, just waiting to haul your ass off to jail for the most minor of offenses?"

As I listen I start to formulate the speech I want to give. "You're looking for some oratory to tell the police that we aren't going to be intimidated, we aren't going to sit idly by while they whitewash events and our community?"

"I expect you to climb to new heights tonight, Reverend Lindo. And I know you're more than capable of doing just that," and Kesha is gone. I hang up as well, still pulling threads together.

Kesha outdid herself. The park is filled with angry voices, trying to be heard above the others who are all trying to express their states of disbelief, outrage and personal affront. There easily has to be more than twice the number from the other night.

Now I'm not intending to ask people to speak tonight. If I do my job, they won't need to do anything other than agree with me with their applause and shouts of support.

I'm pleased to see placards scattered throughout. Kesha let people know that tonight is not going to be just another walk in the park and statement of expectations. The city has already ignored us once. They will not be able to ignore us after tonight.

As I walk through the growing crowd, I stop to shake hands and recognize members of my congregation. If they're not all here, most of the regulars in attendance on Sundays are. That's gratifying. "Hello. Thank you so much for coming out tonight."

"You going to give them hell, Rev?" is the response of more than one.

"Fire and brimstone, brother. Fire and brimstone. 'Cause that's where they're goin' if they don't listen to us."

I find Kesha with nearly the entire lay council on the corner nearest City Hall.

"Evening all. It would appear you have struck a chord with our friends, brothers and sisters, they would all join us in this cause. Were the signs a suggestion or is that spontaneous?"

Kesha has a twinkle in her eye, "I think I may have mentioned something about this being a sign-friendly event when I talked with my friends today."

I look at my phone to see what time it has gotten to be. Six-forty-five. The designated time, expecting a fifteen-minute march. "Then I think it's time to begin."

Kesha moves to my right and the rest of the lay council members form a line across the street. Those closest to us fall in behind and we start down the street. I glance over my shoulder and notice the number of signs is much greater than I recognized. I deliberately don't turn further, even though I would like to read them. I'll have plenty of time to do that once we get to City Hall.

"Fine evening for a walk," Kesha notes. "Perfect weather to foretell the coming storm."

I look up at the sky. She's right. Storm clouds are gathering. "I may have to keep this short or we may all have our enthusiasm dampened."

"You go as long as it takes, Rev," Kesha responds with a determination behind her smile.

I'm thinking about the allusions I've considered for my speech. Kesha has brought to my attention just now that there are others I should work in. I just need to decide where and when they will fit.

That's never been a problem for me. Once I get going, things seem to just flow. And the longer I go, the more I raise the temperature of my expression.

As we get closer to the steps where I intend to deliver my remarks I see there are camera trucks parked nearby. Cameramen and reporters have set up to ensure they get the angles they want. I see Tex Anthony already making notes in his phone, head down, working his thumbs much faster than I could as he records his initial thoughts and impressions.

This growing crowd has to be noteworthy for his story. That was the idea behind waiting. Get absolutely everyone out here, in the street, marching to a resolution, marching for recognition of our grievances, marching in unity to demonstrate that the white community can no longer keep us down.

The first row of marchers join me at the top of the steps. We turn around and watch those behind us, carrying their signs high, fill the square and streets around City Hall.

Kesha has arranged a speaker system so I can be sure to be heard. I walk towards the microphone and just look out over the sea of signs, some reading 'Impeach Everyone', 'Fire the Chief', 'Justice for Deshaun', and variations on those themes.

Maybe that's how I start. I wait just another minute until the crowd has settled in.

"I want to thank everyone who has joined me here tonight, for we together have a solemn message to deliver. That message is hand lettered on a thousand signs I see amongst you. A message that what has been will be no longer. Look up! Storm clouds are gathering. This will be no prairie downpour. This will be thunder and lightning that's not been seen here since the creation.

"We will turn this city into scorched earth if our demands are not heard. We will ensure that not one person involved in the deliberate assassination of Deshaun Bush calls Fort Christian home when we rest from the long journey ahead.

"These events have served as a catalyst. You have awakened the sleeping giant of outrage that has been growing in the hearts and minds of all of those you see here tonight, and the thousands of others who would be with us if they could.

"We will not go peacefully into the night when this evening is over. We will not take up the routine of living our lives in this city. Nothing will be routine anymore!

"Just today I have been reminded about how long and deep-seated the racism is in our police department. And that is what is just so incredible to me. This is 'our' police department, but they act and behave as if it were not.

"That stops tonight.

"Our police are here to serve and protect us, not just whom they choose, when they choose to do so. The issue is respect. Our police do not respect us.

"Our city council members do not respect us, even though we are the ones who put them into their positions of power and authority.

"Our mayor does not respect us, for she hides in her office while Fort Christian burns.

"Our mayor does not respect the principle of representative government, believing she only has to represent those she chooses to side with in any given discussion.

"We are here to remind the Mayor that representative government means you represent all interests in your community. You do not take sides. You take actions that are in the best interests of all citizens, not just those who live in the rich white enclaves away from the poor, and those of us who do not look just like them.

"We are at an inflection point. Change will occur because the status quo cannot continue. We will simply not permit it.

"I mentioned the signs amongst us state our demands. I hope you are writing them down, for we will be attending every meeting of city government, checking off who listens, who asks questions, who is legitimately trying to understand what life is like in this city for those of us who do not live on your street.

"We are going to note who proposes actions that will deliver justice to the Bush family and demonstrate that the bad old days are over.

"We live in this city together. You've had more than enough time to make it a paradise on earth. But instead, you have made it a living hell for those of us here tonight, and those who live in our neighborhoods.

"Now it will be our turn to end the nightly phantasms of Satan, dancing on the graves of our loved ones, singing siren songs to our children. It is our turn to end the fact that the only way to achieve anything in this city, as a person, is to join those who work hard and leave to find success elsewhere because of your racism.

"You are on notice. We are watching and demand action starting tonight."

18 – THOMASINA 'SINA' JEFFERSON

Flo arrives as I prepare to open the library for the students. Flo is never in this early. She has nearly a half hour before school begins and as T.K. likes to say about her, Flo is a just-in-timer, meaning she rarely arrives anywhere until the very last minute.

I don't know if that's because she's not as organized as most people, or if she's always trying to crowd one more thing into the next five minutes.

"You see what's going on?" she starts right in.

"Morning, Flo."

"They're out in the streets demanding we resign or be impeached or voted out at the next election. Whatever it takes to push us out of the way."

"The report is a problem," I say.

"Problem!" Flo nearly erupts. "You don't know the half of it. People are trying to manipulate a tragic event for their own gain. But in order to do that, they want to turn over the apple cart. Clean house. Start over. But what will that do? I don't know about you, but I don't trust the motives of the loudest voices."

"That would be Reverend Lindo and…"

"The union is actually who I'm blaming. They're screaming for more officers to put more money in their coffers, and manipulating negotiations to benefit from their malfeasance."

"You're using some heavy-duty accusatory language here, girl. This isn't like you."

Flo stops and looks at me with a puzzled expression, "Heavy-duty accusatory? You should have been there last night. You talk about language that was intended to incite a riot?

"I mean Rev Lindo is smooth. If you took a transcript of what he said, there's nothing there that would put him in jail. But he came close to at least endorsing civil disobedience.

"He's sending people to sit in on every meeting we have, to take notes of who says what, what questions each of us ask, what proposals we make. It's like this lynching that's just waiting for the tree to grow strong enough to support the weight of the victim."

"What are you afraid of?"

"I didn't sign up for any of this. You know better than anyone that I ran for office to make a difference. And now my own friends and neighbors are making me out to be racist! Me, a racist?

"Before this is over they intend to drive me out of this city. Make me start over somewhere else with my husband and kids who are bearing the burden of a wife and mother who has been labeled a racist. This just isn't right. How can I possibly see everything I've worked so hard for, my whole life, just be torched by events others are taking advantage of?"

I pull Flo into me and give her a hug.

"Flo, you're the same good person I've known since I started here. You're the same good person I went out and helped get elected to City Council.

"The people of this city know who you are. They know you're not anything like what you're being painted as. You'd be re-elected in a heartbeat. If you stand up in Council and do what's right for the city, for the Bush family, and concentrate on how to make the police department more respectful of everyone, you'll come out of this just fine."

Flo pulls back and looks at me. "Sina, you're my friend, but I don't think you're seeing what's happening here clearly. This is a witch hunt, and right now I'm the witch."

"It's up to us to prove that the accusations are unfounded, then. I'm here for you Flo. I'll help you in any way I can. Just tell me how."

"That's the problem. I don't know what to do. From what the other members of Council have to say, I'm not sure anyone does."

"What are people saying?" I ask.

"More police on the streets is all I get."

"From the Chief?" I wonder aloud.

"Not so much from him as from the union," Flo responds thoughtfully. "That's something I've been wondering about. We don't seem to be getting leadership from the Chief. It's almost as if he has no idea either."

"Or he's just holding on for retirement, hoping things don't get any worse."

A glance at the clock shows her class is going to be showing up any time now, as will my first students of the day. Time to send her back to her classroom. "So, you have a better idea what you've got to do?"

"I definitely need to talk to Regina," Flo shakes her head. "She's been elusive about this so far. Not sure she wanted to say anything to us until the report came out.

"Probably didn't want us saying anything that might be attributed to her. I get that. She's the Mayor and should be impartial until the investigation is complete and the report filed."

"I think you should also do some investigation on your own. Do your homework. Find out what other cities have done when confronted with charges of police racism. Might give you some ideas of what might work here."

Flo nods. “I can do that. Would you do a search too? For me? I always trust what you come up with more than what I find. You’re the research queen.

“Sure. I said I’m here for you.”

I give Flo another quick hug and send her on her way. Why am I seeing behaviors through different eyes all of a sudden? I never would have given it any thought before. Deshaun’s death has certainly brought out the fissures in Fort Christian society.

I knew there were things that weren’t right, but I had no idea so much was just below the surface. This is going to get ugly and none of us will come away the same.

19 – FRANCIS 'DUKE' MARION

The boys are already scrimmaging. Looks like T.K. is letting them play five against the four of us, at least until I can get out there. Since I'm later than usual I have to quickly change.

T.K. hustles by going to the defensive basket. "Nice of you to drop by." He always busts my chops when I'm late just as I bust him when he misses a week or more because he's traveling for work.

Tony works the ball in, runs smack into Shorty, but one of his teammates picks up the loose ball and lofts it through the basket behind Shorty.

T.K. picks up the ball and passes it to me so I can get the feel of it although I usually don't bring it down since nearly everyone else on our team is a better dribbler.

Just a fact, so we have kind of migrated to the things we do best. I'm good at stopping up a lane on defense and good at hanging under the basket for either a tip in or rebound. T.K. can do it all, so I just let him.

When I get down at the top of the key, I pass off to Will, who sets a screen for Randy, who drives for the basket and charges into Tony, who has planted a foot to draw an offensive foul.

Tony is playing smarter. That's good to see. He's emerging as a leader among the kids who are regular now. Think he should make varsity at the high school if he keeps working hard.

Time for me to get back on defense. I need to hustle or Tony will fly right by. I decide to run backwards, which is always a challenge for me. At least I can keep my eye on Tony and make sure he doesn't get past me, or at least slow him down so hopefully Shorty can get back to block a layup.

Tony apparently decides I'm not in the flow yet, so he passes behind him to one of the other kids. I don't know the new kid's name as he just started playing here a few weeks ago. Family moved from Dallas, I think.

I watch as Tony sets a screen for his teammate. As the other player raises the ball to shoot, T.K. comes up behind him, and steals the ball, going the other way for an easy lay-up.

It's good to see T.K. back in the flow. He certainly wasn't last night. I understand how he feels, I miss Deshaun too, but it seemed to just have taken the wind out of T.K's sails. Never seen him like that all the years I've played with him here.

The new kid picks up the ball and holds it, watching something or someone behind me. I turn to see what caused him to hold up the scrimmage and see a very unlikely sight.

A very tall, probably taller than Shorty, Hispanic kid and a middle-age white guy who's built like a Mack truck. They're both dressed to play, but I have no idea why they would be coming out to join us.

T.K. walks towards them like he knows them, then I notice the tall kid is wearing a University of Texas T-shirt under his jacket. Tony and his teammates all flock to the tall kid wearing the UT T-shirt, which makes me wonder if he's a player or something.

Tony is talking with the tall kid, "You had Spencer's number in the Oklahoma State game. No way he was going to get to the basket past you."

I approach them and extend my hand, "Duke Marion."

The tall kid shakes, "Devin Alvarez."

"You play for UT?"

"When they let me," Devin Alvarez responds sheepishly, "I was only the backup."

"You a point guard?"

"When they let me," he laughs, "For some reason they seemed to want me to play center, but I hardly think that's fair… for the other team."

"Welcome," I still have no idea why he's here. "You visiting Boys Clubs or something?"

Devin Alvarez looks at T.K., "I think I was recruited to play with y'all. A charity tournament or something?"

I look at T.K., "First I've heard 'bout it." I extend my hand to the Mack truck. "Duke Marion."

"Brad Jones," he shakes and nods to me.

"What's this… " I begin, but T.K. takes me by the arm and we walk towards the center of the court.

"Brad's my boss. His wife is chair of a charity in town and they got the idea to have a basketball tournament of adult league teams representing different companies. Mine doesn't have a team, so I suggested that I could ask you all, if you'd like to play.

"As you can see, I can get to three of us from the company, but we need to fill out the roster. Since his wife is the chair and the company a major sponsor they wanted a team that could be competitive.

"You're the most competitive guys I know. But if it doesn't work in your schedule or you would rather just not play… that's fine. As I said, three of us could play, although Brad hasn't played basketball since high school."

"Looks like he played some other ballgame -- like golf," I respond. I suspect his style will be more Dennis Rodman than Michael Jordan.

"So he's your boss?"

T.K. nods and glances over his shoulder for just a moment. "What do you think? You want in?"

I look at Devin and realize he would be formidable for an adult league and I have to think we would be able to hold our own with just the five of us who regularly play. "Can we add any of the kids? Or this adults only?"

T.K. shrugs, "They're still working out the rules. I suspect not, but we can ask."

"I'm in as long as I can work my shifts around it. That shouldn't be a problem, but you never know."

T.K. pats me on the shoulder, "Great. It will be a lot more fun if we're all together."

"Uh, one thing." I draw him closer, and whisper, "Who do you have for refs? A couple of the guys on the force have been doing college games. Since it's for charity they might be willing to do it gratis."

T.K. brightens. "I don't know if they've even thought about that, but sure, that would be perfect. I'll mention it to Brad and see if he can work his magic with his wife."

"I take it she's the one who makes the decisions?"

"Her daddy is Tom Morton."

I instantly recognize the name, as he's the Chairman and CEO of Morton Exploration and Production, the company T.K. works for. Didn't know that.

It's also the company Tom Morton took public a few years ago and it just exploded his personal wealth.

Some things about T.K. I've wondered about are starting to fall into place. Like why he's the one that travels so much for the company. He's got an almost straight line to the top guy. Would never know it from his unassuming behavior.

I'm beginning to wonder what I've gotten myself into. The Mortons and their friends never associate with folks like me. I'm not sure I want to be in a freak show for them. "Let me know."

T.K. returns to talk with Brad, but I stay out on the court waiting for them to come back out to scrimmage. The conversation is brief, Brad nods to T.K. and waves to me to show his thanks for the suggestion.

I watch as Devin and Brad take off their warmup jackets and take a lap around the court to loosen up. Shorty and Randy retreat to the bleachers and take a seat to watch. When Devin and Brad complete their lap and warm up stretches we begin the scrimmage.

After about ninety minutes, where we try all kinds of combinations, we find we have a lot of different looks we can put on the floor. Brad is winded and sitting in the bleachers when we decide to call it quits for the night.

"Can I have the ball?" he asks me, since I'm carrying it. I pass it to him and Brad comes out on the court. T.K goes down under the basket and waits as Brad sets up and starts taking shots from around the court with T.K. returning the ball.

"Why don't you let the kids do that?" I suggest.

"They need to get home and get their homework done," T.K. responds as he pulls down a rebound. Then bounce passes back to Brad.

I get it. T.K. needs to work with his boss. Give him personal attention so he can shake off the rust and be at least mildly effective.

I walk over to Shorty, "What do you think?" I ask as we are both watching Devin talking with the kids as if he were the new messiah.

Then I realize that Devin has their attention exactly the same way that Deshaun did. A player who came out of a background like their own who made it in college ball. Who has had the opportunity to play with the big boys and hold his own.

20 – CHIEF CALVIN ANDREWS – FORT CHRISTIAN POLICE DEPARTMENT

I don't think T.K. has ever asked to come see me in the past.

I've kinda lost track of him. He had a great college career. Don't know why he never went pro. He was good enough as I remember.

As T.K. comes in, the smiling face I recall greets me with a head nod and an extended hand. Now that he's here, he's not as tall as I thought he was. Maybe six-three or six-four. Any way you look at it, he's taller than my five-ten, and he's still athletic, with a firm grip.

"Chief Andrews. Thanks for taking the time from your busy schedule to talk with me."

"How have you been? Haven't heard much about you since the NCAA tournament. That was your final game, wasn't it?"

"It was."

"Finals against Clemson. Am I right?"

"You have a good memory, Chief. That's a game I wish I could forget."

"Forget? Hell, you carried your team all the way to the final shot. If that Clemson lad hadn't deflected it you'd of won. You would have been national champs."

"We'll never know."

"How long ago was that?"

"Seventeen years," T.K. responds reluctantly.

"What are you doing now?" I ask.

"Working for Morton, figuring out where to drill wells."

"Must be interesting work," I say,

"I work for a good family and have a great team, so yes."

Team. That's what I remembered instantly. T.K. was a team player. Never the star, but he was right there with all the stars. The term someone used to describe him was an enabler.

He was always in the right place to get the ball to the right person to score, or in the right place to keep the other team from scoring. He was a smart player who saw what was happening and could predict accurately how the play would develop. Not many like him.

"Who did you marry? Someone local as I remember."

"Thomasina Townsend. Her parents are Jack and Marie over on Mesquite Drive."

"Don't really think I've met her. Know Jack and Marie, but guess I'd lost track of their kids."

"You have a great memory, Chief. Not sure I know as many people in town as you do."

"Now that we're all caught up, what is it you wanted to talk about?"

"Deshaun," T.K. responds. "I read the report."

"What's your interest?"

"You may not be aware that Duke Marion and I both work with the ballplayers at the Boys Club. Deshaun was one of the players who we worked with before he went to college."

"I knew Duke was doing something over there, but didn't realize you were working with the players as well. That's commendable. Must take a lot of your time."

"I enjoy it. But I'll get right to the point of why I'm here. The report on the shooting references several failures to follow procedure. The implication is those failures were the primary reason for Deshaun's death."

"That is what the report says," I acknowledge. "So what's your question?"

"Since more than one person failed to follow procedure, what have you, as Chief of Police, done to ensure there will be no further failures to follow procedure?"

"I'm sure this is personal for you, T.K., but we have fired the patrolman who was involved. He was the one who is ultimately responsible. He went out alone in violation of procedure, he left his assigned post and task, in violation of procedure.

"He went to the scene of the events of that night and did not stay in the car as he had been instructed by dispatch and he did not provide the required warnings to the suspect as required by procedure.

"In this case we had an undisciplined raw recruit who was in over his head, and instead of following procedure, obeying orders and instructions, he proceeded to put himself into harm's way and took an inappropriate action in response to an unverified situation. What else can I tell you?"

"That's your professional opinion?" I am not liking what I'm hearing. "That Deshaun was killed by an inexperienced officer who went off on his own and made a series of bad choices."

"T.K., we've both lived in this city a long time. What happened isn't business as usual. If every young black basketball player were killed by a cop, I'd say we have a problem. But this was a one-time incident. A series of bad choices resulting from unusual circumstances.

"If Deshaun had remembered his key, nothing would have happened. If Deshaun's parents hadn't been away, nothing would have happened. If Patrolman Webster's partner had not called in sick, nothing would have happened. If Patrolman Webster had found another officer to go out with him that night… nothing would have happened.

"Do you see where I'm going? A series of unusual circumstances and bad decisions. Most times at least one of those contingencies doesn't turn wrong. On this one particular night, not by anyone's fault, they all did. It created a situation which we couldn't prepare for. It's not in the scenario book, because it's just inconceivable that anything like it could actually happen."

"But it did. And that's what I'm trying to understand. It seems to me that no one person was responsible for Deshaun's death. I'm a systems engineer by education and that's what I do every day. So there must be something wrong with the system if so many failsafe points exist, and yet they all turned the wrong way on this particular night.

"Do you see where I'm going? I'm not pretending to understand your business. I'm not pretending to understand exactly what went wrong that night.

"But all my training and experience tells me that something is fundamentally wrong with a system that has so many check points and still fails, even if it's only once.

"If you were in the grocery business, or renting hotels… well, in those instances if there is a system failure, no one dies. That's what's different about what you do. People's lives are at stake. A systemic failure can't be allowed to persist."

Where the hell is he coming from? I don't give a shit about systems. This is all about discipline.

"I appreciate your perspective. I didn't know you were a systems engineer. I don't have much of an opportunity to deal in that area, so I won't pretend, as you've pointed out, to understand what you do all day. I won't pretend that I have any idea about systems and what that means to Deshaun Bush's death.

"The closest I can come to what you're describing is procedure. We have a procedure book that everyone is responsible to memorize and be able to quote back to any supervisor who asks. We drill procedure. We drill discipline. That's all I can deal with here.

"You talked about the report saying there were failures to follow procedure, not that the procedure was inadequate to the situation. You're the first person to have said that there may be something inherently wrong with our procedure.

"I can't tell you whether there is or there isn't. All I can say is that if the procedures on the books had been followed that night, Deshaun Bush would likely still be alive. That's enough for me."

"You seem to think what happened is an isolated incident."

"It was," I dismiss not only his accusation but his tone of voice which is beginning to annoy me.

"Then why have nearly a thousand young black men lost their lives at the hands of police officers each year over the last several years?

"The Washington Post has been tracking the reported officer-involved shootings that have resulted in the death of a young black man.

"They have reported that if anything, their numbers may be understated.

"That's nearly three every day. Going back years.

"What happened here is not an isolated incident. It's part of a national disgrace. No other nation has as many shootings involving police."

"You don't know what you're talking about." I have to put him in his place. Internet searches don't tell the whole story and that would appear to be the source of his information to make such statements.

"What information can you offer to refute what I've researched?"

"I don't want this to become adversarial, T.K. I like you personally and respect not only what you've done in your career, but the work you've done at the Boy's Club and in your profession.

"I have to give you a lot of credit. An engineering degree? That's not something that's easy. And I'm sure you're really good at predicting where to drill an oil or gas well.

"But that has nothing at all to do with what I'm faced with each and every day. That's not something that would help us better understand how to prevent another officer-involved shooting at some point.

"As I said, we have procedures. If they'd been followed, Deshaun would still be alive. That's enough for me."

"Let's talk about following procedures for a minute, then. How many officers were disciplined for not following orders that night?"

"How many? The patrolman was the one who violated multiple procedures that night."

"Yes, but there were others."

What is he talking about? "Others?"

"Your procedure is that a rookie does not go out on patrol alone."

"Yes. He was instructed to find someone to ride with him."

"The default should have been, no ride along, no patrol. But someone sent him out anyway with a mild caution. That clearly wasn't enough."

"Dispatch had orders to put as many patrols on the street as possible," I remember, but is he saying that I should have disciplined dispatch because they followed my orders? "They were following orders."

"In contradistinction to the procedure."

"Direct orders supersede procedure," I point out.

“And in this case that overruling led to a death… And those who refused to ride along with him? What happened to them?”

“Nothing. No one is obligated to come in to help out a rookie.” This has become tiresome. Nothing I say is going to make him happy.

“But officers knew he was going out alone and simply admonished him to not engage in anything that wasn’t routine without backup.

“That was not a good decision because Patrolman Webster had no compunction to disregard that instruction and several others as the evening went on.”

“That’s not in the report,” I note. Where is this coming from?

21 – THOMASINA 'SINA' JEFFERSON

T.K. and I are walking down our street with a full moon in the sky and streetlights illuminating our path through our familiar neighborhood.

I could probably close my eyes and still find my way home, we have walked this way so many nights, just like this one. But tonight T.K. is preoccupied.

I'm doing all the talking, and maybe it's time for me to quiet down and let him talk, or not, until he is finally willing to share with me.

"What's it going to take?" I finally ask him after we have walked on for probably five minutes without exchanging a word.

"For what?" he finally responds.

"For you to talk with me," I protest. "You're into yourself. I can't be of any help when you don't let me in."

T.K. takes my hand and squeezes it. "I know you're there. I count on you being there. I'm just trying to make sense of things. That's all."

"It doesn't make sense. It never will."

"What are you talking about?" T.K. asks me.

"What happened. It will never make sense. But you have to accept what happened and move on."

"No, I don't," T.K. says teasingly. "I can remain hung up my whole life if that's what I want to do."

"But you don't," I say. "Do you?"

T.K. squeezes my hand and then gives me a sidewise hug, before walking on just holding my hand. "I know I'm not alone on my journey to understanding what happened."

"You're not." I confirm emphatically. "What are you feeling? Can you describe it so that maybe I can help you understand your feelings? Come to terms with what has happened?"

"I guess the one word that summarizes how I feel is helpless. There's nothing I can do to change a thing."

"Why did you come to that conclusion?" I ask.

"I'm just one person living in this town. Elected officials will decide what needs to happen.

"But in reflecting on what's happened all across the country, in this kind of situation, the outcome has always been there is no change. All the factors that led to a needless death remain.

"The rhetoric dies down until the next event, and the shameful truth is there is always a next event. Different people. Different circumstances. But there is always a next event."

T.K.'s just at a loss for how it changes. How it stops. How black kids can finally feel safe in their own neighborhoods. Something we take for granted, but they can't from the day they are born until they move away or die.

"What do you want to do?" I have to ask. "What would allow you to move on?"

"They're not the same. What do I want to do? I want Council to step up and do something with the police department. Make them look at their procedures. Determine what needs to be done so such a systemic failure can't happen again.

"That's what I want to do. What would allow me to move on? I don't know. I failed Deshaun. I don't know how you move on from that."

"How did you fail him?"

"I heard him say he'd forgotten his keys. I should have told him to come stay with us that night. Don't go home. If I'd done that he'd still be alive. When Richie Webster showed up I should have told Duke to not let him go out alone. I could have said that."

"You couldn't have foreseen what was going to happen. You probably thought he would just stay with his girlfriend for the night. He would have much preferred that to our house and you know it."

T.K. doesn't dispute my observation. "There must be something I can do to make sure nothing like this ever happens again."

"Is that your responsibility? No one elected you God. Come back down here where you belong.

"If you come up with a good idea, I'd suggest we call up Flo and invite her over for dinner. You can discuss whatever idea you have with her. That's more than most people can do. You will have the undivided attention of one of the five votes needed to get something through Council."

"Flo's not the person the other members of Council go to for solutions," T.K. points out. Unfortunately I know what he's saying is true. She's the expert in education, but that's only a minor part of the responsibilities of Council.

"She actually has more influence on the School Board since she's a teacher than she does on Council.

"If the idea is sound enough, Flo can sell it."

We walk on in silence, then I stop him, "Are you thinking you're going to fix this all by yourself?"

"Someone has to do something."

"Council is doing something. That's what they do. How long has Fort Christian been a city? Couple hundred years or so?"

T.K. nods.

"This isn't the first Council to have to face a major issue like this. They've been doing it since the first year Fort Christian was a city, and more than likely they had some kind of governing council even before that. So this is nothing new. All the people who lived here before us?

"They had issues with one thing or another. They worked together and found solutions. The city has survived and it will survive Deshaun Bush's death."

"But will I?" T.K. asks. I'm not sure if he's asking me or himself.

"You will. There are so many others at the Boy's Club that need your inspiration. Need your confidence to find their own.

"You have so much to give that you have to. Besides, I'd be really pissed if you left me with the mortgage to manage all by myself."

"We don't have a mortgage," T. K. reminds me, although I already knew that.

When we were first married and bought this house we set out a goal to pay it off in fifteen years. We did that last year. T.K. is nothing if not disciplined. He hugs me and I give him a kiss on his cheek since he's not looking at me.

"Maybe it's time we go somewhere. Just the two of us. Kick back for a week or something. Maybe getting away will make it easier to decide what you think needs to be done."

T.K. shakes his head, "Next year maybe. Right now's not a good time. I have work issues I've got to resolve before I disappear for even a few days.

"Brad's acting real schizoid right now. One minute I think he's going to fire me and the next he's asking me for favors. I can't read the guy, so I'm not going to give him an opportunity to decide he's not happy with me."

"This something new?" I ask, knowing that Tom Morton hired T.K. personally. He's always had a direct line but I know he's never used it.

If Brad were to fire T.K. I would think Tom Morton would step in and fix that. T.K.'s too valuable to them and too central to their investment planning. That's the thing about shale oil drilling. It's not as long lived as the old wells that drew oil from an underground reservoir.

Now they have to continually fracture the stone to release the oil into collecting veins. Still plenty of oil, they just have to work harder and smarter to find it and get it up.

"I can't tell," T.K. responds but doesn't elaborate.

"What's going on you're not telling me?"

"You know me," he begins, "I don't ask questions. People often don't tell me much. But I'm always trying to read between the lines. Figure out what's not being said.

"Something has changed. I can't tell you whether it means things are going to get better or worse. I suspect Tom Morton has an idea of how it's all going to work out. He's probably making plans to ensure he can take advantage of whatever the change will be.

"Does that mean we are going to up production in the Permian area or reduce it? Don't know. There are other reserves we're working that are less work and less expensive to extract. But by the time you add shipping and pipeline fees? Well, it ends up being about the same. So I just don't know. But I can feel something's going on."

"With the company or with Brad," I ask thinking of rumors I've heard he probably has not.

"It's all the same to me. If Brad's unhappy it's probably because Tom's unhappy, and if Tom's unhappy I'm likely going to be the one to have to go fix whatever it is."

"Why didn't you say something?"

"No sense worrying over a feeling."

"You clearly are, and if you are maybe I can help you make sense of what you're feeling, hearing and seeing. Sometimes all it takes it talking it through with someone."

"I don't know what I can tell you that would help you help me better understand the situation."

"There are rumors…"

T.K. displays a quizzical look in his glance toward me. "What kind of rumors?"

"You know how the rich and famous are. Always a scandal here, an infidelity there. Something to spice up their dull lives."

"You talking about Tom?"

"Actually the rumor is that Leticia has grown bored with Brad…"

"You don't pay any attention to that, do you?"

"Word on the street is Daddy has come to the conclusion that Brad just doesn't have what it takes to run the family business. He's made Leticia aware of his dissatisfaction."

"So?"

"Leticia's no dummy." I play the scenario out for him. "If Brad's not the guy, she better find herself a new guy who can pass Daddy's muster or she's likely to not end up with the company."

T.K. stops walking. "That could explain Brad's recent behavior. He's sucking up to Leticia in a way I've not seen before. I mean she's always been in control of that relationship. But now he seems to be singularly focused on making her happy with him, or at least not giving her any excuses to be unhappy."

"By fielding the winning team in her charity tournament, and being a member of the team?" I wonder aloud.

"I was the one who convinced him to play, but he didn't say no when I fully expected him to. Guess I need to keep my head down in the foxhole until the family decides what it's going to do."

22 – T.K. JEFFERSON

I poke my head into Brad's spacious office. I've always liked the white fur rug in front of his oak desk and wood everything else. Even the frames of the pictures on his desk are wood. The paintings on the wall are western art scenes from the 1880s. Steam locomotives. Indians on horseback hunting bison. Cowboys roping cattle.

It all represents a time gone by. A time that was oblivious to the mineral wealth beneath their feet. And yet it was a robust period in American history. A time when people stood together or died alone. Is there a lesson to be learned from that?

"Hey, Brad. Question for you."

Brad looks up from the computer screen on his desk. Can't tell what he's looking at as he hits a button to take him to another screen. When I get closer it's evident that he's now on his email screen. But that's not where he was. "Sure."

"I know we have a policy about making public statements on behalf of the company. All have to be cleared through communications."

"Sounds right," Brad shrugs.

"But what if I wanted to make a public statement that has nothing to do with the company? What if I wanted to make a public statement as a private citizen, totally unrelated to work?"

"If it's not work-related I can't see how we would be concerned. As long as you make it clear you're not speaking on behalf of the company."

"That's what I thought. But I still wanted to discuss what I have in mind because it could be really controversial."

Brad looks at me with a frown, "You going to advocate for universal divorce or something?"

That struck a chord. Apparently the rumor Sina heard may have some substance to it. "No. I've been thinking about the officer-involved shooting incident."

"The what?"

"The cop who shot Deshaun Bush at his back door?"

"The cop… oh, yeah. I remember that." Brad finally gets on the right page. "What about it?"

"I'm thinking of going to the next City Council meeting with a modest proposal for their consideration."

"You're right. Why would anyone get upset with that?"

"My proposal is modest but radical."

"Wait. How do those things go together?"

That's the problem with Brad, it takes him a while to catch up even when he's not stoned, which isn't often. I've actually been wondering if he's going to be stoned for the whole basketball tournament.

"I'm going to suggest the police department needs to change some of their policies and procedures."

"What's the issue? You look at processes and procedures for us all the time. Nothing controversial about process change."

"In this case it's more than a simple process change." I try to explain.

"I can't see how we would care if you're acting as a good citizen and using your knowledge of process to help them do things more efficiently or effectively.

"I may also make a recommendation regarding personnel." I check his reaction.

"Advocating firing the Chief? People do that all the time." Brad shrugs.

"City Council will be taking testimony on what to do with the police department."

"What do you mean, 'do with them'?" Brad's not following as usual.

"They had an internal investigation after the Deshaun Bush killing. The internal investigation made several recommendations that not everyone thinks goes far enough to address the issues that led to the officer-involved shooting that took an innocent life."

"All perps are innocent until proven otherwise by a court. Didn't you know that?"

"Yes, but that's not where I'm going with this. The city has a set of recommendations the police made. They can either accept those recommendations or reject them and do something else.

"They could also accept them and do more than the police suggest," I say. "Or they could do nothing at all, which is what's happened in the past where there's been a similar set of circumstances."

"You're recommending they do something different."

"I've been doing some research. There are models from other countries that are interesting and I think the folks at City Hall should take a look at them. That will be my recommendation."

"How did you become such an expert on all this? You're not a policeman, never have been."

"Never hope to be. But I'm convinced that something has to change in the way that we conduct law enforcement. And since I can't change how we do that at the national level, I can try to do something at a more local level.

"The city is the best place to start because they know they have a problem and with the Deshaun Bush events they are motivated to look at alternatives.

"Is my modest proposal a bridge too far? I have to be honest and say it most likely is. But if someone doesn't put that recommendation on the table it won't be given any consideration. And maybe we don't go that far.

"If we do something different, there's a chance that someone who might otherwise die at the hands of a police officer, might live. And that would certainly be worthwhile."

Brad nods, but I can tell it's not in agreement. It's probably because he's mostly if not totally stoned. Oh well.

"What do you think?" I ask to bring him back into the conversation and my question. "Any issue with me making my modest proposal?"

"I can't tell you not to make it…" Brad certainly doesn't sound like he thinks it's a good idea, though. "As long as it's not an official company position… you know. That would require you to sit down with communications and then the lawyers and then back to communications.

"If you had to go that route, I'm sure the final version would say something like Morton Exploration and Production believes that every American should have the right to decide how they want to burn as much oil and gas as possible."

"But there's nothing about me, as a private citizen, unrelated to Morton Exploration and Production, even though an employee here, that should limit in any way my ability or right to make a public statement that suggests a possible course of civic action in an area totally unrelated to our business or interests."

"I would agree with that, but if you want to speak to legal, I'm sure they would be more than willing to render an opinion." Brad winks at me, "In a month or two. We have them rather busy with the run of the mill mineral rights and government permitting work they do day in and day out."

I nod. "You going to be at practice tonight?"

"Practice?"

"For the tournament. You know… the basketball tournament Leticia is chairperson of? You asked me to put together a team? Has Devin Alvarez on it? You're going to play low post with Duke Marion?"

Brad seems to have no memory of a basketball team, but then something seems to cut through the haze that has settled over his perceptions. "I thought we practiced."

"Once won't make us credible in the tournament."

"Tomorrow," Brad waves me off. "Tomorrow I'll be there. Got lots to do today."

23 – T.K. JEFFERSON

I am reading a report Mustapha put together on expected volumes from a potential well site when the phone rings. I don't recognize the number. When that's the case I usually don't answer, preferring to initiate a call back if it's something important.

But something about the number makes me think I should take this one, so I do. "T.K. Jefferson."

"Mr. Jefferson, this is Mayor Regina Blackwell. How are you today?"

"Madam Mayor, I'm not sure. How am I today?"

"I don't think we've had the opportunity to meet, and I'm sure we will do so soon in any event. I have known of you since your college days and have to say you were a fine representative of our city in those years.

"Now I have a request that may give you another chance to make the citizens of Fort Christian proud of you."

"A request, Madam Mayor?" Flo must have told her of my idea and the Mayor is wanting me to not repeat it, I suppose.

"As you are aware, Council member Lopez recommended you to serve on a citizen's commission on police reform that we intend to create in light of the recent events. Would you be willing to serve if I place your name before Council and they approve?"

"Has Flo discussed the modest proposal I would like the city to consider?" I put it out there as I don't want the Mayor to appoint me and regret it almost immediately.

"Flo and I discussed your dinner conversation. I must say, I had a similar reaction as Flo. But I am also of an open mind as to how we must deal with the situation.

"So I would also recommend that you chair the commission. Now, that may actually make it harder for you to advance your ideas, and it would be my expectation you would seek to advance only the most workable and beneficial proposals.

"Flo told me you've read the internal investigation report.

"Apparently you had a similar impression to most of us on Council. And that is the exact starting point I think is important so this commission can do meaningful work."

"That would be an unexpected honor, Mayor Blackwell," is all I can think of to say, wondering if I would really be the best person to chair this commission. But I've already discussed the idea with Brad and he encouraged me to state my mind.

"Good. You may wish to attend the Council meeting tonight, as that is when we will be acting on the recommendation to form the commission.

"And that would give you an opportunity to not only meet the Council members who will be counting on you to provide leadership on this issue, but also to understand their thoughts about it as we begin."

That night I'm sitting in the Fort Christian City Council chambers at 7:00 pm sharp. The audience seating is full, others standing along the wall and in the back with mostly black faces I'm not sure I've ever seen before.

I continue to look around as Mayor Blackwell calls the meeting to order and moves through the standard agenda. The creation of the commission is the first item of new business.

"I have a resolution to create a Fort Christian Citizen's Commission on Police Reform. Would a Council member move this resolution for consideration and debate?"

Flo responds, "Madam Mayor, I would like to move the consideration and debate on resolution 12-3-1712- SPC as presented."

Roxanne speaks up, "Madam Mayor, I second the motion to consider and debate the resolution."

"All in favor signify by saying aye?"

Flo, Roxanne and Alvin all say "Aye."

"Opposed?"

No response.

Mayor Blackwell then turns to Council member Peter "Petes" Cochrane, a local attorney who handles mostly civil work for local businesses. He is also white. "Council Member Cochrane, I take it you wish to abstain?"

"I do," Petes Cochrane responds.

"Would you provide the rest of Council insight as to the reasons for your wish to abstain?"

"Commissions are often a waste of taxpayer money. I want to know more about the charter for this commission before I commit to support it. If it's just a witch hunt, we can save the people a lot of time and money by firing the Chief and getting on with life.

"If it's a look at what this body can do to ensure we better safeguard all who live in our city, such as the consideration of whether to put more officers on the street, or providing enhanced training and upgraded body cameras, those seem to me to be recommendations that I would be willing to consider.

"Recommendations that I think the voters would recognize as positive in regards to their safety."

"Council member Lopez," the Mayor recognizes Flo.

"I discussed the concept of a commission with each of the other members of Council and the Mayor before drafting this resolution you have before you.

"There was agreement that this Council needs input from a diverse representation of our citizens to ensure we consider a range of options. There was general dissatisfaction with the recommendations of the internal investigation.

"They were generally seen as insufficient to bring about meaningful change.

"So the charge to this commission is

- to solicit inputs from whatever sources the members of the commission wish to obtain,
- to have a robust debate about how to transform our police department into a model for the nation, and
- to set forth a set of recommendations to not only effect that change but at the same time build in safeguards such that the recent tragic events cannot possibly recur."

Flo has honed that presentation until it was crisp and very clear while not alienating anyone other than maybe the police officer's union, who will be cautious about the word transform.

"Council member Williams," the Mayor says.

Roxanne looks uneasy as she gazes out at the full auditorium and the Reverend Lindo, who is sitting right down front. I can't see his expression from where I'm sitting, but it is apparently upsetting Roxanne.

"The scars from the recent tragic events will not soon heal.

"I seconded this resolution for consideration and debate because this Council must consider any and all ideas our residents wish to put forward. And it's not just ideas, as some will be workable and others just not appropriate for Fort Christian.

"We must gather as much verifiable evidence as to the success of the ideas advanced in other cities in Texas, and possibly elsewhere, as possible.

"We must not do something just to do something. We must have reasonable justification, reasonable expectation, and reasonable assurance that whatever actions we take as a body and as a city to change the way we protect our citizens and enforce the laws of our city, state and nation will result in an improvement."

Alvin Hill is the other member of Council who has not yet spoken. The Mayor simply nods to him.

"I support the creation of this commission for the same reasons Roxanne and Flo have given. I'm a small businessman. I live and die by all of you coming to my restaurant. If you don't feel safe in doing so, you won't come.

"For me, it's essential that we do whatever is necessary to ensure we adequately supervise our new recruits, properly train them and demand strict adherence to procedure.

"That's what I got out of the report, even though that didn't end up in the recommendations.

"And I also think we need to do a better job of selecting our officers, but that's a personal opinion.

"I'm anxious to see what recommendations this commission makes to us, the debate we will have about those recommendations and then doing something to make our city safer."

"Now that the Council members have had an opportunity to provide initial thoughts about the resolution, I would like to open the floor to those in attendance who would like to speak to the resolution and whether it should be adopted by this Council."

Mayor Blackwell has chosen not to speak to the resolution from the chair. I need to keep that in mind if they create this commission and I end up as chair.

Reverend Lindo rises and nods to the Mayor.

"Please come to the microphone, state your name and address for the record and then you may make your comments."

"Reverend Leroy Lindo, 17 Linden Street."

I note he has used the address of the church and not the home the church provides for him. Curious.

"I am pleased that Council has heard our calls for action and is soliciting input from a broad spectrum of our community before taking action. This can only have a beneficial effect in that you will have the opportunity to consider actions you might otherwise not think about.

"As you know, I have been very critical of your response to date. I am still not comfortable that the commission you propose is more than a whitewash. And I use that term very deliberately.

"I and many of those who are in the audience tonight have made the point that the negative effects of this police force are disproportionately impacting the black community.

"It is our children who are afraid when a policeman approaches them. It is us, who wonder if our children will come home when they go out with their friends.

"We have fears that are more immediate than those of the rest of you. We do not have the ability to change who our policemen and women are, but you do. That's why we are here tonight, to make sure you are putting the right people on this commission.

"To make sure that people who will make substantial recommendations to you are appointed. And that is why I have risen to address you tonight.

"As I have pointed out, the impact of the negative behaviors of our police are disproportionate. The black community lives in fear of the people put in place to protect us. That must end. The black community is not adequately represented among police officers. That must change.

"The black community has little say in the policies and procedures of the police department. That must change.

"And finally, the black community must feel safe once whatever changes are made go into effect. Those are the minimum expectations we have.

"But as I look at your proposed commission membership, I do not see enough representation of the black community. That must change.

"I also object to the chairman being white. I am not suggesting that Mr. Jefferson, who I do not know personally, is unqualified to serve on the commission, I just believe the chairperson should be from the black community.

"For that reason, I ask Council to add me to the commission membership and appoint me as chairman. That is the minimum it will take for the black community to have any faith that the commission will be more than a whitewash."

As I think about the Rev's request, it should have been obvious he would want to be on the proposed commission and chair it. I understand why Flo and the Mayor would not have wanted that, feeling that the larger community would have seen it as caving in to his demands.

And since he stated his minimum expectations tonight, it will be hard for anyone to believe it would be anything other than capitulation to make him chairman.

If they don't accept his demand, then the black community will react negatively.

They're damned if they do and even more damned by the newspapers if they don't. Maybe this will be a lesson in leadership for me to observe. What will they do?

"Thank you, Reverend Lindo. Would anyone else like to address

Council on this matter?"

A petite black woman comes to the microphone who had been sitting next to the Rev. "Keshia Foster, 29 Linden Street. For the record I am the chairman of the Lay Council for the Second Baptist Church here in Fort Christian.

"I think it is important for you to understand that connection as I am going to support everything that Reverend Lindo has spoken to this evening. I have a son. He's sixteen. He is more responsive to the command, 'spread 'em' than he is to 'wake up.' That's not right.

"He has been stopped by the Fort Christian police on eleven different occasions. On none of those occasions was he doing anything other than minding his own business and either going to a friend's house or returning home afterwards.

"He does not go to movies. He does not go to clubs or bars, not only because he's underage, but he knows the police watch those establishments, waiting to stop and search the black boys, looking for drugs, mostly, but sometimes they're looking for weapons.

"I constantly fight with my son about when he needs to come home because I want him home before dark. Do you know the reason why? Because the police in this city are like vampires. They wait for the sun to go down and then they swoop down and haul innocent young men off to jail, just to give them a record of arrests.

"Do you know why they do that? Because when that boy gets caught with something minor, they can send them away for a longer period of time. As the Reverend Lindo said, this must end.

"And this most recent assassination of Deshaun Bush? That destroyed the hopes of my son. He didn't know Deshaun other than as a member of our congregation, but Deshaun was a role model.

"Someone who came from this community and was making it out there. Someone who could grow up here and be bigger than Fort Christian good. He was America good.

"Your police department took away a hero from all the children of Fort Christian. You have forever shaped the expectations of my son. He now believes that he shouldn't work hard to be the best because if he succeeds someone will find a way to take away his success. You've taken away his hope. This too must end."

Keisha Foster stops for a moment and regains control of herself. "Reverend Lindo is the only person I know in this community who will fight for us. He is the only voice that has been heard saying 'enough'.

"That's why it is imperative that he be the chairman of your commission. He is our only hope at the moment for meaningful change."

"Thank you, Mrs. Foster. Anyone else?" the Mayor asks.

A taller black woman who has been sitting next to me stands up and goes to the microphone, "Rebekah Winston, 9901 Elm. You all have heard my story from before.

"You know I'm not bashful about making a ruckus when things aren't right. So tonight I'm making a ruckus. Rev Lindo and I are kindred spirits. We both like fried chicken, although for everyone else that's a stereotype and so we don't admit that in public.

"But come on over to Popeyes on Twelfth Street on Monday nights late, like eleven. You'll find us both there, talking about how we need to find a way to make things better in this city.

"Now I'm not one to want to sit on a commission and listen to all the BS. That's just not me. I cut to the heart of things and don't have patience to listen to ignorance.

"I also don't have patience for people who don't listen, and I've found more of them than people who do. That's a shame because the Rev here, he's pretty much convinced me that you all up there? You're in that first category and not the second.

"Now tonight, you have a chance to change people's minds about you all. You have a chance to listen to those of us who came out tonight. A chance to consider the real problem in the police department isn't anything to do with procedures or discipline, Mr. Petes.

"If you think that's all that's the matter, you got your head up your ass. You need to come out and see what's going on in your city. You need to ride along with a police officer, listen to the calls, observe how dispatch works, and see how your officers talk with folks.

"I'm sure it would be eye-opening for all of you.

"On the other hand, if you came to my neighborhood, came to dinner at my house when I have neighbors in and listen to what they talk about? I assure you that Keisha's experience would not seem out of the ordinary. There are a lot more stories where that came from, trust me."

Rebekah Winston nods and turns around to look at those who are listening to her, nods again and turns back to look at the Council members.

"Do we look like people who are happy with the job you all are doing? I mean look at us! We're out here telling you that we aren't going to stand for another half-assed attempt to put off you making a decision because your police are a bunch of racist vigilantes.

"You know, those of us in the black community? We're like frogs in the proverbial pot of increasingly hot water. We have been sitting in this pot for a long time, watching the temperature rise, feeling the effects.

"But because the temperature has been rising so slowly, we haven't jumped out yet. We have our reasons for staying put. We have family and friends here. We know things were worse when we were slaves.

"Things were worse after the Civil War when we were no longer slaves, and those who provided for us abandoned us and made us fight every day just to survive, with no money, no land, and no homes. And slowly we've fought for and gained rights, and we've even gained middle class status in many cases.

"But we still have a long way to go to reach equality.

"Now I know most of you think we have it good, because we can get jobs, we can go to the same schools and some companies promote us.

"But at the same time, there are many that won't even hire us except to exploit us. So I'm here to tell you, Rev needs to be the chairman of your commission, because it must be our commission, too."

About midnight, after a long progression of stories like Keisha's and Rebekah's, the Mayor closes the public comment period and asks for discussion amongst the members of Council.

Petes raises his hand. The Mayor nods in his direction.

"Since I have my head up my ass, I guess that means I would not if I agreed to put Reverend Lindo on the commission. Let me just say, I won't be insulted, and I won't accede to your demands. I move the adoption of the resolution with the recommended membership."

The Mayor asks, "There is a motion on the floor to move the adoption of resolution 12-3-1712- SPC as presented. Is there a second?"

Silence.

"The motion fails for lack of a second," The Mayor nods to Roxanne Williams.

"I had a long discussion with Council member Lopez when she came by to talk about who should be on the proposed commission. I raised Reverend Lindo as a potential candidate to be a member, and we talked at length about whether he should be chairman.

"Council member Lopez convinced me that if I support him as chairman, the perception would be that the Council is simply rubber stamping his demands, which would prevent others from coming forth with ideas, thoughts and suggestions.

"While I think that some, although not all of the actions he has demanded of us, could have a beneficial effect, I recognize the need for broad community input. I am afraid that making Reverend Lindo the chair would limit that."

The Rev stands up to respond, but the Mayor zeros in on him.

"Reverend Lindo. You may not address the Council during this part of our meeting. You have had your opportunity to say what you will about us, and we now have the opportunity to say what we will about your request and your demands. Please sit down or the officer in the back of the room will escort you out."

The Rev turns around, sees Duke standing in the back and sits down. I hadn't noticed Duke being in the room previously.

"Council member Lopez, this is your resolution."

Flo looks directly at the Rev as she speaks. "I have listened to many members of the congregation of the Second Baptist Church speak this evening on behalf of their Pastor. I have listened closely to the heartfelt fear, anger and apprehension about the world they are delivering their children into because of the way our police force has interacted with them.

"I recognize that the events that led to Deshaun Bush's death have crystalized the nature of race relations with the police in this city.

"While it is tragic that Deshaun's life ended as it did, I am looking for the good that can come from that tragedy. I firmly believe the proposed commission is our best hope of beginning to change the nature of race relations.

"I am a teacher, and many of my students are teenage black boys. I have been asking for their stories in the days since Deshaun's death. I regret I didn't ask those same questions earlier.

“I hear the concern that there may not be sufficient representation of the black community on the commission. In our attempts to create balance I can see that maybe we overshot, given the disproportionate impacts.

“So I have no objection to adding Reverend Lindo to the commission, but I do not recommend that he be named chairman.”

Alvin Hill raises his hand. “I am a member of the congregation of the Second Baptist Church here in Fort Christian. Reverend Lindo is my pastor and a good friend. I too support the request to add him to the commission as an additional member, and frankly am torn by the request to appoint him as chairman.

“As we all know, he is a strong personality and may have a tendency to believe his solution is the only one.”

Petes Cochrane raises his hand and Mayor Blackwell nods to him.

“I don’t support changing the composition of the commission membership as you know, having not seconded my motion. So it’s inevitable you’re going to put him on.

“So to split the baby, so to speak, why don’t you name him vice chairman? That way everyone wins and you’ve still put someone in place who will have to ensure we get a balanced set of recommendations.

“Now I have met T.K. Jefferson, who is here tonight, and is the recommended chairman. As a basketball fan, I also know that T.K. worked with Deshaun at the Boy’s Club for a long time.

“I don’t know if any of you ever watched Deshaun play or watched T.K. when his team went to the NCAA tournament. But I saw how much Deshaun learned from T.K. They were both incredibly talented and selfless players who worked to make their teams better.

“If he can work his magic with this commission the way he did with Deshaun? I think we will get the right set of recommendations.”

"Are you making that motion?" Mayor Blackwell asks.

"I am."

24 – T.K. JEFFERSON

I've never been to the Second Baptist Church of Fort Christian. I attend the First Baptist Church on the other side of the city.

That's where my parents went and that's where I was baptized. I've been a member ever since, not because I ever thought about where would I want to attend services, but because that's where my family has always gone. I wonder now if I would choose differently today.

The church is large, although I can see it could use some repairs. But what church, other than the new mega churches, ever have enough money to maintain their facilities?

I enter through the side door that goes to the Pastor's barren office. This surprises me. There is a cross on the wall behind his simple wood desk and that is it.

My impression was that he would have pictures on every wall of him with another important person. Someone who is always trying to establish his own importance, I had decided a long time ago, tends to seek out mementos of associations with the powerful. The Rev has not done that. Curious.

The Reverend LeRoy Lindo is sitting at his desk as I enter. He is writing something using a pen on a yellow legal pad.

"Come in, please."

I let him complete his focused effort, and in a minute or so he looks up.

"Ah, Mr. Jefferson. Thank you for reaching out first thing. I appreciate that you were willing to take the time from work to come visit during the day. As you know, in my line of work my evenings belong to my congregation, so this is much more convenient for me."

"What were you writing? You seemed to be impassioned in your work," I observe.

The Rev smiles in a satisfied way, "My sermon. I'm pleased you could see the passion I try to bring to my work and to the causes I champion for my congregation. But that's not why you're here. You're here to figure out how to contain my passion, since I am now your vice chairman on the commission."

"Not contain, Reverend that would be a hopeless cause. Rather, I'm much more interested in how you and I together harness your passion, your insights, and your knowledge along with those from the other members to forge a set of recommendations that not only will have the results we all want, but also have the support of Council, the Mayor and ultimately the whole community."

"You have already made a judgment that my recommendations to Council will never be adopted."

"I don't make judgments like that," I respond calmly. "But what I observed is that fear of being seen as a rubber stamp for your recommendations or the recommendations of the internal investigation are the reason I am chairman and you are not."

Reverend LeRoy Lindo blinks several times in succession. I assume he is thinking about my observation. "You would have me believe that my demands are dead on arrival?"

"Reverend, again, it doesn't matter what I believe. I am not the enemy here.

"I intend that you will have the opportunity to present and discuss your thoughts, recommendations and demands with the full commission. You will have an equal opportunity to convince the members that your ideas should be among the recommendations.

"But only an equal opportunity.

"Even as vice chair, you will get no more consideration than anyone else.

"Your thoughts, ideas and opinions will be given no more weight. The report has to have the endorsement of all members or it will be a minority report and therefore Petes Cochrane's typical commission that everyone will ignore.

"I don't have time to work on anything that doesn't have a meaningful impact on addressing the issues," I say.

"I didn't pay much attention when I saw you were the recommended chairman." The Rev sounds dismissive. "Just thought, okay a white guy. The commission isn't going to do anything.

"That's why I insisted they make me chairman. And you just gave a nice talk about doing what's right for the community, but you have to have an agenda or they never would have chosen you.

"You're identified, I was surprised to learn, with helping black kids become better ball players at the Boy's Club.

"White guilt, I suppose.

"I thought maybe I can work with you. But when Petes endorsed you? Petes is owned by the police officer's union. For him to back you tells me you're in the pocket of the union. Says to me: whitewash.

"I sort of got what I wanted, but I'm not sure I'm even going to attend the meetings or support the recommendations because I don't think you're going to recommend anything that addresses the racism."

"For a supposed man of God you're quick to judge," I need an open mind on his part.

"I am a man of God, but I can only turn my cheek so many times," the Rev replies with just suppressed anger.

"You and I come at this problem from different perspectives. I've lived in Fort Christian my whole life except the four years I was off to college. You've lived here for what, six years now?"

"Immaterial. I'm more a part of the community than you are, even with all your years here."

"You come at the problem from a moral outrage perspective. I'm an engineer who delivers results through empowering teams of people to solve impossible problems."

I'm trying to make him see we are complementary but he's just being defensive about the whole thing. Looking to be able to continue his incendiary speeches and keep his congregation in a state of perpetual uproar.

"We are not dealing with an oil well here. We are talking about the hopes and dreams of a new generation, trying to break with the past that limited all of us."

"When was the last time you created something new?"

"What do you mean, something new?" The Rev doesn't know how to respond to my question.

"I'm an engineer. I'm paid to solve a problem, gather facts and data, analyze it, and then go create something totally new, whether that's an algorithmic analysis tool that helps us find oil, or new drills that can pull oil out of horizontal seams of stone. Things that have never been done before. When was the last time you did that?"

"I'm not an engineer," he uses as his defense.

"I'm not a pastor, but I do lead people to discover who they are by giving them insolvable problems to go work. So at the moment let's say I understand your world a lot better than you understand mine."

"I don't entirely agree with you because I don't think you really have any idea what my world is like."

"I do. My Uncle Ken was the pastor at First Baptist when I was growing up and attended services there. He's pastor in Phoenix now, and I see him once in a while."

"Didn't know that," the Rev concedes another point. "You're not black. You can't tell me your Uncle is so you understand what that means."

"No, my Uncle isn't black and neither am I." I leave it there rather than trying to claim any special knowledge of what the black experience may be in this country.

"But I do have a deep sense of obligation to make Fort Christian a better place for all of us to live, work, worship and play. A place that enables each of us to become what we can be in service to our families, friends and each other. That's why when the Mayor called and asked if I would serve on the commission, I was deeply honored that anyone would think I had something to add to the conversation.

"But then I realized I have the opportunity to create something new here, too. A new set of dynamics that will address making Fort Christian a better place for all of us. I have to see if I can help us all get there."

"You're making a pitch for me to accept you as chairman and work with you. I get that. But I gotta tell you, I'm not.

"I will use every ounce of my strength and endurance to outlast you. I will not back off any of my demands. I will see that every one of them ends up in the final set. And I will see that every member of that Council is defeated in the next election to send a strong signal to everyone in this city that the black community is a force to be reckoned with.

"Anyone who assumes they can just roll over us is wrong. We will persevere. We will win this fight and send all the white racist officers to retirement where they belong so they can't harass us anymore."

I just sit there looking at him without comment, expecting that at some point he will hear himself. I'm not sure if that is what happens, or if he is genuinely curious, but he asks,

"So how did you get appointed to this commission in the first place? I've never heard of you in connection with anything relating to the city."

"I travel too much for work to be involved in most things locally. The Boy's Club has been the sole focus on what I try to give back to the community, because that's one place where I can help others. I played ball. I did the work. I figured out how to turn my physical limitations into strengths.

"And I want to communicate that to the next generation of ball players, because so many think if they spend their whole lives just shooting hoops eventually someone will get them a chance to shoot hopes for money. It doesn't work that way."

"What does that have to do with the commission?"

"I get to know ball players because I'm out there on the court with them helping them get better. I put a lot of time into some of them, and not just the Deshauns. They become like younger brothers to me.

"I celebrate their successes and help them deal with the setbacks. I get involved with them as people, not as just some poor kid I spent some time with. I'm not ever going to play in the NCAA tournament again. But some of them could. And if I open a door so they can do the right things to get there? It's worth it to me."

"Living vicariously through them?" the Rev suggests.

I nod. "And also dying vicariously through them, as I did with Deshaun."

I let that sit there with him for a moment.

"I can't tell you how deeply his death affected me. I asked questions of people about why something like this could happen in Fort Christian. It was just insane to me.

"I did some research on how prevalent these kinds of incidents are. I was shocked, so I asked more questions.

"I guess people realized that I would really like to see something happen that would end even the possibility of something like this ever happening again.

"I want to see Fort Christian as a safe haven for all its citizens, a place where growing up is the same for black and white kids. Where everyone is able to become whatever they dream."

"Do you have thoughts on what should be proposed?"

"I do," I respond as earnestly as possible, "But they should only be one set of the many the commission considers. If I can't convince you and the members to endorse my thoughts that should be because the people of Fort Christian want to go a different way, and that's fine."

"You don't mean that," The Rev thinks he's calling me out.

"If you think I'm abusing my positional power in these discussions, I expect you to bring that to everyone's attention. Majority rules, so I have to fall in line with everyone else.

"And on the other hand, you can be sure I will bring it to everyone's attention if you step over the line."

"What you don't see is the assumption that if the Mayor and Council made you Chairman they must think your ideas are what should be adopted." The Rev is point blank in his response.

"The Mayor and I had the conversation that I may have to withhold my ideas as Chairman for that very reason."

The Reverend LeRoy Lindo looks at me misbelieving, or so it would seem. He appears to be out of questions, challenges, and threats for the moment, so I stand,

"I look forward to the two of us and our new best friends finding a path forward for the city of Fort Christian that, when the next generation looks back on what we did, they say, they really got it right, rather than, what in the world were they thinking?"

25 – T.K. JEFFERSON

The first meeting of the commission is held in City Hall in a conference room on the top floor.

I've never been in this room before, but then again I don't make it a habit to visit City Hall for anything if I can help it. Sina has been here for various meetings pertaining to the election when she was managing Flo's campaign, but not much since.

I look around the room and other than Petes and the Rev I don't recognize anyone.

"Good afternoon. Thank you for your willingness to serve the City of Fort Christian as a member of this temporary Citizen's Commission on Police Reform.

"I believe you have all been briefed by the Mayor and her staff as to the responsibilities and limitations on our roles. So I'd like to go around the room and ask you to introduce yourself and indicate if you have any affiliation with the police department, family or friends who are on the police force, or work with or for the courts.

"I'll start. I'm T.K. Jefferson, I'm a Director at Morton Exploration and Production. I do not have any affiliations with the police department, although I do play basketball with kids from the Boy's Club with Sergeant Duke Marion, who also happens to be the president of the local chapter of the Benevolent Order of Police Officers.

"This has been a long-standing relationship, although it is limited to playing ball and working with the kids."

I nod to the slender young black woman immediately to my right.

"Hi. I'm Jenice Turner, I'm a housewife with two young boys

ages seven and five who are a handful. My husband, Terrance Turner is with First Federal Bank here in town where he is a commercial loan officer. We've been here about five years.

"I don't have any affiliations with the department or officers or the courts. I guess I'm here because I have two boys growing up in this city and Roxanne Williams sold me my home when we moved here. I've kind of kept in touch and she asked me if I'd be interested in serving. So that's me."

The next person is a short stocky white guy with dark hair, moustache and wearing a cheap suit. He introduces himself.

"I'm Lenny Evers. I own property around the city, mostly shopping and offices with a few apartment complexes. I don't have any affiliations with the police other than an occasional call when I needed support to evict someone who had stopped paying rent. But other than that? No. Nothing.

"I was asked to be on this commission by Alvin Hill, who is one of my tenants. He has his restaurant in my Northgate plaza."

Next is a well-dressed Hispanic woman, maybe fifty, who wears glasses with darkened lenses.

"Hello, my name is Dr. Maria Molina. I'm an Emergency Room physician at Memorial Hospital. Life-long resident of the city as is my husband, who is an administrator at Memorial responsible for the obstetrics unit.

"Working the ER I know many, if not most, of the police officers who often accompany someone who has been injured or needs emergency treatment for some reason."

"Am I close friends with any of them? No. I may know some by their last names, but generally only because they wear a name badge.

"I have had no involvement with the courts other than periodically providing written testimony regarding a patient. Oh, I was asked to serve on this commission by Mayor Blackwell who has been a friend and neighbor for many years."

The next person is a young black woman who barely looks old enough to be out of college. She has dark shoulder length hair and deep dark brown eyes.

"Hi. My name's Tasha Goodenough. I'm a social services caseworker. Probably enough said about that. I also grew up here, went to the local schools, and got my Masters degree in Social Welfare at City University.

"Working in Social Services, I deal with police officers, probation officers, food stamps, juvenile court, family court and once in a while criminal court. I deal with all those folks on a daily basis, but most of my friends are from my college days so I don't really hang with any of the police or court types.

"Would be too weird to see someone out at night and then have to deal with them the next day, you know? I was nominated to be on this commission by Councilman Peter Cochrane, who is sitting next to me here.

I volunteered on Councilman Cochrane's election campaign and he remembered me. Wow. That was a surprise. Anyway I just may be one of the few people he knew who touches all of those law enforcement organizations in the city. I don't know," she looks at Petes Cochrane.

Next is the Council member who is likely forty-ish, well dressed and athletic in appearance.

"As Tasha has told you already, I'm Council member Peter Cochrane. People call me 'Petes', just as they have since I was in elementary school, although I don't remember this, because I always used to say 'Petes' to anything someone brought into the room.

"The name just stuck, what can I say? I'm the senior partner at Cochrane, Stills and Jones, a law firm specializing in civil and corporate law. We do most of our work for the Electric Utility and that's my specialization, utility law.

"Because I'm working in corporate law, I have few occasions to interact with police or court officials, other than through my work on Council."

The last member is the Rev.

"I'm Reverend LeRoy Lindo. I'm Pastor at the Second Baptist Church with a congregation of almost seven hundred souls. My specialization is salvation.

"From time-to-time I have come in contact with various police officers in the work that I do at the church and tending my ministry.

"I do not have any family members or close friends among either the police department or the court system here in town. I assume you all know that I am the designated vice chairman of this commission."

I'm about to move on to the next item on my list when the Rev starts in.

"I think we all know why we're here. The police department is overrun with racists who are out to humiliate every living black boy in this city so they won't give the white cops any trouble. This has got to stop and I mean right now. If we don't stop it there's going to be a terrible…"

"Reverend Lindo." I put my hand down on his crossed hands before him to get his attention. "You will have an opportunity to express every relevant opinion, thought, idea and recommendation, just as everyone else here will have such an opportunity. But the time for that is not yet. I'll recognize you at the appropriate time."

"Things will be very different on the nights you're not here," the Rev retorts.

I turn to the rest of the commission members, "One of the rules of this commission is that we are a committee of the whole. That means we all meet or we don't meet."

"What?" The Rev explodes, "Nobody told me this. I'm liking this less and less. Whitewash I tell you."

"There will be times when individual members have to be elsewhere," I continue. "They will be permitted to join by telephone as long as they have access to the materials the commission is reviewing at that time.

"It's essential that we all review everything together, we all participate in all discussions and that the recommendations that come from this commission represent the collective thoughts of all of us.

"What that means is if we do not come to consensus on a recommendation, it will not be included in the final report. We cannot put forth solutions that we are not in agreement with. If we cannot agree, we cannot expect Council member Cochrane and the other Council members to agree. Only if there is a unified community effort will we be able to effect change. And by the way, Council member Cochrane is ex-officio, meaning he doesn't have a vote. If he did, he could veto any recommendation. That doesn't mean we shouldn't take into account his perspectives. It just means he can't impose his recommendations on the rest of us.

"To help you understand the task before us, we have just thirty days to complete our work and forward a set of recommendations to Council. That may not seem like much time, and it isn't.

"We could easily work on this task for six months or a year. But in my work, I have found that it is better to confine the task to a shorter time frame. Let the calendar serve as a forcing function, making us come to agreements so we can move on to the next topic.

"The Mayor has provided funding for a researcher who is already assembling data and statistics on the scope and scale of similar issues in other cities around the world, the nature of actions they have taken to address those similar issues and the results.

"That way we will have facts and data to inform us as we discuss alternative courses of action. Now this does not preclude any member from doing independent research and bringing that data in for discussion. However, our researcher will validate member data to ensure we are not biasing our actions based on unverified information gleaned from the internet."

I hand out copies to the other members. "One of the pieces of information we will start with is this report of the internal investigations team that looked into the Deshaun Bush officer-involved shooting resulting in loss of life of the civilian.

"Full disclosure, I knew Deshaun Bush and viewed him as a friend. Just want that on the record so you understand statements I may make as we are going through this report.

"I expect you to challenge me if I say anything about that event that is not substantiated elsewhere. We absolutely must stick to facts and data if we are going to have any chance of affecting the performance of the department."

Tasha interrupts me. "If you were friends with Deshaun, why did they ever put you on this commission?"

"The commission is looking at what can be done to make the police department more responsive to the community, not whether Patrolman Webster is guilty of murder, manslaughter or some lesser crime. You are correct, I would not be an objective juror, but that was not the charge here.

"I am an engineer. My life's work has been finding ways of creating something that many believe to be impossible. I've always worked in motivating teams to perform feats of magic, if you will.

"So I think the answer to your question is that my friendship with Deshaun is a motivational factor for me to help the department find approaches to ensure no one else dies at the hands of a police officer who is not threatening an innocent life."

"Fair enough." Tasha says. "I see now why you're wanting to get something done quickly, but I look at the fact that all of us have demanding day jobs, including Jenice with her two little ones. I can't imagine how we can do what is needed in the few hours we will have to dedicate to this effort over the next month."

"I understand your concern," I answer. "When we get to the end, if you feel we have made a series of inappropriate or unachievable recommendations let's discuss.

"I know none of you have been through a process quite like what we are about to undertake. I do it regularly and am comfortable you will be satisfied with whatever we collectively decide upon."

I glance around the room to see if anyone else has an objection. "Okay, back to the internal investigation report. I know Council member Cochrane has read it. Has anyone else?"

All shake their heads. "I want you to read it before our next meeting on Wednesday. As you read, make notes of any questions you have and fax or email them to me at this address." I hand out business cards.

"I will give your questions to our researcher, who will obtain written answers, which will be provided back to you in advance of our next session. The whole idea is to come as prepared as possible, to not spend time on singular questions, but focus on issues we all identify. Does that make sense?"

I check for nodding or shaking heads or expressions that indicate a lack of agreement. Seeing none I plunge forward,

"The intent is to meet twice a week for the first two weeks and take a week off while a small team drafts the report.

"The last week we will meet every day until we have an agreed upon document to submit to Council."

Petes asks, "What happens if we can't get to agreement?"

"I know not everyone will be happy with everything we put into the final report. I expect there will be things that I may not agree with, but the question will be can everyone live with an imperfect but adequate document?

“Now the other thing that can bog us down is word choice. Attorneys make a living charging by the word, or so it seems to me sometimes. We are going for clear and concise language, not perfect language.

“Anyone who intends to read this document aloud on a podcast is likely to not have many listeners. That is not the audience. We are focused on actionable language.

“Can someone take the statement we make and actually go do what we want them to do? That is the test of clear and concise.”

The Rev shakes his head to Petes, who nods, just once. I decide to call them on it. “I see you two gentlemen are skeptics. Have either of you ever created something that didn’t exist before you tried?”

Petes and Reverend Lindo both shake their heads.

26 – REGINA BLACKWELL – MAYOR, CITY OF FORT CHRISTIAN

T.K. comes up to my office immediately after the first meeting of the commission.

I rearrange a budget meeting so we can talk. I've not worked with him before, so I'm trying to understand how he thinks, how he's approaching this effort, whether he thinks I've stacked the deck against success by adding Reverend Lindo on top of Petes Cochrane.

"Mayor Blackwell, thanks for making time to see me." T.K. seems deep in thought.

"I put you in this position, the least I can do is make sure you can be successful. What did you want to talk about?"

"We concluded the first meeting just a few minutes ago. I now have a better feel for the people part of this process." He sounds cautious. Is he going to want me to change out commissioners? That won't be easy after the other night's ambush by the Rev Lindo and his congregation.

"What's your read?"

"The people part of it will be challenging, but put any two people in a room, even if they're family, they're going to disagree.

"So that part isn't a concern as of yet. If any of them don't do the homework, it could affect the timetable, but so far I haven't felt like that's going to be a problem."

"Something's on your mind or you wouldn't have come by."

"What will the city do if I can't get to a set of recommendations that all members endorse?"

"I know how difficult things have become since Council gave in on the Rev's blackmail. I just want you to do the best you can, submit a majority report with minority opinions noted."

I watch T.K. process that suggestion. He apparently isn't happy with it. "What are you thinking?"

"You gave me the chairmanship with the expectation that I will deliver a set of recommendations that will make a difference. If we have minority reports within the report, that will make it almost impossible for you to get a united Council and united citizens to back what you want done.

"That's not good enough."

"I hear you, T.K. I've been working with the city government for a lot of years now.

"Perfect is the enemy of good.

"We have to start and not expect to transform in one fell swoop. Getting to unanimous consent on our agenda with only five members of Council almost never happens.

"You are blessed with a commission that on the surface may not seem to be representative of our city, but it is. If you trust them, they will exceed your expectations.

"Every one of them has stepped up in the past, some under great duress. You have the chance to do something that this city has needed for decades and probably longer.

"A truly independent look at how we enforce laws in our jurisdiction.

"How our law enforcement officers work with the people of the city.

"How we become one united community working together rather than blaming others when things go wrong.

"And things always go wrong from time to time."

"I can see determination in the room, but at the moment that determination seems focused in different directions to address different agendas…" I observe.

"And that is your opportunity. You can bring those agendas together.

"I know what you can do, even though you don't think I do. I watched your championship season on television with my older brother who just thought you were the best thing ever to have come out of Fort Christian.

"Took me a long time to convince him I was actually interested, but I finally did. I watched you play those games, seldom showing off your skills, always working in the backcourt to set people up, draw a foul if needed, dish off as you went to the basket and took more than your share of elbows to the face for your team.

"I've just given you another team. I expect you to work you magic with them in the same way."

T.K. considers my comments, "I'll do my best."

"I understand your desire to get something done, but think about the approach of a minority set of recommendations, but don't inform the members of that approach until they have proceeded as far as they can. That way you should be able to contain the Rev and Petes."

"You know it's Petes who worries me more."

"I'm surprised. Why do you think Council member Cochrane is a bigger problem?"

"Petes was primarily supported by the police union. How can he support anything they would not be in favor of? Anything that changes how the department is run, or how the policemen do their job is a threat whether in fact or just an impression."

"Like not following procedure?" I ask, expecting T.K. to have a ready answer. But to my surprise. T.K. just shrugs.

"What are **you** looking for, coming out of this exercise? Just insistence that the police department follow its own procedures?" I ask.

T.K. grimaces, "I'm looking for a different city to emerge from this examination of who we are and what we've become. A different city that values everyone alike."

"I'm looking for fundamental change," I shake my head without even knowing I am, but I see the frown from T.K. "I don't know what to think about the ideas you shared with Flo.

"There may be something there that is that paradigm shift in people's attitudes. But then again, maybe not. I put you on the commission as chairman because you're not trying to protect anything.

"At the same time you're not trying to make a circus out of the whole thing to benefit personally.

"The one thing I do know is that you're going to take on sacred cows on both sides of this discussion. I hope something different emerges. A path forward if nothing else."

I watch T.K. consider my thoughts. The expression on his face conveys the seriousness with which he is contemplating this exercise and that is all the tangible evidence I need to know I picked the right person.

Only time will tell now as to whether he has the ability to deliver a paradigm shift.

I have to give him the opportunity to succeed -- whatever form that takes -- although I think that for the most part it will be air cover from the media and Council members who are getting reports that the commission isn't getting to the core issues.

I fully expect that. I just hope I don't get ambushed by the Rev dialing up Roxanne and Alvin and suddenly colluding with Petes.

I just don't trust his motives. Everyone has pointed to his support from the police officer's union, which is why he's not on the negotiations team, even though he has asked repeatedly to be added.

Interesting that T.K. is more wary of Petes than he is of the Rev, who is firing at anything that moves. I wonder what experiences he's had that are telling him to be more cautious of those who aren't shooting than those who are.

T.K. starts to get up. "You're very busy and I've taken too much of your time already."

"Sit down, T.K." I motion to him realizing that maybe I'm the problem here because I've pushed this conversation too quickly -- because I'm feeling I should be in the budget meeting rather than here.

"You're feeling alone and afraid knowing you're about to get sucked into a shoot-out on the frontier.

"Let me assure you that others have walked this way previously. Some have actually lived to tell about it.

"Now, I get the sense that you're smarter and more introspective than most of those folks. So I have great confidence that you will emerge from this exercise not only with an actionable set of recommendations, but that those recommendations will transform the department in a positive manner."

T.K. looks at me with a puzzled expression. "Is this a pep talk?"

"Of sorts," I acknowledge. "Being an elected official is the craziest job anyone could ever want. You spend all kinds of money you don't have, you call on every friendship you ever had and some you never thought you would, to go out and campaign for you.

"Day-after-day of going door-to-door, sending innocuous tweets and Facebook postings so that people will even know you exist.

"Endless meetings, honing messages, learning how to dodge questions about identified groups who won't like the first answer that comes to your mind. Learning how to smile when your stomach is fighting another civil war. Or learning how to carry on when your head is pounding from a headache that just won't quit.

"And then you get up and do it all again -- until either the polls tell you it's hopeless -- or they don't." I pause for a breath.

"I tell you this not because I think you might be crazy enough to want to run for office. Way too many people do so for the wrong reasons. I tell you this because I know I'm asking you to take on the impossible task of making us better than we are.

"I'm asking you to help us see who we could be, even though our heads are down, looking at our cell phone screens, rather than engaging in a meaningful dialog with any other human being." Again, I pause for breath.

"The world is spinning off in some unfathomable direction. I don't know what is going to change next week, let alone next year. But, in any event, what I did to get elected last time? Totally irrelevant.

"The Facebook posts I spent so much time on last time? Nobody is reading Facebook anymore. We've moved into a world of pictures. That's all anyone cares about.

"Who is with who? Where are they? What is so and so wearing? Where in the world did she buy that? Nobody talks to anyone these days. That can't be a good thing."

"You're telling me what?" T.K. asks.

"Not to worry. The rules you think apply to the situation you are taking on…? They don't.

"You're out on the frontier. No landmarks you recognize. The tumbleweeds cross your path as the winds kick up, but still you don't have a bead on the direction your horse should follow.

"Do you know what you need to do? No. Is that a problem? Only if you let it be."

"Damnedest pep talk anyone has ever given me," T.K. responds.

"Maybe so, but don't take it personal. I do this to every new commission chairman I have the Council approve."

"How many commissions have you authorized in your term?"

"You're the first."

"So we're both Christopher Columbus, sailing the unknown, towards a place that isn't where we think it is, and unfortunately we won't recognize -- even when we get there.

"We mistakenly call native Americans Indians because we think we are someplace else."

"Things could be worse…" I tease him.

"How?"

"You could be taking on a hopeless task, with a group of unreasonable parties who have no interest in coming to agreement because they only succeed if you fail."

"I thought that describes the commission members rather well…"

"No one I gave you is unreasonable, not even the Rev. You just have to discover what it is that will drive him to agreement. There is something that will do that, I'm quite certain. Or I never would have agreed to put him on the commission."

T.K. rises. "Again, thank you for making time for me. I can't say as I have any clearer idea how we get to the desired outcome. But it's early in the process.

"I have a friend who never watches baseball before the 8th inning or football before the 4th quarter. He tells me that's the point at which it becomes interesting --- because until then it's all random."

27 – T.K. JEFFERSON

Wednesday arrives all too quickly. I have to shift work I'd normally do to Mustapha to keep things moving. I don't like doing that, because then he gets less time at home with his family.

But this is a surge. And we often have surges at work. I'd just rather it be routine surges than something that really has nothing to do with the company.

I'm writing instructions to my team on an analysis that has to be completed tomorrow when I look at the clock.

Oh shit, I'm going to be late for my own meeting.

I finish the sentence and then the thought, hit send and shut down the computer as I race for the door and my car.

I arrive at City Hall exactly at the time the meeting is scheduled to begin. I wonder if the Rev is sitting in my chair, hoping to commandeer the meeting.

I take the stairs two at a time rather than wait for the elevator. When I get upstairs everyone else is there. They, almost as a group, look at the clock as I walk in. I nod to everyone and take my seat.

As I look around the room I ask, "Has everyone read the internal investigation report and submitted your questions?"

Nods all around.

"And you received satisfactory answers and clarifications?"

Nods from two members, apparently the only ones who submitted questions. That tracks with my remembrance.

"In that case we have the facts of the matter. So I recommend we go around the room and tell us how you feel about what has happened in a single word."

We start with Jenice, "Appalled."

Lenny has to think before answering, "FUBAR."

Jenice asks, "What?"

Lenny shakes his head, "Not something I care to repeat in polite company."

"Then why did you use it?" Tasha asks.

"It summed up my feelings about the situation."

"Then tell us what it means." Tasha is adamant.

"Fucked up beyond all recognition – FUBAR."

Maria shakes her head, "Disappointing."

Tasha shakes her head, "Outraged."

Petes offers an explanation, "I don't remember my first feeling as I've slept a few times since then, but I guess it was more incomprehension, not understanding how something could get out of hand like that."

The Rev offers his standard, "Whitewash."

"I think it's important that we deal with our feelings about the precipitating incident before we start into the hard discussion about what is needed to make those negative sentiments about the department into positive feelings."

"What was your feeling?" Petes asks me.

"I felt loss."

"Could you explain?" the Rev asks me.

"I felt and still feel a personal loss of a friend and someone I was mentoring. I feel the loss of trust in the police and the loss of respect for some of the men and women of the police department that they would enable something like this to occur.

"Most of all I feel the loss of faith in each other, that together we can rise above these horrible circumstances and find a shared path forward for ourselves, our families, our friends and neighbors and all those who live, work and play in this city.

"My expectation is that the commission will rectify the situation."

Heads nod, although neither the Rev's nor Petes'. "I'd like to go around the room again. This time I would like you to share your opening opinion of how best to restore trust in the police department and faith in each other."

Jenice begins as we have apparently decided this is how we will respond, "My opinion…" Jenice thinks a moment longer,

"As a mother of two young children I think I'd like every officer to have to spend a year in an elementary school, becoming friends with the kids, getting to know them and letting the kids get to know them as people, not just someone who is enforcing the law.

"Maybe if the officers and the kids can build trust in each other, we can bridge this divide that is so evident in the report. Does that make sense?"

I type into a spreadsheet: A mandatory year in an elementary school for all officers.

Lenny is next, "All new police recruits go through Marine Corps basic training and Military Police training before they can go on patrol in a civilian city. Instill procedure and discipline."

I type into the same spreadsheet: Mandatory Marine Corps basic and MP training.

Marie is writing a note to herself on the pad before her. "I like to organize my thoughts in writing. It helps me be concise.

"Anyway, I think a year in a hospital and surgical suite, putting people back together after being shot. Working with them through rehab. It would give them a perspective on what a bullet does to someone and what it takes to recover. I think it would give them pause."

I type into my spreadsheet: Mandatory year in hospital and surgery suite.

Tasha is looking at me as if she doesn't want to say what she's thinking,

"I think being a police officer is so stressful that there should be a time limit for how long they can patrol or be on the streets. Twenty years maybe.

"Some time limit so burnout doesn't become a factor, and so the officers can be young enough to relate to much younger citizens and recruits."

I type into my spreadsheet: Time limits for service.

I look at Petes and wait, "It seems to me that the key problem in the report was the lack of discipline. If the patrolman had simply followed direction, the events never would have occurred.

"So I'm somewhere between what Lenny suggested and maybe just a severe fine for anyone who fails to follow procedures. Maybe a suspension for egregious behavior. Something along those lines."

I type into the spreadsheet: Fines or suspension for failure to follow procedures.

The Rev has been waiting for this.

"Fire the Chief, fire all officers, hire only black officer replacements, create a community police oversight board, Recall the Mayor, Recall the Council…no offense, Petes… enforce discipline and invest in proper training for all officers.

"I'm not talking just weapons training. I'm talking conflict resolution, de-escalation, and negotiations, skills that makes non-lethal encounters the rule and weapons the last resort."

I type: Fire Chief, all officers, hire only black replacements, community police oversight board, recall Mayor, Council and invest in training.

The Rev asks, "And yours?"

"I'm seeing a possible solution in the different parts of what each of you have proposed. I'm not nearly as eloquent as you have been, but I agree, discipline is a core issue in the report and needs to be addressed.

"But the kind of training Reverend Lindo has described has a lot of merit. I've asked for the current training requirements and records of which officers have failed that training or failed to attend it.

"And I think Jenice, Maria and Tasha have hit the nail on the head that many officers don't know their communities and the communities don't know their officers as people.

"Tasha suggested limits so officers could better relate to younger people. Maybe the solution is that officers must live where they police on the local level. Become part of that community so they are responding to their friends and neighbors. That's another core problem.

"So I'm a little earlier in thinking this all through than you are. But one question I have, and no one touched on it, is what role does the weapon play in law enforcement?"

"Are you suggesting we need to take the weapons away from police officers?" Petes demands of me.

"I don't know the answer to that. I've asked our researcher to look into it, gather some statistics. See what we can find out.

“The reason I wonder about the weapon is if Patrolman Webster had not been armed, he might have been more willing to wait for backup. He might never have gotten out of his car.

“I also look at what most officers do all day. Weapons simply aren’t needed. So I’m asking for some data on that as well.

“The Council, including you, when you established this commission, directed us to look at any and all data, information and proposals, to talk to anyone we deem appropriate, and to think creatively, especially when it comes to potential application of solutions that have been proven elsewhere.”

“Police officers are armed everywhere,” Petes responds.

“I really don’t think this subject merits a lot of discussion at this stage because it’s just a question. But just to be clear, your statement is not accurate.

“There are a number of countries where officers don’t carry guns, to include England and Wales, Sweden, Norway, New Zealand, Iceland and others.”

“Not countries where people have easy access to guns like here,” Petes says.

“I look at it differently,” and wait for everyone to look up at me. “Officers don’t carry weapons in countries where the people don’t want them to, because they will accept responsibility for themselves and their community.

“Now, at the moment I think it’s fair to say that no one has asked the people of Fort Christian if they want to live up to their name as being willing to embrace Christian principles in their conduct with others, or leave it to the government through their police officers.”

Petes dismisses my arguments. “You’re right. Not worth discussing now because it would never happen. This is Texas. Open carry is the law. Anyone of age can get a license and carry a gun. So the police have to have an equalizer.”

Reverend Lindo looks at me thoughtfully, but says nothing.

"Good," I say, moving on. "You each have a notebook of reading for our next meeting on Monday. This is a compilation of data, statistics and information about incidents where fatalities have been the result of officer-involved shootings.

"It is also information about our department's training requirements, profiles of the last ten years of recruits to the department in terms of not only prior training and experience, but also department fitness reports.

"You also have information on disciplinary actions for the last ten years. The nature of the incident, the disciplinary action taken and information on subsequent disciplinary actions including warnings and notes to file."

"This is all highly confidential," Petes notes for everyone.

"You all signed confidentiality agreements to be on the commission," I say primarily for Petes. "You are not to make copies of any of this information, share it in any form with anyone not on the commission, nor discuss it even in abstraction with the media."

I look directly at the Rev, who nods back at me. "This is where things turn gray. I am hopeful we can have a substantive discussion on Monday.

"Thanks," I say, concluding the meeting.

28 – T.K. JEFFERSON

I have to work through the weekend to keep up at work and get through all the reading for the commission, but as the data and statistics inform me, I'm convinced that the initial suggestions have a good chance of forming the outline of a workable set of recommendations.

Mayor Blackwell was right about the members she appointed to the commission. They think the right way. Only Petes seems to want to keep the status quo. However, even he was willing to be somewhat critical.

I just need to find a means of driving the extremes to the middle and convince even Petes that some things have to change.

And now I'm hustling back up the stairs at City Hall, carrying my notebook and laptop, realizing I'm going to be a few minutes late again. Not a good precedent and hopefully I can get my act together for the next meeting.

I come into the room and find Petes and the Rev are not there.

"Afternoon, everyone." I take my seat, look up at the clock as I open up the laptop so I can record the information from the meeting. Five minutes after the hour. I'll give them until four-fifteen and then send everyone home.

But then the Rev appears. "Sorry, I know I'm late. Got stuck in traffic and then couldn't find a parking spot and had to circle."

The Rev comes over and sits next to me in the same seat. He too looks up at the clock as he opens his notebook where I see bookmarked pages. Good. That means he's come prepared to discuss specifics.

We wait in silence until ten after the hour. Petes appears, doesn't say a word, takes his seat next to the Rev. I begin.

I plug in my laptop to the overhead projection system so I can display my spreadsheet as I begin the meeting. "Did everyone have a chance to review the materials?"

Everyone, even Petes, nods.

"Good. I spent nearly a whole day over the weekend trying to absorb what we have here. I'm not sure I really have a good handle on it.

"I'm hopeful that as we discuss our takeaways you'll be able to help me better understand some of it. So let's get started.

"I'm going to display the initial suggestions you all made last week. And I want to focus us on those suggestions and discuss them in light of what we read.

"I'm doing this because we could spend a month going through all of the data and be no further along other than in just understanding the data.

"That's not the objective. The data is suggestive and will also validate actions, but our focus has to be on actions or we will not complete our task within the thirty day limit because we are now in the second week."

Maria raises her hand seeking to be recognized. "Yes, Maria."

"Are you suggesting that we're not going to go through all of the material we read?"

"Not as a group. This process demands that we do our homework and apply our takeaways to the problem at hand.

"As we discuss, we will use the facts and data to validate what we want to do and in that process we will come to clarify our understanding.

"Does that make sense? I want you to apply what you read and learned rather than just confirming it."

"That's a big assumption. That we're ready to apply what we learned."

"You will surprise yourself, and find that the other members have takeaways that in some instances will be very different than yours.

"That's when we go back to the data and have a discussion if needed to come to a common understanding of something we want to use to validate whether to do something or not."

"I see what you're wanting us to do, I've just never…"

"Been held accountable for following a procedure?" I suggest. All of a sudden a lightbulb goes off for everyone in the room, but I see Petes look at me, not at all happy that I've simply asked the commission members to do what any police officer is required to do.

"No." Maria responds. "As a surgeon I am required to follow a procedure or my patient may die."

"As a patrolman, either that person follows procedure or an innocent civilian may die," I respond.

Maria nods and I check with everyone else visually. Each one is thinking about this little exchange, which is exactly what I want them to do.

"If we're ready to proceed?" I turn on the data projector and my spreadsheet is displayed on the wall screen.

"I have taken the liberty of summarizing your initial suggestions in the left column, which I've labeled as department and I have created a column to the right which is blank, but labeled community.

"I added this column because I believe -- and as we go through this exercise we may discover together that I'm wrong -- but I believe there are going to be actions that the community must take in order for the change we are seeking to occur and sustain.

"I'm not interested in having the department do a whole bunch of things that after a year have had no effect and are discontinued.

"I think it's incumbent on us to design a set of recommendations that may be hard to implement, but if successful, will permanently change community policing in Fort Christian."

I see Lenny and Maria nodding to themselves. The Rev just looks at me. I'm not sure if he thinks I'm crazy or going down a hopeless path. "So are we ready?"

All eyes move to the screen. "Okay, the first suggestions came from Jenice.

"As you can see she suggested that all officers -- she was not specific if they were new hires, or any time during their career -- but that all officers spend a year in an elementary school, getting to know the kids, and letting the kids get to know them as people.

"What else would you like to say about that, now that you've looked at the facts and data about officer-involved shootings?"

Jenice is hesitant, finally looks back at us rather than the screen.

"What I was thinking was that officers should work in a school for a year during their first five years on the force. First year would be ideal, but they may need to get more generalized experience before doing so.

"However, my husband took the kids over the weekend to give me time to read and reflect on the larger issue. How it's played out in other cities and countries. That really struck me.

"This isn't an isolated incident. It happens everywhere. So last night I was thinking about that summary you did of our suggestions last week. How you pulled the different ideas together.

"I can see just one thing isn't going to make a whole lot of difference. Putting officers in the schools is a good idea, but it's not the whole solution."

"Does anyone have anything to add to Jenice's suggestion?" I ask.

"Data from cities that have tried putting community police into schools for a tour to get to know the kids and vice versa? I know some cities have school police officers in the schools, but they work for the school district and not the community.

"I would think -- and there may be evidence to refute this observation, but I didn't see it in our binders -- that school police versus community police working in the schools have less effect in reducing community and police relations issues."

"We have school security officers, is that the same thing?" Tasha asks.

The Rev speaks up. "Yes and no. From what I've read, some districts arm their security teams and then they become sworn officers.

"Others, like ours, aren't armed. They aren't sworn officers, they don't have the same level of training, but also don't have the same level of enforcement authority. Their job, if things get out of hand, is to try to quell the disturbance until the regular police officers can arrive."

"Is that how it works in countries where the officers aren't armed, like England?" I ask.

Tasha tentatively responds, "After you raised that issue, I did some research on what they do there. Actually, in England they have very small special weapons and tactics teams. The only officers who carry weapons as a matter of course are the Nuclear Constabulary.

"Those are the police who protect the nuclear power plants. That's a special case, but it kind of goes to what T.K. was saying.

"That it's an expectation of the community that the police will enforce laws without needing to resort to weapons, so they don't carry them. Armed police are only summonsed in the events of terrorism or active shooter scenarios."

"But people don't own guns in England. Not to the extent they do here. So there crime is a lot less violent," Petes notes, returning to the same point he made last week.

"We have to understand the cultural differences," I say. "I agree with Council member Cochrane that England is a different cultural environment than ours. Weapon ownership is a lot less common.

"The statistics bear out that there is much lower violent crime in that country. What role the lack of common weapon ownership plays in that would be a question we might want to investigate further."

Again I see the Rev giving me a curious look.

"Lenny, you had a very different suggestion." I turn to the property owner member.

"I did. I suggested all new officers need discipline, and going through Marine Corps basic and advanced training seems to be a way of instilling that discipline.

"As I read the report it appears the discipline to follow procedure is lacking beyond just the new recruits, so there would need to be something to remind everyone of the need for discipline in following procedures.

"Fines or suspension without pay, as Council member Cochrane suggested, those kinds of things might be adequate, but in reading the material this week, it would appear that the union is in the middle of disciplinary actions, so I don't know how you make something like that work.

"That's a question I'd like us to explore. What is the appropriate role for the unions in disciplinary actions? If the police are like teachers, who once they have tenure you can't fire them, then we have an issue there we need to make recommendations on."

I turn to the group, "Thoughts?"

"The unions have a legitimate seat at the table," Petes responds immediately.

"They absolutely do," I agree to set up my next question, "But Lenny raised an interesting question on which we need data." I type in next to Lenny's suggestion: Data on Disciplinary Action Modifications

"What are you trying to get at?" Petes instantly reacts.

"Facts and data. Lenny asked a question and we need to get facts and data to understand the answers to all our questions, regardless of what the area may be. In this instance, Lenny wants to know if the union role in modifying disciplinary actions may be contributing to a willingness to disregard procedure.

"I don't know if the department has any data on that, or if there is any data from some state or national source. But it is clearly worth investigating.

"It may lead to a recommendation in that area, although until we see the data I have no idea what that recommendation might be."

"Why are you going after the union?" Petes drills me.

"I'm not. I'm simply saying we need to look at the facts and data. There are no sacred cows here."

"You know you can really be annoying…" Petes responds, clearly without thinking.

"My wife says the same thing," I observe and am greeted with laughter from everyone but Petes. "Okay, does anyone have other observations about Lenny's modified recommendations?"

I am greeted with silence until the Rev notes, "I'm still thinking about Lenny's idea of Marine Corps. training for new officers.

"I agree that lack of discipline was clearly a major contributing cause of the recent events. I think we need to find a means of making discipline an assumption and not a sometime reaction amongst our police.

"I'm just not convinced Marine style training is the key. I think on the one hand we're noting that our children and families need to get to know police officers as people and vice versa.

"Marine style discipline means responding to orders immediately, and if necessary, without thought. I'm not sure the two are compatible.

"Now I've had the privilege of knowing some fine young men who have chosen to serve in the Marines. When they are not fighting on our behalf, they are respectful and engaging. They tend to genuinely care about civilians and are willing to help in a time of need.

"But they are stiff and formal. Do you see what I'm driving at? I don't think stiff and formal works for a police officer. I think it comes down to a perception of what I would call controlled violence.

Marines are taught to be disciplined but ruthless fighters who will protect their own in the face of overwhelming odds. I think of the Spartans and their stand against the Persians. That kind of attitude, and self-sacrifice. Again, I'm not sure that's what we want in a police force."

"You've raised a good question: What is it we want our police to be like?" I look at Petes.

He looks away, but after a moment reengages.

"We want rugged individuals who aren't afraid to go into a fight and break it up, who aren't afraid to go into a domestic dispute and defuse it, and who aren't afraid to pursue someone in a high speed chase, if necessary, to bring them to justice."

I nod, "Anything else?"

"That's kind of the top line for me," Petes responds.

"Anyone else?"

"I think there's a lot more to it," Jenice offers. "As I think of it what the Council member has suggested is kind of what got us where we are.

"I think of the report and how that could happen. The kind of person you just described? That's the kind of person who would do what happened that night.

"But I think of my boys. That's not the kind of person I want them to encounter when they come home from a friend's house -- as I heard from, what was her name the other night?"

"Keisha," Tasha responds instantly, "Keisha Foster."

"That's right. I don't want my boys to live in fear. I want them to be whatever they want to be and not feel they can't stand up for something because the police may come and take them away."

"So what should the police be like?" I ask generally.

"To me, they should be concerned citizens who want to help resolve disputes first." Tasha responds. "People who want to help people first.

"If we can get to the point that the police officers are seen as people who want to help us first, then the instances where you break up fights and all that? It becomes a secondary part of the whole experience.

"Maybe if we can rely on the police to help, then maybe we become more like England, where we don't want to keep guns in the house for protection."

Lenny nods to me that he'd like to speak.

"You know, we have this built-in conflict when it comes to law enforcement.

"The courts say you are innocent until proven guilty and you have a right to have that determination made by a jury of your peers.

"I had to study all this when I became a citizen. I was born in Ireland and moved to London first and then here when I was seventeen.

"So I guess maybe I have a different perspective."

“What do you think about the police not carrying weapons?” Maria asks almost immediately. “You lived in a place where that was the norm.”

“I did, but as has been pointed out, that’s a place where essentially the only people with weapons are bad guys. So it’s different. Did I prefer that? It took me a long time to accept how things are here, but there’s so much more opportunity than in London, at least for someone like me.

“So I came to accept that people here kill each other and don’t think much about it. Is it right? Not in my mind, but I’m willing to go along to have the life I want.”

“So you prefer the officers to be unarmed?” Maria asks.

“Absolutely. Is that something we could create here? I’d love it, but frankly I doubt it’s possible.”

“Talk to us about the conflict in the role you started exploring,” I say, bringing everyone back to his original point.

“Oh, that’s right. How is a policeman or woman supposed to do their job when everyone they encounter is innocent until proven guilty?

“If you think about it, for the most part they must observe someone breaking a law in order to arrest them.

“And In some instances detectives gather evidence, then send officers out to arrest someone based on evidence gathered after the fact.

“But they are only arrested. The judge or jury must still convict them before they are punished.

“So we put officers in this natural conflict. They can’t do anything unless they observe someone breaking a law and even then must presume innocence until proven guilty.

“I don’t know how you do that job. It’s not the storm-into-a-bar-and-break-up-a-fight kind of thing. It’s more the traffic cop who sees you speeding and gets you on radar.

"It's more the reckless driving, or endangerment kind of situation. The whole notion of arresting someone is literally stopping someone from continuing to break the law or continuing to create a dangerous situation for themselves or others."

"What kind of person do we need to fulfill that role?" I ask.

"What I'm seeing in my mind is one of those three circles kinds of pictures, where the circles intersect. Do you know what I'm saying?

"An officer has to be Council member Cochrane's macho man, Jenice's caring adult, the Reverend's disciplined -- he didn't say this but it's kind of where I think he was going -- neighbor who's looking out for you.

"Maybe that's really what I'm thinking -- that it should be a disciplined neighbor who was in the military a long time ago, so they know what to do and won't be afraid to help. Does that make sense?"

"That's what you see at the point of intersection?" Maria asks.

"I think so," Lenny reflects. "I'd be comfortable with someone like that on the force."

"But that's not who is on the force today," Tasha responds. "Not according to the data we looked at."

"Just to be clear," I say, "while the Reverend has expressed a different opinion, I personally think this commission has the right to propose either immediate changes as he has suggested, or we can propose changes in policy that would implement over time.

"To Tasha's point, what we are describing is not who we have today. When we get to the point of writing our report and recommendations, we will need to decide which approach we believe is most readily achievable, balanced against what is most important for the people who live here."

"Thank you for acknowledging my position on that subject," The Rev responds.

"And as you say, just to be clear, we can't afford to wait one more day to remove the racists from our police force. So an incremental approach to change is not something I'm willing to consider."

"And we will have that discussion at the appropriate time," I affirm. "Does anyone have anything they would like to add to our desired police man or woman?"

"They must be Black," the Rev asserts.

Maria nods to the Rev, but then responds. "What I heard from Lenny is that the people we want don't exist. We have to create them or grow them or train people to be what we want in a policeman.

"The issue is that the people who are training the next generation of officers aren't the people we want training them, because they're not the people we want as policemen either.

"Do you see what I'm saying? Lenny said the role has a built-in conflict. That's not something most people can readily negotiate without training, support, experience and the proper mental attitude.

"And I don't want to overlook the mental part of this whole discussion. I may not be a psychiatrist, but the mental stress on a law enforcement officer has to be enormous.

"Someone once said that being an airline pilot was hours upon hours of boredom with two minutes of extreme stress while they try to land the aircraft.

"I think being a law enforcement officer is much the same. Hours and hours of boredom, filing reports, walking beats, giving out traffic tickets, with unpredictable extreme stress where there is a fight, or robbery or domestic dispute or worse.

"So I like Lenny's three-circle diagram. We're looking for people with a core set of abilities around routine procedures, who can pull on unique skill sets to address the extreme situations."

"That goes back to Reverend Lindo and Lenny's initial observations that training has to be a big part of our recommendations," Tasha asserts.

"To some extent we must recognize that the ideal police officer isn't born as such. She or he becomes ideal through the training, experiences and attitudes they employ."

"What makes for the ideal police officer in your mind?" the Rev asks me.

"A Girl or Boy Scout," I respond without hesitation.

The Rev does a double take. "Are you being facetious?"

"Not at all," I respond neutrally. "I think of Girl and Boy Scouts as anyone you meet on the street. Someone who wants to be helpful, carry groceries and look in on sick people.

"Someone who will respond in an emergency, and practices to prepare to answer the call. They are curious, and achievement-oriented -- especially in completing the studies and tasks to get their merit badges.

"So, yes, I think of the Boy Scout oath: 'On my honor, I will do my best, to do my duty to God and my country and to obey the Scout Law; to help other people at all times; to keep myself physically strong, mentally awake and morally straight.'

"Doesn't that seem to be what we're talking about?"

"So that's the Scout Oath?" Lenny asks. "I was too old to be one when I came to this country."

"There's also a Scout Law. 'A Scout is: trustworthy, loyal, helpful, friendly, courteous, kind, obedient, cheerful, thrifty, brave, clean, and reverent," Petes responds. "I was an Eagle Scout. I've also been a Scout Master for my son's troop."

"What do you think about T.K.'s thought that police should be Girl or Boy Scouts?" Jenice asks.

"It has merit," Petes admits, grudgingly since it is so far removed from his description.

"I think we need to get back to our original solutions," I suggest. "Maria, you're next. You suggested our police officers need to spend a year in a hospital and specifically a surgical ward to see what it takes to put someone back together physically and emotionally after being shot. More thoughts on that?"

"I like where we've gone with this discussion," she responds.

"When I read through the material you provided, it opened my eyes to the much larger issues we are dealing with. It's not just our police department where these kind of incidents occur.

"I guess I've known that right along, but have never given it much thought until now. Much like your summary at the end of the last session, I'm seeing threads now. And I realize we aren't going to solve all those societal issues here.

"But what I do think we have is an opportunity to do something different.

"We shouldn't fall into the traps that the police are professionals; that we don't understand what it takes to be a policeman or the stresses they face; and most importantly that they are the law and so should not be subject to it.

"I was pleased that the district attorney took what I think was appropriate action in regards to Patrolman Webster. In doing so, she sent a clear signal that the police are not above the law.

"That's a good first step. But now it's up to us to write the rest of that new narrative about our city. That what has gone before, is gone. Today we are making a change for the better and this is how."

"How would you change what you initially suggested?" I ask.

"It seems one of the things we have danced around is the need for our police officers to walk in our shoes, if even for a little while. You said something about Tasha's suggestion. You said that officers needed to live where they work. They need to be part of the community they patrol.

"That struck a chord for me. If someone is your neighbor, like Lenny described, they know you and you'll trust them more. You know they're there looking out for you. If you need help, they will respond. Do you see what I'm saying?"

I draw a diagram with three circles on the computer. The top circle is: 'A part of their micro-community'.

"What are the other circles?" Lenny asks before anyone else can.

"Do you have a suggestion?"

"Disciplined," he offers.

"But discipline goes hand in hand with training and experience," Maria responds. "You don't want someone to be so disciplined that they blindly follow an inappropriate procedure, or orders from someone who is not on site.

"Officers need to be trained and experienced and know why following the procedure is essential to keep everyone safe."

"I agree with that," Petes chimes in.

"So how would you label that?" I wait a moment, but no one comes up with a proposed title. "I know it's hard and we can come back to this after we've had a little more time to think it through.

"But I agree with you. Discipline is integral to training. Knowing what to do, how to do it and when to do it. Then doing it when appropriate and essential."

"How about essential skills, knowledge and training?" Tasha offers.

I look around the group and a few head nods. No one is clearly opposed, so I add that to the second circle. Everyone watches my attempt to spell knowledge correctly. Luckily spell check keeps me from showing my literacy strengths or lack thereof. "We have two circles. Anyone want to suggest the third?"

"Fresh blood?" the Rev suggests and waits.

"Could you explain so we all know what you mean?" I respond, biting my tongue to make sure I don't dismiss what I know is coming.

"We need to fire everyone on the force today and bring in all new officers. That's what it would take to do our first circle anyway. I can assure you Duke Marion isn't going to come live in my neighborhood and only patrol my streets.

"So let's get rid of those old white racists who sit behind their desks at City Hall and wait for an opportunity to go shoot some more black boys."

I decide to overlook his attempt to be inflammatory.

"You've had an opportunity to read the disciplinary reports for the last ten years. I hope you have been able to form an opinion about a few things. First, is there a problem where officers are disciplined regularly for not following procedure?"

"The average has been about one hundred disciplinary actions a year," Petes offers. "Not what I'd call a Wild West ethos with three thousand officers."

"That's actually less than the officer-weighted average of large cities in Texas," Jenice informs us.

"Is there a pattern where one or two officers are repeat offenders?" I pursue.

"I noticed that," Tasha looks directly at Petes. "They tried to hide it by nesting it under a single offender. If you look at it quickly it looks like it's only been seventy to a hundred and fifty over the last ten years, but in reality, there are fifty to one hundred and twenty officers who have multiple repeat violations each year.

"Nearly two hundred officers were dismissed from the force, or left on their own. The average I calculated was closer to two hundred violations and disciplinary actions each year, which would be higher than the numbers we have for Texas large cities."

"Still not Wild West," Petes proclaims.

"Let's look at some other statistics that might go to the direct charge the Reverend has made."

I pull up a chart I knew I'd get to at some point in this session. "Racial profile of arrests, broken out by sex and age."

"That's not adequate," the Rev instantly responds. "The police are harassing black boys, profiling them. Those incidents are much more common than arrests."

"We don't have facts and data on harassment, so let's focus on what we do have," I insist.

Maria summarizes the chart for us. "This data would suggest that black youth are arrested three times more often than whites, but Hispanic boys are arrested about twice as often as white. What's the relative proportion of blacks, whites and Hispanic in the city?"

"Forty percent white, thirty percent black. Twenty-five percent Hispanic and five percent Asian and Other." Petes rattles off the numbers. Guess he knows that from being on Council.

"Clear indication of police discrimination against blacks and Hispanics," the Rev almost shouts at us.

I put up another chart. "What's this?" the Rev asks since I've not responded to his claim.

"Socioeconomic status of the racial segments in our city," I tell everyone. This chart breaks out the numbers of individuals in each socio-economic bracket by racial group.

"Am I reading this right?" Tasha asks. "It says there are more poor white people in our city than poor black, and the same for Hispanic. What are you trying to show?"

"If one makes the assumption that criminal activity is derived from economic status, namely that poor people are more likely to commit a crime, then this chart would indicate that there should be more young white men than either black or Hispanic that are arrested."

"I told you," the Rev almost jumps out of his chair. "Proves my case. Fire every last one of them."

"Hold on," I say as I put up still another chart.

"What are we looking at here?" Lenny asks as he squints at the chart's tiny legend.

"Comparative data, for Fort Christian and nationally. What are individuals under the age of thirty arrested for by ethnicity.

"What it shows is blacks and Hispanics are more likely to be arrested for gang involvement and drug sales. The drug use data looks almost inverse.

"Users arrested are much more likely to be white. However, the numbers are much smaller. That's most likely because police have targeted those who sell drugs over those who use them.

"We can debate why police and courts have made that decision, but it is probably because of the legalization of marijuana in so many states and a policy in former administrations to not prosecute users."

"Where are you going with this?" the Rev demands.

"Maria referenced threads. What I'm trying to show you is that anyone can look at one chart and draw a conclusion: racism in the department.

"Look at two charts and you say, okay you've just proved my

case.

"But when you add a third, all of a sudden it's not so clear cut. What you are seeing may not be for the reason you thought."

"This is ridiculous," the Rev says. "The police here don't harass white kids like they do black kids, and that's a fact. I don't care what the charts say. "

"Well, the last chart would indicate that police believe black kids are more likely than white kids to be dealing in drugs or are active in gangs, which might involve illegal weapons.

"In fact, their arrest data would validate that the officers, as we noted earlier, can't arrest someone just on suspicion. They have to have some evidence, or have witnessed illegal behavior, like busting up a drug sale, or breaking up a gang fight."

"You're saying black kids are more involved in criminal or gang activity than whites," Petes says.

"I'm not saying anything. I'm simply presenting you with data and letting you draw your own conclusions."

"And the conclusion you have drawn from the data is that while our police officers arrest a disproportionate number of black and Hispanic kids, it is because they disproportionately engage in criminal or gang-related behavior." Petes interprets.

"Whitewash," the Rev pronounces. "Who puts that data together? Some deskbound white statistician in the police department. There are lies, damn lies and statistics. I've heard that said, but you just showed it."

"Actually, if you look at the chart you will see that the proportions have been relatively the same over the whole twenty years of data. During that time there have been four employees of the department, and these are civilian employees, not officers.

"Three were black and the fourth was Hispanic.

"So no whitewash. All four statisticians had college degrees in either Social Science research or Mathematics. No one has challenged this data because it is required to be sent to the Department of Justice each and every year.

"Now I know you were all focused on the Fort Christian data, but look at the national data. A little variation, but consistent."

"I will not agree with you that the police in this city are not racists…"

"Reverend Lindo, please tell me when I said that?"

"Your charts. You've just tried to prove it with your statistics."

"I've not tried to prove anything. I said, I'm simply presenting you with data and letting you draw your own conclusion. You just concluded that the data says the police aren't racist.

"The data doesn't say that. It can't because that wasn't the question asked.

"The data merely suggests that criminal and gang-related violence leads to more arrests for people of color and Hispanics. One could infer that is because white kids are richer, but the data on the prior chart says that's not true either.

"Some are, but some black kids are richer and some Hispanic kids are richer than those that generally engage in criminal behavior or gang-violence. And I'm not asking anyone to determine whether we need to fire every officer as you have recommended. The group recommendations will be in our next session.

"Today is to convince everyone here that the question is what do we want the new Fort Christian Police Department to become?

"It will be a new department because just from the two circles on our diagram, if we define a roadmap to get there, it will be substantially different than the one that exists today."

"I think you have convinced me that Fresh Blood is not the term we want to use for the last circle," Tasha says. "It's getting late for a Monday and I've got a day packed with home visits because I'm spending so much time reading and researching this.

"So I'd like to ask if we can sleep on that third circle? Sleep on this whole amazing discussion, as I need a little time to process it all."

"We only got through Jenice, Lenny and Maria's initial recommendations." I say, seeing Maria start to gather her things. "But that led to defining two circles on the diagram. Maybe now we can go through the others on Wednesday and determine what the third circle should be.

"What we will discover in that discussion is whether three circles are enough."

Lenny asks, "Why weren't the three charts in the reading material?"

"They were. However, they were in separate articles and reports," I respond. "Taken in isolation you miss the big picture. But pulling threads is what I do for a living, so I was just trying to be helpful in calling it to your attention. See you Wednesday."

29 – THOMASINA 'SINA' JEFFERSON

Nona's Restaurant is always busy right after work on a Tuesday.

You would think Friday or Saturday would be the big night, but they are closed on Sunday and Monday, so everyone who is in need of an Italian fix after two days of beef or chicken goes here.

Reasonably priced, it seems to be comfort food for a lot of people in Fort Christian. Brian and Sandi join us here frequently if Brian and T.K. are both in town. Otherwise it's just Sandi and me.

"Baylor picked up a kid from San Angelo," Brian is talking sports with T.K., which they often do if it's college basketball, as that's the only sport T.K follows. "He's been sitting on the bench the whole season, but now it's like where did he come from?"

"San Angelo?" T.K. asks.

"Mission High School, I think. The crazy thing is he wasn't a starter there. Played sporadically and didn't show much. The team wasn't very good the last few years and maybe that's why no one noticed him.

"What he's really good at is spreading the floor and getting the ball to a player who's in position. Could be in high school he'd get the ball to the player, who couldn't put it away."

T.K. nods. "That happens."

"Anyway, they lost momentum there for a while, but now they seem to be coming alive. The only question is whether they've lost too many games. They must be right on the bubble."

"From what I'm seeing, Texas has a chance this year," T.K. responds as he puts down his menu, apparently having chosen what he's going to have. Probably the chicken, spinach lasagna. That's what he gets here, and cioppino at Ferrari's but never here. Strange how he has favorite dishes at different restaurants, but seldom tries a favorite elsewhere.

"Texas?" Brian says. "They haven't been good since you graduated. They've already lost how many games? Four or something?"

"Three, but they were all before their two shooters and big man came back. From what I've seen they can play with anyone. The question is whether they can stay healthy until the tournament."

Sandi touches Brian's arm. "You guys can talk sports any time. Why don't you talk about something we can all join in on?"

Brian considers his wife's request. "Okay, you got yourself appointed to that commission. You whip them into shape yet?" Brian turns back to Sandi. "Happy?"

"I'm sure Sina has heard all she wants to about the commission." Sandi tries to steer it off to something else, not sure if she doesn't want to talk about it or she really thinks I've heard all I want.

"It's okay," T.K. responds. "The answer to your question is no. I've not had to whip anyone yet. It's a small commission, there's only seven of us. So everyone is really involved.

"But we're still trying to understand the situation, exploring concepts and ideas, you know, the kinds of things that have worked elsewhere and what's not, that kind of thing. So we're a ways from getting to recommendations."

I note that Steve and Cylla, neighbors down the street, are getting up from their table and head towards us. Cylla says hello, but Steve stops to talk with T.K. "What did you do wrong to get appointed to a hopeless task like chair of another city commission?"

"Hey Steve, we're good, how are you?" T.K. responds.

"Better than you, I'm sure. So what's the secret? I'm trying to make sure they don't pull my name out of the hat the next time they want a citizens advisory anything."

"Secret is, I told some people what I thought of the situation."

"That was enough?" Steve sounds worried. "Who did you tell, the Mayor?"

T.K. shakes his head. "Flo Lopez. She's our Council member but also just a friend. Wasn't expecting anything to happen, but just wanted to share some ideas."

"Well, you see about making something happen over there at City Hall. I'll bet you could fire a cannon down the main hallway at two in the afternoon and all you'd do is wake up one or two of them."

"You been over there recently?" T.K. asks, apparently knowing the probable answer.

"No. Not exactly a place I want to visit, except to vote. Then you don't see anyone except those folks manning the voting booth."

"I hope to exceed your expectations."

"That would indeed be a good thing, but my expectations are so low anything might be feasible."

Steve looks to see where Cylla has gone to, sees her waiting at the door and turns his attention back to T.K.

"Just make sure you don't handicap the cops. They need to do whatever it takes to keep everyone safe. These things can turn into a witch hunt. They indicted the rookie who shot the black kid. It should be over soon."

"It'll never be over," T.K. responds, still looking up at Steve.

"You sure you're the right person to chair that commission? I'd feel better with a different set of answers."

Cylla opens the door to tell Steve she's ready to leave. Steve notices. "Cylla. She don't wait for no one, and me in particular. You take care, T.K., and remember what I told you. The cops are your only protection so you don't want to get on their bad side."

Steve nods to the rest of us and soon disappears out the door just behind Cylla.

"What was that all about?" Sandi asks.

T.K. shakes his head and asks Brian, "You took a recent trip?"

"We did, Argentina. What a wonderful place."

"Did you go find the grave of Evita?" I ask. "It's amazing. Crypt is right in line with a whole lot of others, but they say her remains aren't there and they actually poured concrete down into the grave to keep people from ever finding out."

"We did." Sandi responds. "The Casa Rosada tour, the stadium where Maradona played, steak dinner, the whole thing."

T.K. asks, "Do any wine country tours?" This is something we like to do once in a while. T.K. will research the wines and then we find a guide who can take us to the off-the-beaten-path kinds of places.

"Went to Salta since everyone goes to Mendoza for wine," Brian says.

"What's the difference there?" I ask.

"High desert rather than the Andes range kind of vineyards. The grapes just have a different flavor. Particularly like Malbec for red and Sandi really likes the Torrontes for white," Brian answers the question.

Another neighbor, I scarcely know them as they only recently moved here from somewhere else. Where was it? Kansas City, maybe? They stop at the table.

"I'm George and this is Marti. We wanted to thank you for taking on the task of figuring out what to do about the police. That was just awful what they did, shooting a young man in his parent's back yard.

Just unbelievable. Anyway, I'm sure you'll come up with recommendations that will make sure something like that can't happen again."

"That's the objective," T.K. responds as he shakes the man's hand. George nods to us and they make their way out.

"This happen to you a lot?" Sandi asks.

"Only since I was appointed," T.K. responds with resignation in his voice.

"Seems a lot of people are wanting to see something happen, but when I ask them what, I generally just get blank stares. It seems everyone knows there's an issue, but no one has a plan, or suggestion, or anything.

"Now I don't know if that's because people don't really spend a lot of time thinking about the police, so they haven't studied the issue, or what.

"But I can understand why so few communities have tried to change the narrative around police and community dialog. Seems those who aren't directly affected don't have time to get involved.

"The result is that when something happens it seems only the black community, or the Hispanic community or the Asian community is in complaining and that turns everyone else off.

"And the next thing you know no one is talking about it anymore and nothing fundamental has changed."

A young black man, with an apron around him, carrying a wet mop comes up to the table, "You're T.K. Jefferson, aren't you?"

T.K. nods, "Who are you?"

"I'm Deshaun's cousin, Demetrius. I didn't play ball like Deshaun. I wasn't fast enough to play football. So I always had to just work, make a dollar or two, 'cause I wasn't going to be no dealer, you know what I'm sayin'?

"Now Deshaun? He was cool 'cause he knew he had a gift. He could play ball like no one else, except you. He told me that. Said you taught him how to be the best player out there. You showed him that defenders always go to the ball, whoever's got it.

"So if you see the whole court, you see everyone, what they're going to do? You can get the ball to the one they least expect.

"That's never you because you got the ball. I remember that. Be someone who puts everyone else in a position to make the play.

"That's what I do. I help everyone get their job done.

"I don't ask for nothing. But I know if I keep helping without being asked, someday someone like you will see what I'm doing and do something good for me. Just like you did for Deshaun."

"You work here, Demetrius?"

"I do everything they ask me except cook. I'd do that too, but someone has to teach me first."

"Is that what you'd like to do? Cook?" I ask because it doesn't seem to be consistent with what he's saying.

"I always thought I was going to be a cop when I grew up, but I didn't graduate high school…"

"Why not?" T.K. asks with a frown.

"I lost interest in all the classes I had to take. I just couldn't understand how any of what they wanted me to know had anything to do with being a cop."

"You still want to be a cop after one was responsible for Deshaun's death?" I can't believe T.K. is asking this question. I don't think he's going to like what he hears.

"More than ever, but that's not going to happen," Demetrius looks away, back to the kitchen where he came from.

"The only thing keeping you from what you want to be is the choices you're making.

"Listen to me for a minute. I know you need to get back to the kitchen, but you can keep your job here and get your high school diploma by taking a GED test.

"Once you have that, you can still work here or wherever you want and take college courses, one at a time, if you want. It will take a while, but if you want it badly enough, just like Deshaun wanted to be a player badly enough, well, you can succeed the same way he did.

"Here's my business card…" T.K. hands it to him. "You call me and I'll meet you at the Boy's Club. They have someone there who will help you get ready for the GED test so you can get that behind you. And once you've done that? There's no stopping you. Got it?"

Demetrius looks at T.K.'s card, "Why would you do that for me?"

"Because you came to talk to me, and just like you, I'm trying to get the ball to the open man."

Demetrius wipes his hand and shakes with T.K., then he shakes with Brian and nods to Sandi and me.

"Wow, Deshaun's cousin," Brian says. "He's got a great attitude. I hope he follows through with your offer of help with the GED.

"I'd forgotten that's an equivalent diploma and he can get into college with it. Not Harvard certainly, but the local community college? They have a Law Enforcement curriculum, I think."

"They do," T.K. confirms. "Boy Scout."

"What are you talking about?" Sandi asks, puzzled by his comment.

"I was talking earlier with the commission members how we need Girl and Boy Scouts to become police officers. Demetrius is exactly the kind of person I had in mind. Just didn't realize that people like him would need the help of others to get there."

30 – T.K. JEFFERSON

I can't believe I am a whole three minutes early to the fourth session of the Commission. Today will be the last discussion day, as next week we start writing our report.

As usual I take the stairs two at a time until I reach the top floor and breeze through the door to the conference room as the clock strikes four o'clock.

Lenny's footsteps follow me into the conference room and I turn to see Maria and Tasha coming off the elevator. Jenice is setting up her computer and Petes and the Rev are heads together, quietly discussing something.

This is my last chance to produce the evidence needed to get those two extremes to entertain a middle ground. I'm actually surprised to see them talking as I thought they would not want to share anything with the other.

We all take our seats, I plug in my lap top to the data projector and turn it on.

"Thanks everyone for being prompt, including me.

"Today is an important day because today is the last day we are going to look at data or consider new questions before we start writing our report and recommendations next week. And that's an important reminder for me.

"Next week a smaller group of us will draft the report. The small group will meet every day until the first draft is complete and the draft will be sent to everyone.

"Then the following week we will meet just once to review and make changes to the document. The changes will be made and submitted to the Mayor and Council."

Everyone is quiet. I'm not sure if they are daunted by the task before us, relishing it, or hoping they will not be part of the small group of writers. Hopefully that will be clear in a few minutes.

"I wanted to tell you all a story about the dinner I had last night at Nona's."

"You bragging?" Lenny asks.

"After we finished our meal a young black man came out from the back and approached our table. He introduced himself as Deshaun Bush's cousin Demetrius.

"What I learned is that Demetrius dropped out of school and would do any job asked at the restaurant. He did every job to the best of his ability, and would readily help anyone else do their jobs as well.

"He asks for nothing in return. He is hoping someone will teach him to be a cook, as in the restaurant business that's where he can at least make a living wage.

"So I asked if that's what he really wanted to be. Do you know what he told me?

"He had always wanted to be a cop.

"Even after a cop killed his cousin that is what he would rather be.

"The only thing I could think of was Boy Scout. Demetrius is who we want policing our city."

The group is listening intently, as I had hoped. Even Petes seems to be thinking about my story.

I bring up the spreadsheet. "Tasha, you recommended time limits in the job. Do you have further thoughts?"

"I think you caught the essence of where I was going the other day," she begins. "Trying to find a way to ensure the officers can relate to the public they are serving.

"There's so much talk about how the different generations relate to each other differently. And that was what I was thinking.

"If parents can't relate to their kids, how are we supposed to expect a sixty-year-old cop to be able to communicate with a seventeen-year-old who never communicates with anyone other than on social media he carries in his hand all-day, every-day?"

"Do you think we covered this with the first circle on the diagram?" Maria asks.

"Not completely. A cop in the neighborhood is a good idea, I'm all for that.

"But the different styles of communication are an issue I don't think we can solve. We need to think about how we might address it.

"Training maybe? When I was in college they used to have the residence hall counselors participate in sensitivity training. Maybe that's part of the training we require.

"Something that helps the police understand how kids communicate, so they can communicate with them better."

"Does anyone have anything to add to Tasha's initial recommendation?" I ask.

"Not a circle on the diagram," Petes notes for all of us.

"Your turn," I pass the floor over to Petes. "You suggested the root cause of the recent shooting was lack of discipline and that fines or suspensions for failure to follow procedure should be adequate.

"What are your thoughts after reviewing the data and the subsequent discussions?"

"I don't think anyone would disagree with what I suggested, do you?"

"It's incorporated in the second circle," Jenice responds. "But it's not enough to make meaningful change."

Petes bristles at Jenice's response, "I don't understand why you all think we have to recommend a whole lot of changes." He stops before he says something he evidently thinks is not a good thing to say on second thought.

"Look, one rookie cop makes a mistake…"

"A whole lot of mistakes, made when others in the department didn't decide to intervene," the Rev clarifies testily.

"I would disagree with the characterization you're making. Aren't you the one who described it as having a Wild West ethos?"

"In my opinion that is exactly what we have been dealing with," the Rev responds.

"Gentlemen," I interrupt. "We need to return to facts and data. Personal attacks won't get us to a set of recommendations that anyone will approve."

"Especially since I'm one of the approvers," Petes says, in an apparent effort to try to sway the group.

"One of five, as I remember," I point out so the other members will remember he does not have veto power.

At least I hope that's what the members will assume I'm trying to say.

"Let me ask this, what else do you think may be necessary to achieve a state where young black men are not told to 'assume the position' when there is no verifiable precipitating event?"

"I don't know what you're asking." Petes almost dismisses my question.

"Mr. Council member, I think you know exactly what I'm asking. Along with the rest of the commissioners, you voted…"

"With one exception." Petes notes in regards to the Rev.

"…to appoint, thereby entrusting us to propose tangible actions the city can take to ensure no similar incident ever occurs again."

"Ever is a very long time, Mr. Jefferson. I don't deal in absolutes…"

"That's because you're a lawyer and always looking for words to obfuscate what you mean to say...

"And so you have wiggle room if you ever end up in court before a jury of your peers." I instantly regret my response.

"Touché," the Rev slowly claps at my performance.

"Council member Cochrane, I am sorry for my characterization of you as an attorney-at-law.

"But we must absolutely get back to facts and data. If we do not, we may fall into the same irrelevant state as our many predecessors.

"I believe you don't want that -- I know I don't and I doubt any of the other commissioners want that. So back to my question.

"What do you believe the city must do?"

Petes looks bewildered, unsure if he came out okay or is still the bad guy in the view of the other commissioners. He glances around before he begins.

"I think there is merit in increasing the training we require of our officers at all levels. Given what Tasha has suggested, it seems like we should probably increase the sensitivity training == particularly for officers who have been in the department more than ten years."

I don't ask for further comment on his recommendation since I would expect the Rev to just rip him apart. So I go on.

"Reverend Lindo. You had the most extensive list of recommendations."

I read them from the list on the screen before us.

"Fire Chief, all officers, hire only black replacements, community police oversight board, recall Mayor, Council and invest in training. Do you have additional or different thoughts given our discussions to date?"

I'm expecting a fiery retort, given the fiasco of the last discussion, but get a measured response instead.

"I see no reason to change any of my minimum demands, or recommendations as you would prefer to call them."

"No change?" I seek confirmation as my heart sinks, seeing this whole exercise about to implode between the Rev and Petes.

I was hopeful they would listen to reasonable changes, but apparently even this process is not going to get us where I hoped we would be at this point.

"Let's talk about them," I suggest, hoping that he will soften his demands if we go through them in light of the discussions we've been having.

"You still think that Chief Andrew should be fired?"

"Absolutely. The man is useless. Worse than useless. He impedes progress and perpetuates racism in his department. I mean, what else do I need to say?"

"Then who should be the Chief of Police?" I hope he will see that there is no one in the police community ready to take up that responsibility who will champion the change he is looking for.

"Someone like you should be the Chief," the Rev responds. His comment is met by dead silence. No one saw this coming, particularly me.

"I have a job," I respond, weakly stunned by his comment.

"That's the problem with all you white folks. You think this is all someone else's problem. All the time you're not realizing you are both the problem and the solution.

"You go out and hire a black Chief, and then emasculate that person. That dog don't hunt. Can't hunt. Because you all throw the problem over the wall and expect that black Chief to take care of your problem without giving him or her anything to work with.

"Give the new Chief a union dominated by white officers who won't make any kind of change."

The Rev stops to let his tirade sink in. "The only person in this room who expressed the loss he felt personally in what happened is you. The only person here who was able to reach out to the victim's family was you. The only person here who saw in a raw young person the qualities needed for the kind of police officer who would make a difference was you.

"The city needs someone who personalizes what's happening. Someone who deeply feels loss when someone needlessly dies. Someone who isn't looking at the issues as insolvable."

I'm stunned.

"According to your rules there are no bad ideas, so write it down," Petes instructs me.

I reluctantly add this surprising notion to the spreadsheet, although everything I know tells me this is not my fight. This is not who I am.

"Just so you know, I would not be a good Chief. I don't know anything about police work."

Petes whispers loudly to the Rev. "The union would never accept someone like him."

The Rev responds in a loud voice. "All the better."

"What about your recommendation that the city fire all officers?"

I want to move beyond the discussion of someone like me becoming the Chief. That will not be in the final set of recommendations.

"We have come up with an interesting alternative," the Rev responds.

"If we hold firm to the idea of officers who live in the community they police, I actually think that might be more effective than having black officers residing in white, Hispanic or Asian neighborhoods."

What? The Rev has budged? I didn't see this coming.

"It will require a wholesale change in the officers recruited, trained and deployed by the department, but I can see how it would be a big improvement from where we are today."

I'm seeing a crack in the wall of opposition to change. Maybe there is hope after all.

"What about a Community Police Oversight Board that would provide citizen input to Council and the Mayor about issues that are not being resolved by the department?" I ask.

"We are here because such a board does not exist," is all the Rev will say to this one.

"Unless there is opposition, this is a keeper," I note on the spreadsheet.

"We can't deal in this forum with your demands to recall the Mayor and Council members including Council member Cochrane who is sitting next to you. So let's go on to the last recommendation, which is invest in training.

"As I remember, you were focused on de-escalation, conflict resolution and similar training as opposed to qualification with weapons."

"Correct," the Rev responds. "The only thing I would add there is I think Tasha has a great point about the generational divide, and how we all communicate.

"Sensitivity training or generational communication training, anything that will help officers be able to communicate better and resolve situations peacefully has my full support."

I highlight that with a note about generational communications training and look up.

The Rev looks at me and says, "What about your recommendations?"

"My responsibility is to deliver a report to the Mayor and Council that reflects the consensus of your recommendations.

"If I give you a set of recommendations that are mine and mine alone I have done a disservice to the city. If I influence your recommendations unduly, that is an abrogation of my authority.

"That's why in our prior meetings I sought to draw threads from all of your thoughts and asked questions you did not.

"The fact that as we walked through your original recommendations you did not seek to include the answers to questions I have asked indicates to me that those questions are not relevant to the set of recommendations we will make.

"So at this time, it would be inappropriate for me to introduce new recommendations."

"Bullshit, pardon my French," the Rev responds. "You have clearer insight into what will transform this police department than anyone else here.

"You can't hold out on us, because we and the Mayor and Council are depending on you to share your thoughts. I'll even surprise myself by saying you are the most objective of all of us."

"But if you're full of shit we will have no hesitancy in calling you on it." Petes observes.

I pull up the diagram with the overlapping circles on the screen. “We need to agree on the third circle,” I point out as a way of not answering the Rev. I type in ‘Peace Officer rather than Police Officer’.

Petes almost jumps out of his seat. “WTF?”

“I come back to Maria’s point about attitude.” I stop and look around the room to determine how the members of the commission are reacting. I see curiosity rather than hostility from everyone except Petes. Just as I anticipated.

“We have documented that an officer only needs a weapon on rare occasions. Minutes a year versus the hours per day they are on the job.

“Nineteen of 197 nations do not routinely arm their police officers according to a CNN poll I discovered.”

“I knew it! You’re coming after our guns. Not going to happen, T.K.,” Petes declares.

“Hold on. One percent of 197 nations are able to make unarmed police work. Why should I think Fort Christian is among the one percent?” I push back on Petes assumption.

“You make my case.” Petes responds.

“Hold on,” I continue my thought. “I believe that the people of Fort Christian have never been given the opportunity to elevate their game, and join the elite few that don’t need a police force to meet the barbarians at the gate.

“To assume the role of enforcing community norms rather than simply hiring mercenaries to do their dirty work.”

Petes shakes his head. “Cops aren’t mercenaries. Besides, you have no idea what life on the streets is like.”

“Maybe not, but neither do you, so I find it particularly disturbing that you’re lecturing me about what this community can and cannot do.”

"I'll fight you every inch of the way. You'll never disarm our police. I couldn't sleep at night knowing we are sending our young officers into the lion's den without a weapon to defend themselves."

I have to bring down the rhetoric or this will implode right here.

"Council member Cochrane. Let me ask you a question. What is the scenario you most fear?"

"Terrorists," Petes responds.

"Okay, we allow officers with more than ten years of experience to have weapons in the trunk or to work as an armed SWAT team. They respond at the first indication of armed insurrection. Next most fearsome instance?"

"Active shooter," is his next test case.

"Also weapons in the trunk or SWAT team that responds."

"Traffic stop is met with a weapon."

"Senior partner in car who can access trunk weapons in response if the officer who goes to the car is unarmed. Which means the incident is not police incited."

"Gang violence," Petes says.

"First officer on the scene starts with moral authority. If beyond reason, bring in backup in car, or SWAT."

"Bar fight," Petes is getting desperate.

"Same scenario. Try to reason, if endangerment, bring in the backup."

"Domestic dispute." He's giving up.

"Never approach with weapons. Always seek resolution with moral authority."

"You've made your point," Petes concedes, although he is very reluctant. "What am I supposed to do with this insight?"

"Use your influence with the union to convince them they should support a different standard operating procedure, one that should over time reduce their exposure to altercations with weapons involved."

"You can't guarantee that," Petes pushes back.

"No, but by the same token you can't show me with any certainty that it won't work."

I've fought Petes to a standstill. He's expended all of his arguments and none have carried the day. I can see him wondering how to reinforce his position, but it's clear to me that he doesn't have a good strategy.

I'm convinced he will be consulting with Duke and Walter as soon as we adjourn for the evening. That should remind me that even though I intend to get to the basic recommendations tonight, they may well change by the end of next week when we have our first draft complete. That means even more revisions than I'm used to.

"Okay," Petes responds. "What do you mean by peace officer?"

"You suggested the Reverend's use of Wild West ethos was not appropriate."

"I still think it's extremist rhetoric," Petes says, looking at the Rev warily.

"I'll not dispute your opinion since I'm only focused on facts and data," I shoot back.

"So let's look at definitions: New York State makes a distinction between peace officers and police officers. Employees who have only peace officer status are often limited to writing citations/summonses and may not be allowed to carry firearms.

"Does that sound like what's being suggested?" Jenice asks. "That we put peace officers up front and keep the police officers in the background to address the extreme circumstances?"

Petes responds, "I don't think New York State sees the distinction in quite the same way you're proposing."

"That peace officers are the first responders?" I press him. "In New York City that may be the case. But I don't think anyone on our Council, including you, see Fort Christian as being a community with quite the same values as New York City."

"I would agree with that," Petes finally concedes.

"You know, I think Fort Christian is more ready to embrace home rule than you give it credit for."

"Home rule? Home rule is partitioning a part of a state for local governance rather than the state. What you're suggesting has nothing to do with that."

"Other than a determination by local citizens that they don't need someone else governing them, they can do it themselves, thank you. That's what I'm proposing here. That the community will regulate its affairs rather than expect the city police department to do all of that for them."

"I just don't see how we get there," Petes complains.

"What about the rest of the commissioners?" I ask. "Is this community ready to take responsibility back from a dysfunctional police department?"

"Hell, yes," the Rev doesn't mask his pleasure at the nature of this conversation.

I look at Maria, whom I perceive as probably being the most by-the-book person amongst us, given she's a doctor and has all kinds of regulation and peer reviews to deal with.

"The people want something different. Is the disarming of police officers, or at least some of them the answer? I don't think many will have an informed opinion one way or the other. But they will have an opinion."

"So the third circle label is: Peace Officer vs Police Officer??" explodes Petes. "What about 'staff department to full manning table?'"

"Which represents?" I ask, not sure I know what that level would be.

"The manning level that represents union recognized best practice." Petes blurts out only to realize afterwards that probably wasn't the best way to describe it.

No one agrees with Petes. I look at every other member and all shake their head.

"Looks like Peace Officer vs Police Officer is the best label available," I say, closing the discussion -- although I know it's just the beginning of a long conversation with the police union.

Not how I wanted to end what otherwise was a very productive day.

31 – T.K. JEFFERSON

Two weeks later.

All Commission Members are gathered in the small City Hall conference room that has been our place of meetings since that first Monday, which seems to have been a year ago.

Maybe it's because I haven't been able to stop researching points that were made in our deliberations or what.

All I know now is I'm very tired. And that's not a good thing when the fruits of your collective labors are under a full-scale frontal attack from within. Petes in particular is unsettled with the recommendations, and he is one of the five votes we have to address.

"I can't agree with this document," Petes says to everyone. "The only thing that was on my list is the training in mediation and de-escalation, but that was only part of the training I and Tasha recommended.

"What happened to the firearms training? There's nothing here that would make me feel safer. Nothing that would prevent cops from getting shot in the line of duty. This is recklessness. How can a group of Texans even remotely consider what you're suggesting? It flies in the face of reason."

The Rev stands up and addresses Petes: "You're just upset because for the first time in the history of this city a set of recommendations is coming out that fundamentally changes the playing field.

"Cops can't get away with demanding law-abiding citizens to do what they want when there's no probable cause. Cops have to actually talk with folks, try to understand a set of circumstances, and de-escalate first. No more shooting from the hip."

Petes responds, "The recommendations will make it impossible for Fort Christian to recruit officers. No one will want to live here, because the police won't be able to deter crime."

I have to intervene. "The recommendations require the people of Fort Christian to maintain order.

"The peace officers are the first line of contact. They are there to mediate and find solutions to situations of conflict. Senior officers who may be armed and SWAT teams will address endangerment situations, but that will not be the majority of the officers."

Petes explodes, "I won't be a part of this travesty."

"That's too bad. As ex-officio, you have the right to note your minority position on the recommendations. If you simply walk out, that will get lost in the report that goes to the Mayor."

Petes shoots back, "I could care less about the Mayor. I will use my position on Council to lobby the other members to reject this set of recommendations as craziness."

"Council member Cochrane, I have always respected your pragmatism," I say evenly to garner his attention.

"Is it more beneficial to be on the wrong side of this Council and be seen as the lone naysayer to progress, knowing that the Reverend Lindo and the local media will hammer at your retrograde outlook?"

"Retrograde?" Council member Cochrane responds with confusion.

"Try backward," Tasha suggests. "He might understand that term."

Petes looks at Tasha as if he's surprised at her comment.

"Remember the generational communications discussion?" I suggest. "You're clearly on the other side of that, at least to the folks here listening to you."

“Backwards?” Petes shakes his head. “The Council will see the merit in an evolutionary as opposed to revolutionary approach to the one incident Council wants to address.”

“Where were you when Council took up this matter?” the Rev asks. “I was in that room as you were. You even voted for the measure. The Commission was supposed to determine what actions will make the police department more, and I underline more, responsive to the community. If we only recommend the few token actions you propose, the community will storm City Hall and demand your ouster.”

“Like you did before,” Petes acknowledges but with defiance.

“Yes, like we did before,” the Rev stares Petes down. “Since this may well be one of your last official acts as a Council member, you may want to rethink which side of this issue you wish to be seen on.”

“You probably don’t have more than two hundred votes in my district, so I’m not overly concerned by your rhetoric. Save that for Alvin and Roxanne. They have a lot more exposure to your congregation than I do.”

“But Tex Anthony has a lot more readers in your district than you can survive. If the paper endorses your opponent, you’ll have a lot more difficulty returning to Council,” the Rev cautions.

Since Petes had the endorsement of the newspaper last time, this threat gives him pause. I watch him processing. He finally re-engages us with more conciliation. “Remove the whole peace officer section and I’ll consider the rest. That’s an absolute no go.”

“Why are you concerned about officers carrying weapons? You have stock in some firearms company?” Lenny asks.

“I just look at how many police officers are shot in the line of duty,” Petes responds with the defense I can hear Duke giving him.

“The statistics say there are twenty times as many civilians killed by police officers as police officers killed by civilians in the line of duty. That doesn’t seem like a fair fight even for a Texan,” Reverend

Lindo retorts with sarcasm.

"Those are bullshit statistics. You said yourself that statistics lie," Petes is trapped and he knows it.

"Reputable sources like the Washington Post and a website sponsored by police officers? Bullshit statistics? I don't think I'd want to make that accusation in front of Tex Anthony. You just might end up wearing them for Christmas next year." The Rev chuckles to himself.

"You're enjoying this, aren't you?" Petes accuses the Rev. "You have most of what you want in one form or another, so you've won. Probably should have listened and let them name you as chairman. Then none of this would have any credibility."

"And neither would you for caving in to me, or was that someone else who said that in the Council meeting?"

I need to end this sparring and give Petes a win he can take back to the union. I know if he doesn't he's toast, because without the union support he can't get re-elected and if he votes against a set of recommendations he helped formulate, he won't have the support of the newspaper, which is an even more likely death knell.

"What if…" I say to get everyone's attention. "What if we recommend a differentiated pay scale, that when an officer transitions from peace officer to armed senior officer that there is a substantial pay increase. Recommend that we implement that differential now for officers with greater than ten years of service and are qualified in all training requirements?"

Petes looks at me, confused.

"Why would you make a recommendation like that?" the Rev asks also confused. "Doesn't that create an incentive for more officers to want to be armed?"

I have to be careful how I answer this, so I start slowly, "Stay with me for a minute. I'm still working this out in my head. There are probably at least a couple ways of looking at such a scheme. One way could be as you describe, an incentive to want to be armed.

"But I think it could also be framed as an acknowledgement that someone who has kept the peace for a decade without a weapon should be rewarded. Any peace officer, who has been relying on their moral authority and skills in human relations, may wish to take on the added responsibility to be authorized to use a weapon that is kept in the trunk of their vehicle except in response to events of jeopardy is seen as adding value to the community."

Petes jumps in. "I thought the peace officers could access weapons to respond to events of jeopardy, as you've described them, as long as they have qualified with that weapon and are under the supervision of an armed senior officer."

"Meaning one with more than ten years in the department," Maria seeks to clarify.

Petes nods. "That's what I thought you were talking about."

"But you want that whole section removed from the recommendations, so what difference does it make?" Lenny asks, with a tone in his voice that he thinks there may be a solution here. I hope he's right.

"Approximately sixty percent of the men…, er, of the officers in the department have at least ten years in." Petes informs us, a fact I had researched but not mentioned.

"That would be the first substantial pay raise for them in nearly a decade." Petes thinks about this further. "I don't know… maybe there's an opportunity to do something."

"I would propose that such a recommendation be discussed conceptually with the Mayor and Council members individually before we submit the report and recommendations.

"Would not want to discuss it in an open meeting for the first time, and neither would I want us to propose something that has no chance of adoption," I respond, although not directly to his comments.

Petes looks at me cautiously. "You would do that as chairman?"

"I think it should be the chairman and vice chairman who have those conversations, so as to ensure there is no ambiguity about what we are proposing or the reaction of the voting members of Council." The Rev glances at me, apparently surprised again.

"You have no idea how disruptive this set of recommendations will be to the police officers of our community." Petes backs off the opportunity, apparently thinking about the discussions he's probably been having with Duke and Walter.

"I fully expect if you even put this report on the table there is likely to be a job action, which will put lives in danger and make the community less safe," Petes continues. "I can't support something that would have that outcome. I can assure you either way the members of Council will be gone, and this will either never see the light of day, or if adopted for some unfathomable reason, it won't last one election cycle."

"You seem to forget I've said the same thing since the beginning, but for the opposite reason," the Rev reminds Petes. "If we don't take these actions, I'll be leading the nightly marches on City Hall, I'll be finding well-qualified candidates to run against each and every one of you, and you will be gone.

"And not only that, we will ensure that your successors take out what I'd call the sweeteners T.K. has managed to work into this package because the new Chief will fire every last one of the officers in the department.

"At that point Duke and Walter will be off on some lake fishing, 'cause they won't have nothing to do. You seem to forget there is a big red R on the door to the police station.

"And at the moment, what I see in this package doesn't erase that big old red letter, but it makes the department function in such a way that those attitudes won't be what drives behavior."

I can't tell where we are. If Petes is right his supporters will ensure that even if we see our recommendations approved they will be reversed by the next council that will have his allies in place. And if the Rev is right, I'm not sure he has the support to keep the current Council members in their jobs to protect the gains we've made. Why put the community through the disruption that it will take to make the community responsible, when the community may not really want that? Maybe I'm forcing something that should be left alone.

32 – THOMASINA 'SINA' JEFFERSON

When T.K. told me about the tournament his company was sponsoring, I thought it would be a good diversion for him. He needed to put a team together, to practice and to see how much of his former prowess he's lost.

Besides, a tournament would be fitting as it could be an opportunity for some small shred of redemption for that shot that was tipped away so many years ago.

But the commission work has just crushed his time. He's been putting in weekends at work to stay afloat, nights reading and researching for the commission meetings. And this last week he has spent a half day every day at City Hall, drafting the report.

Nevertheless, he's worked in a two-hour practice at the Boy's Club every third day. Time has been just too precious to do more. He needs to keep up with his job and at the same time produce a report in which he can take pride.

It never occurred to me that the tournament would happen over the weekend after the report was submitted. It hasn't been released and won't be until the Council members have had a chance to read it and determine whether they will accept it.

They have the option of sending it back and asking the commission to change parts of it or all of it before it is accepted. But once it's accepted, it will be released to the public.

So for the two days of the tournament, T.K. actually has the opportunity to focus on just one thing, rather than three, and I know that gives him hope they will at least be competitive.

The last thing he wants is to be seen as nowhere near the same class as the other teams, some of whom have played each other regularly.

I'm sitting in the stands with the petite and perfect Leticia Jones. Her smile dazzles, and her hair is a stylist's dream. Her designer jeans and shimmery soft silk blouse broadcast her multi-thousand-dollar shopping event earlier in the week.

Even though she's the chairman of the event, she wanted to sit with the crowd since Brad, her husband, is playing on T.K.'s team. I've spoken with Leticia on a few occasions, but I don't really know her. She tends to travel in different social circles, which is fine, but it makes it difficult to know what to talk about.

I don't sense she's really into the games that are being played. This is more an opportunity to be seen supporting her husband and his team.

"Duke doesn't seem to be himself," I remark to Leticia.

"Which one is Duke?" she asks quietly.

"The one who is back in the far corner. That's just not a place where he can take a shot and it's kind of out of the flow T.K. is trying to set up."

"Which one is T.K.?"

"The one standing at the top of the key with the ball in his hands."

"Oh, him," she says with a limp-wristed wave of her well-groomed hand. "Brad says he was a really good player, once. He hopes he will be able to find some of that this weekend."

T.K. doesn't see an opening, steps back and drops the ball through the hoop for three points. That brings his team back into the lead by a point with three minutes to go.

Leticia offers a golf clap, very soft and proper. I wonder if this woman ever attended any kind of sporting event other than tennis or golf in her life. Clearly not a beer drinker.

T.K. guards the member of the other team who is bringing the ball back down the other way. He's pressuring him, apparently looking for a steal so he can go back the other way.

I notice Duke is coming up along the sideline, but hanging back. Not sure why he's not setting up to defend. It's almost as if he expects T.K. will get the ball back and lob it down court to him.

Maybe he will do just that, but this is a close game and a stop would be better than letting the other team score two or three points.

T.K. sees his opportunity, pushes the ball away from the other player into what should be a bounce pass to the trailing Duke, who isn't paying attention.

The ball goes out of bounds off T.K., so the other team keeps possession.

"That wasn't a very good pass," Leticia observes. "Maybe they should put Brad back in."

"Might be a good idea," I respond, checking the clock. "Probably not enough time left, but let's see what they do. They can win this one with just a little more hustle."

"Hustle?" Leticia looks at me like she'd never thought of that. But then she clarifies her confusion. "Isn't that a dance they used to do a long time ago? I think my dance instructor tried to teach it to me once. But it's just not a step I use all that much. It's the music. Doesn't go with modern music."

T.K. is all over the player who is trying to inbound a pass. Blocks an attempt at a bounce pass and the ball immediately goes out of bounds.

Still off T.K. The ref retrieves the ball and hands it to the opposing player, who immediately passes it in over T.K.'s jumping reach. But the ball has so much arc on it that Shorty is able to step up and snatch it out of the air over the player for the other team.

Devin, the new kid Brad brought in, is loping towards the basket, picks the pass from Shorty and hardly needs to jump to dunk the ball.

"That's good, isn't it?" Leticia asks as she repeats her soft golf clap.

"Very good," I respond and add, "Devin is the player who works for your company. He played for the University of Texas in some big games. Your husband recruited him for this tournament."

"Which one is Devin?" Leticia asks.

"The tall one who just made the basket."

"Is that when the ball goes through the hoop?" Leticia looks at me earnestly. "Tell me if I have this right. Brad tells me I constantly confuse things. If they are close to the hoop, it counts as two points, and if they are farther away it's three points. And they call that a touchdown?"

"They call it a basket, and that's where the name basketball comes from."

Leticia nods at me as if she's repeating that to herself in her head. "I think I have it. Brad used to score touchdowns. That's right. This wasn't this game, because he played outside in a bigger place. A lot more people watching.

"Maybe we should do a football tournament next year. We might get a lot more people to come out and watch, although we'd have to let them Watergate in the parking lot. I did that once, but they burned the food and we couldn't see the game from there so we went into Daddy's box and had them bring us wings."

Time is running out. The other team brings the ball back down and sets up.

T.K. is on the point man for the other team, watching the passes. Quick as a flash of summer lightning, he throws out an arm to knock one away, but is too late.

The player for the other team catches the pass and moves past T.K. towards the basket, but Devin is waiting and knocks the ball away.

T.K. has recovered and waits as Randy picks up the loose ball, begins to bring it back, but passes off to T.K. who collides with Duke, who is just standing there. T.K. falls, dazed and surprised that he didn't see Duke.

T.K. gestures like 'Isn't that a foul?'

The ref shakes his head. "You collided with your own teammate," he says.

T.K. reacts immediately, scrambles for the ball, and gets to it at the same time as a player for the other team. They wrestle for control.

"Jump ball," shouts the ref.

Shorty stands in to take the jump and Devin is positioned on the offensive end. Shorty is easily able to tip it to Devin, who relays it to Will, who drives in for a layup.

They are now up by five with a minute to go. I see T.K. go over to Duke, ask him something and Duke pushes him away forcefully.

I see T.K. gesture like 'why did you do that?' But then he shakes his head and returns to the game.

The other team races down the floor. The player with the ball passes to a player who sets up for a three-point shot, but Shorty is right there.

The player passes off since he no longer has a shot. Will tries to steal the pass, but the ball bounces off him and a player for the other team picks it up and lays it into the basket with a half spin.

Margin down to three points.

T.K. grabs the ball, and motors down the court towards the other basket like his hair is on fire.

He drives the lane and the other team's tallest player steps up to try to block him,

T.K. dishes a backwards pass to Devin, who has stepped into the lane behind T.K. But Duke backs into him as he is about to loft the shot, giving the other team a chance to tie him up and foul him.

Devin gets two free throws.

He easily makes both baskets, up by five and less than thirty seconds to go. If they simply play smart, try to slow the other team down, they should win despite the sloppy play.

T.K. again tries to press the ball player who is bringing the ball back down, but the player quickly passes off and T.K. is now behind the ball.

The other team player picks up the pass, steps up and lofts the ball towards the basket in a beautiful arc. It drops through for three points and it's now a two-point game again.

Clock restarts as Will inbounds to Devin who brings it part way down and passes off to T.K., who spins around the defender and drives towards the basket.

This time Duke deliberately steps into T.K., knocking him down.

The ball gets loose.

A player for the other team picks it up and, seeing no one down court, starts dribbling that direction, waiting for his teammates to get back.

Shorty and Devin set up just inside the three-point arc to block corner shots while T.K. and Will press the players closest to the key.

Duke moves under the basket to cover the other team's center, knowing that a pass into the young man would not win the game unless he were fouled and the resulting free throw counted.

The clock ticks down and the player with the ball has just about run out of time.

He fakes a pass to the corner, but holds the ball a little too long.

Finally, he tries a bounce pass to the player Will is covering. But T.K. sees it coming all the way, goes for the pass and picks it up as it comes out of the other player's hand.

He races the length of the court and drops it through as the buzzer sounds.

Final score is 62 to 58 in favor of T.K's team.

Duke walks off the court without saying a word to anyone. T.K. watches him go, shakes his head, just once, then goes over and congratulates the other players on his team. Leticia and I come down from the stands.

"Good game," I congratulate them and notice Leticia moving a little further away from the players, apparently offended by the sweat.

I go over to T.K. and give him his well-earned kiss. "What's up with Duke?"

"Said I'm no friend," T.K. responds.

"What does that mean?"

"Means Petes has been feeding him the recommendations."

He rubs his temples, then continues.

"I think the only reason this didn't happen earlier was that I always couched them as possibilities -- something we needed to consider but needed consensus on -- before moving forward.

"When we got to consensus -- minus Petes -- the other commissioners elected to go ahead and let Petes file a minority report.

"So Duke just found out what the recommendations are going to be -- and he doesn't like them one damn bit."

33 – THOMASINA 'SINA' JEFFERSON

The kitchen is dark save the one light that illuminates our breakfast table, where we often eat when we want to have a quiet conversation.

It's convenient to the food preparation area and the sink to clean up afterwards, so we often open a bottle of something, either red or white depending on our moods, and just talk.

Since T.K. accepted the role on the commission, we have not been able to have dinner together. He has been either working late to get caught up, or upstairs pulling research reports from the websites of vetted organizations.

The last thing T.K. wanted was to make a proposal and find that the basis for his proposal was from compromised sources. But now the draft has been submitted to Council and the Mayor for consideration.

From comments he made that last week as he tried to negotiate a unanimous endorsement from the other commissioners, I know he wasn't happy with compromises that were agreed to -- last minute fixes that were actually counterproductive.

He apparently gave Petes, the lone member of Council on the commission, the chance to file a minority report, but in the end Petes elected not to do that and simply refused to sign the final document.

I don't know if that was what deflated him or if it's something else, but he's been remote. I'm hoping he will open up about what's bothering him tonight.

So a special red. One of his favorites. And a slow cooked vegetarian stew that he likes. See if I can get through to him. Help him understand that life as we know it isn't over.

If Council accepts his report, he will have done everything he possibly could to make the city a better place. And then it will be time to focus on his work, playing ball with the guys and the kids at the Boy's Club, and reading another scientific treatise to expand his thinking about the world of the possible in oil exploration and production.

T.K. finishes the last spoonful of the stew with an expression that tells me he enjoyed it. Seldom does he say something specific, but I always know when we have something he likes more than the usual choices.

He sits back as he scoops up the half-full glass of wine and looks at it for a long moment, apparently appreciating the color. He swirls it and looks at the legs that show themselves off as the wine settles back. I see a nod, so he has decided this bottle is acceptable.

"Chocolate?" I ask, thinking I know the answer. We often will have a few pieces of dark chocolate when we are drinking a good red.

I rise and go to the cupboard where we keep it, search through to find a version containing either mint, sea salt caramel or raspberries. Those tend to be his choices, although I'll admit they're mine, too.

I break the bar into small pieces and then unwrap it so he can pick out whatever size appeals to him tonight. I've noticed that when the meal is larger he tends to go for smaller pieces. If it's a lighter meal, like tonight, he seems to search out larger pieces.

And if he doesn't follow that logic, then I know he's preoccupied and just running on autopilot.

"You still thinking about Duke trying to sabotage the game?" I finally ask, since nothing is forthcoming and he has taken a small piece of chocolate.

"He wasn't trying to do that. He's just upset."

"I watched the game. He did everything he could to slow you down short of tying you up and setting fire to the rope."

T.K. looks at me sharply, but then I see him retreat again into his mind.

"I take it he thought since you've known each other all these years that you would keep the status quo? Just because you know him? I certainly wouldn't call you friends. I don't think you've had two words with the man all these years that weren't on the basketball court…"

T.K. looks at me like I'm wrong about that and then I remember, what he's thinking.

"Except that one time. At Christmas two years ago, when Deshaun came home, defeated. You called Duke and asked him to help you help Deshaun."

"And he did," T.K. responds. "I asked him and he stepped up. And the one time he expects me to do something for him, I don't."

"This is totally different," I say. "You're applying your engineering mindset to re-engineer a department of the city that's hurting the kids you want to help.

"The fact that Duke works in a department that's hurting the kids that he comes out to help at the Boy's Club is a problem in and of itself. It says he doesn't believe in what you're doing for those kids. It means he does it for himself, not them.

"He's not your friend. You don't owe him anything."

T.K. shakes his head in disapproval.

"I know I've not spent countless hours with Duke, like you have. Probably not many more than you spent with Deshaun, if you want to know the truth.

"You weren't out there for Duke, though. You were out there for Deshaun and all the others like him who want someone to show them the way to making it in this world.

"For most of them, there is no role model. You're the only one they have. Just like Demetrius…"

T.K. frowns. "I haven't helped him… at least not yet."

"You have. You don't know the effect you have on those kids. They see what you do to make yourself and them better. You never stop, you never quit.

And just like in the game today, when you collided with Duke? You checked with the ref, looking for a call.

"But when you didn't get it? Who got to the ball that set up the final jump ball? Who stole the final pass to set up the final points?

"And I know the only reason you took that last shot was because nobody was down there to take the pass from you. I'll bet if Duke had been under the basket, you would have passed to him for the final shot, despite his attempts to throw the game.

"Why didn't you pull him? Put Brad in? He would have at least stayed out of the way."

I hear a car backfire, twice, in rapid succession, close by the house. At least that's what I think it is until I hear the window shatter in our living room.

T.K. looks at me, listens, then is on his feet,

"Stay put!" he barks. His voice is strained, but determined.

I watch him approach the hallway that leads to where the glass shattered and he disappears down the short corridor.

I listen, holding my breath until I can't any longer, but try to keep my heartbeat under control. It's not cooperating either. Then I hear the front door open and a moment later it closes, apparently behind him.

I can't stay here not knowing what's going on. I go to the hallway and look down. He's not there. He must have gone out.

So I approach the door and reach for the latch just as the door opens into me. I have to step back quickly. T.K. comes back in.

"I told you…"

"Bullshit. What happened?"

"As best as I can determine without turning the lights on, which I don't think is a good idea at the moment, someone shot out our window." He comes across as more annoyed than frightened.

I'm the one who's frightened.

I hug him and just hold on until I feel his strength transferring to me. I finally let go and just stand there for a long moment gathering myself before I go into the living room. I see the broken glass on the floor.

"I need to clean this up," I say to myself, more than to him. "What do you have to put over the open window?"

"Plastic. It's out in the garage. I'll get it while you sweep up. Be careful. That's a lot of sharp glass."

"Before you go, what did you see when you went out on the street?" I have to know if he went to chase away whoever did this.

"Car was down at the corner turning right. Couldn't see the license plate or even anything that would have indicated what kind of car it was.

"That street light's been out for a week or more. If it had been on I might have seen enough for a description of the car, but not tonight."

"Well, I'm not happy. Whoever shot at the house could have still been out there. You going to call the police department to report this?"

T.K. looks at me and I instantly know what he's thinking -- that it was probably an off-duty officer, who got the word that T.K. is trying to screw up his world.

I wonder if whoever did it was brazen enough to have used a

service revolver, knowing they would never run tests on the bullet.

"I'll call when I get the plastic up. No hurry now that the person responsible is gone."

"How do you know?" I'm shaking again. "He could come back."

"Not likely. The message has been sent," he says, which confirms what I thought he was thinking.

T.K. goes to the garage and I start sweeping up the shattered glass. In only a minute he's outside with a staple gun and a roll of plastic. I can hear the ka-chunk, ka-chunk of the staples going through the plastic and into the wood.

He completes his task just about the same time I complete sweeping up the glass. I check the front door after he's back inside, to make sure he's locked it behind him.

T.K. looks at me and shakes his head. He doesn't have to tell me that if someone wants to get into the house there's only plastic to stop them. I know, but I'll feel a whole lot better if I know someone can't just walk in through an unlocked door.

We go back to the kitchen and our wine and chocolate. Well, that mood has been ruined. I listen as T.K. makes the report.

"Yes, T.K. Jefferson. 250 Lilac Lane. Yes, this is a good number to call me back on." He listens for a few seconds and then says, "Yes, I want to report vandalism."

There's a short silence on his part and then he continues. "Someone shot out the picture window in my living room about a half hour ago."

Another brief silence and then, "Well, what would you consider it?" He nods, "Okay, that works for me. Classify it any way you'd like. All I know is I have a bullet in the opposite wall and no glass."

Again he listens as the officer taking down the report talks to him.

"I don't know who might have done it. No, I can't think of anyone who would do it deliberately. No, if it were a pellet gun it probably would not have shattered the glass. No, I'm not a forensics expert, but I am an engineer and I know physics. Do you?" I see T.K. shake his head. He's upset with himself because he made an inappropriate remark about whoever is on the other end of the line.

I see T.K. roll his eyes as he listens to the police officer. "Are you going to send someone out? No? So you're not going to investigate the discharge of a firearm in a residential part of the city, resulting in a bullet hole in my wall? If I or my wife had been sitting in that room, we could have been wounded or worse."

He listens for a moment. "No the light was not on in that room. I understand that means to someone who might want to take a shot at the house that it was most likely empty, but I often go into that room to retrieve one thing or another without turning on a light."

Another period of listening to a discussion that doesn't seem to be getting to closure.

"I did, and in fact I'm surprised you didn't ask before. I went out to the street. I did not see anyone carrying a weapon, and yes, I know Texas is an open carry state and it would have been legal for someone to be carrying a weapon on my street as long as it wasn't concealed without a concealed weapon permit. Got it.

"When I got out there all I saw was a car a block away making a turn. No, I did not get a license number because it was too far away and the street light's out.

"What other excuses do I have? What kind of comment is that? What's your name?"

T.K. looks at me. "He hung up on me."

34 – T.K. JEFFERSON

Just an awful day at work is ending perfectly, I decide as I approach my house.

Sina is standing on the front porch with Tex Anthony, a newspaper photographer who is taking pictures of the front window and a television news crew from channel seven, Fox News, of course. My favorite pseudo journalists.

I get out of the car and start walking towards them when I notice Butterscotch, our Maine Coon cat, apparently sleeping under a bush. As I get closer I realize she's not sleeping.

I stop where I am and look up at Sina whose eyes are red. She's a little flushed and I know she's really upset now. I don't want to embarrass her with the media folks swarming so I go up and simply take her hand and hold it tight.

"What's going on, Tex?" I ask trying to sound calm.

"That's what I was going to ask you, but your wife has been giving me the details. I'm sorry about your cat, by the way. I have one… cat that is. Mipsy. A tabby cat we picked up at the Humane Society when she was a kitten. We call her that because she has white feet that look like mittens and she kind of walks like she's tipsy."

I nod, not interested in his cat, but concerned about Sina. "So what else do you want to know?"

"Who and why would be a good start," Tex looks down at his cell phone notes. I notice the reporter for the television station gets closer, apparently wanting to hear my answer.

"I was hoping you could tell me," I respond calmly, deciding the less said the better.

"I called over to the police station after I got the call…"

"Call? From who?"

"Don't know, the person just said they had a tip that someone shot up your place and they hung up."

I look back down at Butterscotch. Now I can see the bullet hole in her side. It wasn't a small bullet. I close my eyes and understand why Sina is so upset. Someone deliberately blew away our cat. This was no random act.

"Did you check with the police department before you came over?" I ask out of curiosity.

"That was strange, too. They said they had a partial report from you, but you didn't complete the report and didn't come by to follow up and sign the statement." Tex seems interested in why I didn't complete the report.

I nod but offer no explanation.

"Has anything like this happened to you, or anyone else in the neighborhood?" Tex presses.

"Not to us. You'd have to ask the police department to be sure, but no one has ever said anything to me about anything like this." I feel Sina shaking, so I put my arm around her so hopefully she will relax. But she doesn't and just keeps shaking. I try to hold her closer, but still no change.

"You're an uncontroversial person," Tex notes. "The only notes I had on you were going back to your college days. Now all of a sudden you're the chairman of this commission to address race relations in the city. How did that come about?"

"You'd have to ask the Mayor," I say.

I can see he's getting annoyed that I'm not just dumping my suspicions and making wild accusations that would make for a sensational story.

"Look, Tex, I'm probably the most boring person you've ever met. I really don't lead a noteworthy life. I'm just doing my job, helping others when I can. That's all I do."

"Obviously you've done something someone is unhappy about," He's not going to accept my plain vanilla story. "A stray bullet takes out your window. Not in this neighborhood. A stray bullet hits your cat? Again, not in this neighborhood. So I have to make an assumption. That can only lead me back to the commission report you filed with the city on Friday.

"Yeah, yeah, I know you can't talk about it and we can't see it until Council accepts it, which at the earliest is going to be Wednesday. But I think I have enough of a story here that a lot of people are going to want to read that report."

"I would expect so in any event," I say, hoping he's done, but the television reporter is waiting and they're going to want a statement as well.

"Sina, why don't you go on in, I'll be along in a minute." She clearly doesn't want to leave me, but neither does she want to stay out here or answer any more questions. Reluctantly she goes inside and closes the door behind her with a last look towards Butterscotch.

"Are we done? It looks like the people from channel seven would like a statement."

"One last thing." Tex isn't going away just yet. "Council added Reverend Lindo at the last minute and then made him the vice chairman. Did that make coming to consensus hard to achieve?"

"I have no comment about the commission, the report or the relationships of the people on the commission other than to say every single one of them went well beyond what was required.

"Just in accepting this assignment from the city, each and every one of them contributed to our collective understanding of what happened, what others have done to address similar situations, and were open-minded and creative in arriving at a set of recommendations, which we presented to Council and Mayor Blackwell."

"Did you ever write press releases for a living?" Tex asks out of the blue.

"No."

"Sounded like nearly every press release I've ever read."

I just shake my head and walk over to Fox News. "Hi, I'm T.K. Jefferson."

"Melissa Mackey, Channel Seven. Would you be willing to give us an on-air statement about what happened here?"

"Do you want to put your entire audience to sleep early?" I respond.

"What do you mean?" Melissa Mackey says, apparently confused.

"I can't tell you what happened, because I didn't see it. I can't tell you why it happened, because I have no idea. And I can't even suggest a suspect who might have a motivation to do something like this."

"Apparently the person who called it in to us thought there was a story here."

"I'd call them back and ask them," I suggest.

"That would be difficult since it was an anonymous tip."

"Ah, Ms. Anonymous, she does have a reputation of being a gossip, now doesn't she?"

I'm about to go in, when Melissa Mackey asks, "How did you know it was a woman?"

I must have a puzzled expression because Melissa Mackey says, "You didn't know… Well, it was a woman who called it in. We tried to track her down, but it came from a lobby phone at the Holiday Inn Express at the Main Street exit from the Interstate."

"I take it no one at the hotel saw anyone on the phone?"

Melissa shakes her head. "Not likely it was a guest. That would have made it possible to track the person down."

I nod and get ready to leave again, and again Melissa Mackey hits me with the unexpected. "There's a rumor that your commission's report is going to be sandbagged by Council."

"Is Ms. Rumor, Ms. Anonymous' cousin or something?"

"Have you had any contact with city officials since you turned in your report?"

I shake my head as I try to put that piece of information together with what I know for sure, which at the moment is not much.

"Is that a no?" Melissa Mackey wants a confirmation. She apparently doesn't trust me. Why would she not trust me unless she's wondering if I spread the rumor?

"I never respond to rumors," I reply.

But, I think to myself, from my individual informal discussions with Council members, sandbagging didn't seem to be an option. Mayor Blackwell told me they were under too much pressure to not take some action. But she could not give me any assurances until she had read the report and discussed it with the other members of Council, which she would do individually before the Council meeting.

"Then try this one on," Melissa Mackey is studying my reaction and has apparently concluded I know more than I'm willing to share.

"Council member Cochrane is going to announce that he is running in the primary against Mayor Blackwell. Now, the interesting thing here is that apparently the police officer's union is backing him over the Mayor, ostensibly because the Mayor has refused an across the board raise."

"Ms. Rumor certainly is getting around this evening," is all I'll say in response, but I wonder if this all came about because of the commission report.

Duke and Walter must know what's in it, particularly after the way Duke played on Saturday. I've never seen him like that. But if Petes has been painting a picture of doom and gloom coming out of the report, it could be that Duke is feeling he might not get re-elected as president of the union local. He's had that job for a decade or more.

"I have one more rumor," Melissa Mackey seems to really enjoy rattling my cage. "The other rumor I'm trying to track down is that the Mayor has cut a deal with Council member Cochrane to not accept your report on the condition that he not run in the primary."

"Has he done that before?" I can't help but ask.

"Done what?"

"Spread baseless rumors that you report on so that he can back someone into doing what he wants when he knows he can't get it any other way?"

Melissa Mackey thinks about that question. I see she has the answer, but isn't going to share it. "Let's pack up," she calls to her cameraman. "We're chasing the wrong story." She turns to me, "Be sure to tune in at 10."

35 – T.K. JEFFERSON

About noon on Monday I'm reading a report and keep having trouble concentrating.

I decide that I need to go down to the courthouse and listen in on the trial of Richie Webster. I call Mustapha.

"I need to put off our 2:00 o'clock review at least until tomorrow. What problems does that create for you?"

"No problems. Have Brad at 4:00 o'clock."

"I'll sign off on everything except the tables now, so just bring them tomorrow, with your footnotes so we can make sure they pass the smell test and both the footnotes and tables track."

"Can do."

It takes me about forty-five minutes to get downtown, find a parking spot and then find the right court room. Didn't know they have metal detectors to get into the Court House now and a second outside the Courtroom. I notice the second is a portable unit as they don't have them outside the other courtrooms. Someone must really be nervous about security for Richie Webster.

When I slip into the back row of seats, I find a courtroom packed with visitors. One section is apparently friends of the family, and then I notice Mr. and Mrs. Bush sitting in the front row behind the prosecution.

The jury has been seated and they are apparently past opening remarks because the dispatcher is on the stand. She looks to be about fifty, a little overweight, but not obese. Her clothes are too tight fitting in an unpleasant way. The long dark hair is apparently an attempt to make her look younger, but the gray streaks makes that impossible.

The tall prosecuting attorney takes off his glasses and cleans the lenses with his handkerchief as he asks his questions.

"In this earlier incident you've described for us, what was the attitude of former Patrolman Webster? Was he cooperative, was he defiant, or was he just cavalier?"

"What do you mean cavalier? I've not heard that expression before."

"Arrogant or condescending," the prosecutor responds.

"What exactly does that mean, arrogant? I mean I've heard people say so and so is arrogant, but I don't think I really know what they mean, do you?"

"Yes, I do know what arrogant means. A synonym you might recognize is cocky or someone who thinks they're better than you."

"You mean like you?" the dispatcher covers her mouth and looks around at the jury.

The prosecutor just looks at the dispatcher. "Please answer the question."

"Did Richie Webster ever act like you? Yeah, minus the big words. And the time I'm tellin' ya about, he was arrogant. Didn't think he had to follow procedure so long as he got the collar."

"Made the arrest, that's what you're trying to say?"
"Yeah," the dispatcher nods more to herself than the prosecutor.

"So you have confirmed that former Patrolman Richard Webster ignored procedure on more than one previous occasion in his eagerness to make arrests."

"He was arrogant more than once. Yes."

"And that he failed to follow procedure more than once."

"If you say so," the dispatcher is clearly tired of the prosecutor's attitude towards her.

"A simple yes or no?"

"Yes."

"That's all. I have no more questions for this witness."

I'm surprised that neither the prosecution nor the defense called me as a witness since I was there when Richie was told by Duke not to engage in anything non-routine without backup.

Does that mean that Richie Webster thought investigating a break-in and subsequent confrontation of a suspect was routine? I doubt the defense will use that line of defense.

But what is even more confusing to me is that I reported what happened between Richie and Duke to the Chief. It should have been picked up by someone.

But then again, it was the fox investigating the foxes' den. Why would they report it unless they thought their defense was weak without it?

I read the transcript of the dispatch call Richie responded to and even she told him to wait for backup and that warning was recorded. Stronger than a witness statement I guess.

And the Chief? Apparently he intends to keep a low profile since he clearly takes a part of the blame for not enforcing stricter adherence to procedure.

The prosecuting attorney calls his next witness: "Your Honor, I call Sergeant Francis Marion to the stand."

Duke? Are they asking him about his conversation with Richie? Duke, in full uniform, hair more slicked back than usual, is sworn in and takes a seat.

"Sergeant Marion, you were the chief investigator of this incident, were you not?"

"I was." Duke is playing it straight. Of course he would. I didn't realize he was the one responsible for the factual part of the report. I wonder if he drafted the recommendations. Wouldn't that be a conflict of interest in his role as president of the local chapter of the union?

"You investigated the scene on multiple occasions?"

"I did." Clearly Duke has given testimony previously.

"Are the facts of this incident consistent with what was presented here? That would include facts drawn from what you found on those multiple occasions when you visited the site, asked questions of the defendant and inspected the physical evidence?"

"Yes."

"When you first arrived on the scene, did you find that the deceased was in possession of a weapon of any sort?"

"No."

"What did you find?"

"A cell phone and a knapsack."

"Where were those items?"

Duke points to a photograph of the scene after Deshaun's body had been removed, but with a chalk outline of where he had fallen on the concrete pad. In the photo, the cell phone is still where it had fallen.

"You can see the cell phone near the outline of the victim's head, right there. The knapsack you can see next to the door, right about there."

"So if the cell phone fell straight down, as it would have if the victim had been holding it at the time he was shot, it would have fallen about where we see it now?"

Duke nods, and then remembers they are making a transcript of his testimony and responds, "That would be a reasonable conclusion."

"Of course, someone could have placed it there after the events, but it is reasonable to conclude it fell from the victim's hand."

"Yes."

"Did you inspect the contents of the knapsack?"

Duke hesitates before responding, "Yes."

"And what did you find?"

"Change of clothing, toiletries, and a college calculus textbook."

"Nothing that would indicate the victim had a weapon of any kind, or that he was attempting to do anything other than be away from the college he attended for a day or more?"

"No."

"Let's go back to your first visit to the scene. What time was that?"

Duke looks at the clock on the back wall. "Around one am."

"Within an hour of the events."

"Approximately, from the records from dispatch and the arrival of back-up."

"You were able to see the scene, approximately as former Patrolman Webster saw it, were you not?"

"I believe so, yes."

"You believe so, could you explain?"

"By the time I arrived, the backup team was on site, with flashlights, and a camera man had arrived to photograph the scene. That picture you're using would have been one of his photos, I believe."

"So there were other people present, doing things on the site, so not a one-on-one in a dark backyard?"

"Correct."

"But apart from those other elements, from the position former Patrolman Webster entered the backyard, approximately here…" the prosecutor points to the photo of the site. "Looking towards the house and where the victim was standing, here…" Again the prosecutor points to the photo. "Was there sufficient light that it would have been possible to distinguish what the victim was holding in his left hand?"

"Possible? Yes, depending on the size and shape of the object." I'm surprised, Duke is not trying to shade the response. "But given the object discovered, which is small and about the size of a small handgun, like a Berretta or similar weapon, it is reasonable to believe the defendant could have mistaken it for a weapon."

"You mentioned a Berretta. Why did you suggest that particular weapon?"

"Gangs in town have been found to be carrying weapons by that particular manufacturer. They are about the size of one of the current larger cell phones. They are small enough to easily conceal, but powerful enough to kill someone at close range."

"Would former Patrolman Webster have been aware of the presence of those weapons in town?"

"Yes."

"Why would he have been aware of them?"

"He was present on more than one encounter with the local gangs where we took such weapons from them."

"To prevent gang violence?"

"Yes."

"And how do you know this to be a fact?"

"I was present at those events as well. I conducted the searches of the gang members where those weapons were discovered."

"Would you say that former Patrolman Webster was justified to be concerned about what the victim was holding in his hand?"

"Concerned? Certainly. It had been less than a week since the last time such a weapon had been removed from gang members in town."

"Sergeant, if it had been you investigating a possible break-in at this site, under those conditions, do you think you would have made the mistake of believing a cell phone was anything other than a cell phone?"

"No." This response surprises me, I would have expected him to give Richie more cover.

"Why?"

"The suspect had not entered the premises. He was overheard talking with someone, and yet there was no other person present that could be seen. Given that he was talking quietly, anyone else present would have had to be very close to be heard and therefore observable.

"I would have clearly identified myself as a police officer and asked the victim to keep his hands up and move away from the house and into an area where I could see his movements more clearly, which would have given the added light needed to identify any threat."

"Is that the standard procedure?"

"Yes."

"The standard procedure which former Patrolman Webster would have learned, but failed to execute that night, and which was the primary reason for the victim's demise?"

"Yes."

"No further questions."

The defense attorney, a young woman, maybe mid-thirties, Hispanic and wearing a well-tailored dark gray suit steps forward.

"Sergeant Marion. You were aware on the night of the events that former Patrolman Webster was on patrol alone, in violation of the department policy that recruits are not permitted to patrol alone until they have passed all of their proficiency tests and performed on the job in the presence of another officer for at least six months. Is that correct?"

"Yes."

"Why were you aware of this violation of policy and why did you not prevent former Patrolman Webster from going out alone that evening?"

"The defendant contacted me to see if I would ride along with him that evening."

"Could you tell the jury why you did not?"

"I had a prior scheduled meeting with city officials I had to attend."

"And you attended that meeting?"

"I did."

"Why didn't you stop former Patrolman Webster from going out alone in violation of department policy?"

"The defendant explained that his usual partner had called in sick and he had been told by the desk Sergeant that the Chief wanted everyone out on patrol that evening. He was also told to try to find someone to come in and ride with him, which he did."

"So former Patrolman Webster knew he was violating department policy, but had been given instructions that the policy was suspended for that evening."

"Not explicitly."

"But implicitly."

"Yes."

"And it was because he was given an opportunity to comply with the policy and unable to find someone, including yourself, you thought it appropriate for him to patrol alone."

"The department has multiple open positions it has been unable to fill because of budgetary constraints. Since we are not at full staffing, we frequently find ourselves not complying completely with policies and procedures."

"Would you say that the staffing shortfall is a primary contributor to the tragic events of that evening?"

"Yes."

"And you referenced this situation in your investigatory report?"

"I did, on page sixteen and again on page thirty-seven."

"Would you say that the city's refusal to add officers to your department has created a public safety concern?"

"That would be an opinion better expressed by Chief Andrews." Duke just threw that bomb at the Chief.

"While our questioning has been in regards to the investigation you conducted and the report you filed with the department, you also serve as the president of the local chapter of the police officer union, is that correct?"

"Yes."

"You have been the president for a long time, if my information is correct."

"Yes."

"Is staffing levels one of the items subject to collective bargaining?"

"It is."

"Is it a subject of the current negotiations?"

"It is."

"Is the position of the union in these negotiations that additions to staff are needed?"

"It is."

"Has the city authorized any additions to staffing during your tenure as union president?"

"No, in fact, we have been not permitted to fill all vacancies as officers retire."

"How many vacancies do you show at this time?"

"Two hundred and twenty-one."

"Out of how many officers authorized?"

"Three thousand and ten."

"So a little less than seven percent of the entire staffing is vacant. Now if those positions were filled, would a single officer calling in sick for his shift have resulted in a rookie patrolman not being able to find a substitute partner for the evening?"

"It would have been much easier to find someone, yes."

"Let me summarize your testimony if I might. You have testified that because the city has not fully staffed the police department you frequently are forced to 'work around' policies and procedures. Is that correct?"

"Yes."

"You have also testified that former Patrolman Webster attempted to comply with an instructed workaround to a policy."

“He did.”

“And that since work arounds were frequent, former Patrolman Webster would logically feel that he had a certain amount of discretion in how he followed procedures?”

“He willfully ignored two sets of instructions that night, from me and from dispatch.”

36 – REVEREND LEROY LINDO

"Nice to meet you, Melissa Mackey of Fox News Channel Seven," I respond to the young blonde who has stuck a microphone in my face and had her cameraman turn on bright lights so it's hard for me to even see her now.

"Reverend Lindo, you are demonstrating outside the Court House this evening with what looks like more than three hundred other individuals. Could you tell our viewers why?"

"We are here seeking justice for Deshaun Bush, assassinated by a member of our city police department in his own back yard."

"Justice for Deshaun Bush. Why do you think justice may not be done?" Melissa sets me up nicely. We could have rehearsed this, but apparently there was no need.

"The district attorney is apparently colluding with the defense. She has allowed the jury to be stacked against conviction. Just look at the color of their faces. None of color, no Hispanics, no one who has suffered at the hands of the racists who control our police department and patrol our streets, harassing innocent black boys and girls because of racial profiling.

"How can we expect justice for Deshaun when the jury has no experience with the racism we suffer every day?"

"Why would the district attorney permit a stacked jury?" Melissa pitches another soft toss.

"Because she's in bed with the folks at City Hall who just want this whole thing to go away.

"As far as they're concerned the kid screwed up. So their solution is to fire him and let him leave town and be someone else's problem.

“What the kid did was expose the racism and the reckless endangerment that department and city policies have caused to be the situation.

“The kid has exposed the fact that white people in this city can commit murder and not suffer the consequences that any black man or Hispanic man or Asian man or Muslim man would suffer -- in fact anyone who doesn’t wear a uniform, but who assassinates someone in their own back yard.”

“These are pretty strong accusations. What evidence do you have of a conspiracy at City Hall?” Melissa Mackey seems to take a left turn for no reason.

“Evidence?” Where is she? She’s not listening to me! “Evidence? Deshaun Bush is dead.

“We have a report of an investigation of his assassination. The report was written by the president of the police officer union.

“Hello! The city accepted that report and fired the kid, who made the mistake that led the world to see what’s going on behind the closed doors of the police department and City Hall.

“And now they’re having a trial to whitewash the whole thing. Bring the kid in, we’ll give him his hall pass to leave town and never return. He killed an innocent black boy. He admits to it.

“But this is just like everything else in this city… he’s not responsible for his own actions? It’s everyone else. It’s no one else. Who do we blame here if not the kid who pulled the trigger?

“Murder is murder. Deshaun Bush is dead. His parents are devastated. His friends feel his loss every day. Nothing this court does will bring him back to his family and friends.

“But this court can sure send a loud and clear signal to all the other racists on the police force and in City Hall that if someone kills someone in this city and it can be proven that they pulled the trigger, they should be held accountable.”

"That's a bit long for a fifteen second spot, but I'll try to work with it," Melissa Mackey explains to me. "What do you think will happen if the defendant is found not guilty?"

"The lord will look down on this city and bring destruction and death to every last one of those who have transgressed.

"He will strike down all incumbents on the Council and the Mayor in the next election. He will see that someone who understands what is going on here is elected. That person will fire the Chief of Police and hire a transformative leader in his place.

"He will see that every last officer in the department is fired for blatant racism and failure to follow department procedures and policies. He will hire new police officers who can see people as people, not as racial profiles that demand different responses based on the color of your skin.

"He will hold the people of this city accountable for the actions of their government and government departments and judge each and every one of us when our time comes."

"What will you do?" Melissa apparently didn't like that response.

"I will be out here every night, leading this protest so that the people in that building know we are watching, and we will hold them and everyone else involved accountable.

"And if the verdict is not guilty, you will see my name on the ballot for Mayor in the next election. Someone has to stand up to the racism, the incompetence, the malfeasance that is this government."

"Thank you, Reverend LeRoy Lindo, Pastor of the Second Baptist Church of Fort Christian,"

The microphone is taken away and the camera light goes out. I still can't see a thing.

36 – T.K. JEFFERSON

Brad is sitting behind his desk when I enter his spacious office.

His head is down, looking at something on his computer screen. It's never a good day when Brad asks me to come to his office, so I hope I can get this over quickly and get back to work.

Even with all the weekends and later days I'm still behind. Going to the trial yesterday was something I thought I needed to do, but I walked out of it depressed and feeling guilty that if I'd only said something to Deshaun before he left the Boy's Club, maybe…

"Leticia was happy to meet your wife. Said she had a pleasant conversation with her. Oh, and Leticia said she learned a lot about basketball."

I see the trophy our team won at the tournament on the table behind his desk, so apparently he was satisfied about that.

Duke never came back after that first game, so we were able to concentrate on just the other teams and that worked out. We got into a tempo. Devin and Shorty seemed to dominate the play right through the final game. Devin made all the difference.

"Sina enjoyed talking with her as well," I respond politely.

"I understand the Mayor released your commission's report this morning, even though Council hasn't formally accepted it. Guess that's just a formality at this point."

"I hadn't heard that," I respond. "I've had my head down here since early this morning."

Brad nods, "And I saw you on the news. Sorry about what happened there. Have the police figured out who was responsible or why?"

I shake my head.

"Hope they do. I'm sure you and Sina both will be more comfortable when you know who was behind it."

"Sina's still not comfortable being home alone in the evening," I say. But there's something on his mind and he's not getting right to it. I wonder what.

"Tom's gotten some calls."

"About?" I'm not following him. About my work? The project I'm trying to complete? What?

"Tom was at the club yesterday, some of his golfing buddies were making remarks about your television appearance," Brad begins, but I already know where this is going. "Something about that's not the kind of publicity the company needs."

"I didn't identify myself with the company,"

"The newscaster made that link when they broadcast the interview segment at 6:00 am."

"I was already here, so I didn't see it."

"Not important. But I saw the old man this morning and he asked me to have a little talk with you about your outside activities."

Brad waits for me to say something, but I don't.

"Tom thinks there may be some link to what happened at your house and your community work. There's certainly nothing you're doing here that could have resulted in something like that."

"I can think of no reason what happened is at all related to my work for the company," I know I must sound like a robot or something, but I don't want him to think the wrong thing.

"Then we agree it must have something to do with your community work."

"Or a random event. We do have gangs in this city…"

"But why your house?"

"As I said, a random event."

"Tom doesn't think so," Brad almost sings this response to me like I'm a kid.

I can't react to his taunt. "He may be right, I can't tell you, because I don't know anything for sure."

"Let's talk about your work on that commission."

"It's over. The report has been filed and the commission will not be meeting further unless requested by Council. At the moment I'm not expecting that."

"You know, Tom said you'd probably say that." Brad lets that sit a moment. Clubbing me into submission by using the owner's name in nearly every sentence. Apparently Brad doesn't think I would accept his guidance, and he's probably right.

"But he asked me to talk to you about the negative impact your continued association with that commission may have. Tom said he got a call from several of our larger shareholders about an hour ago. Said your commission has made some controversial recommendations. They expressed concern that the fallout for the company will most likely not be good."

"I understand that if Tom had been the commission chairman and stood in front of the media to discuss their recommendations, there would undoubtedly be some association with the firm. But I'm not the owner of the firm, I'm merely an employee.

"The community doesn't identify me with the company as anyone who can influence things the way that Tom could. He can donate money, time and gather support from his peers to take on some community charity or cause, just the way Leticia did this past weekend.

"Nobody reported on my involvement or your involvement. We merely played basketball. It's much the same thing. You and I supported the cause, helped raise money by participating in the tournament."

"Not how Tom sees it."

I have to remember, Brad has already had the conversation with Tom and the outcome has already been decided. Any defense I may offer doesn't go back up to Tom and Tom is simply expecting Brad to tell me to somehow distance myself from the commission and the report. There's only one way I can think of to do that.

"The most important thing that Tom said is no more interviews, period. If anyone wants a quote it should be to refer that person back to the Mayor."

"Just so you know I have not given any interviews to anyone including the newspapers about the commission."

"Really? Tex Andrews attributed statements to you about the commission's work."

"In the context of the vandalism at my home. He came by and wanted me to speculate. I refused. I haven't read his articles as I've mostly been here."

"You need to take the time to see what people are saying about you." Brad considers whether to say something more and then apparently decides to do so, "Even your basketball buddy isn't happy with you."

"Duke?"

"Walked out on us in the middle of the tournament. I think that was a pretty loud statement."

He's right, but I can't say that. How do I explain how important this commission is to me? It provides a chance for meaningful change in how our city grows together rather than being divided by ancient attitudes.

"You can assure Tom that I will not make even a 'no comment' to anyone from any media about what happened at my home or the commission, the commission report, or the Webster trial."

"Tom will be glad to know that you are concerned about the reputation of the company and will fully embrace our desire to limit our leadership role in the community to civic and cultural affairs.

"He wants you to know that we have no interest in treading into the politics of the city and was looking for an assurance that neither do you, either now or in the future."

"Let me ask a question, Brad," I lean forward to emphasize my point. "We have at least a dozen employees just here in Fort Christian who serve on various boards and commissions for the city. They are generally Planning Boards, or Zoning Boards, or Parks and Recreations Commissions. Things like that. They are governmental advisory boards, just like the one I serve on.

"How do you tell me to walk away from serving the community in the same way as those other employees without making it a blanket direction to all of them both here and everywhere the company has employees?

"In fact, I think if you look into it, we have people who hold much more responsible governmental elected posts, like school board. I think our Permian director is a Council member in the city where he lives and worked for more than a decade on the campaigns of others to get support for his run.

"Tom would need to provide the same direction to each of them, even though their community service creates good will in the drilling activity we have in those communities.

"Is Tom really willing to disrupt community relationships where we have operations because a few shareholders were concerned about community perception where we don't even drill?"

Brad doesn't know what to say. I didn't think he would. And now I've created a problem for him.

Clearly Tom expects Brad to handle this situation. Now he has to go back to Tom and tell him he can't just shut me up. He would have to remove a whole bunch of others, some of whom actually directly benefit the company.

I decide to make him squirm a little more, "If you remember, I came in and had a conversation with you before I discussed my thoughts in public about what the city needed to do in this instance.

"You gave me a speech about how it is my civic duty to express my thoughts if they will help the community. You approved my public involvement in this debate.

"Now, I don't want to hold you to that, because I actually took a different tact. I didn't discuss my thoughts with the media. I have not and will not. But I am associated with a group of individuals who spent a month of their time examining that issue and making a series of recommendations.

"The recommendations can in no way come back to the company because I was the chairman and did not even vote on the recommendations. So how can they reflect negatively on the company?"

Brad gives me a little hand wave, like he's said enough.

"Tom is asking you to sever your ties with the commission. Do whatever you need to do so there can be no blowback on the company."

I know I would normally just do as Tom Horton asks, because he's been good to me, giving me my first real job after college. But if I resign from the commission it will hit the paper and the television news.

By simply resigning, I'll be cross-wise on not drawing further comment about my involvement. If I resign, that means the Rev will be the one who has to go before Council and with his calls to defeat them in the next election the report will be dead on arrival. The Council can't approve the recommendations without appearing to cave to the Rev.

And in that case Petes will get what he wants. The department will continue to selectively intimidate young men of color and Hispanic ethnicity in racial profiling.

The city will continue as two cities in one; two life experiences that couldn't be more different. One of hope and aspiration. The other of despair and too often seeking to be a bad somebody rather than a good nobody.

I think of Demetrius, Deshaun's cousin. That was what he was looking for -- the determination that Deshaun had not to be a victim of his circumstances and to rise above it.

Many hands helped Deshaun become what he could be. All too often those hands aren't there for the kids I play ball with at the Boy's Club. For all the others who don't even make it that far.

I can't simply walk away from the work the commission has done, which can change the trajectory of relations within the city. I have to be there for them and open the door to a better life for all of them.

Don't I?

37 – T.K. JEFFERSON

Flo is meeting us for dinner, without Daniel, her husband… again.

I'm starting to think he either doesn't like what we like to eat or doesn't like the eventual political discussions we always seem to end up getting into. He never participates in her campaign activities, saying that's Flo's thing not his.

Anyway, we're meeting at Café Momentum, which is downtown and only a few blocks from City Hall. When I suggested it as a place to meet her, T.K. gave me a funny look, but then agreed. I don't know what that was all about since he is usually the one to suggest we come here.

Café Momentum isn't a typical restaurant. It's only open four nights a week.

The kids who work here, learning skills that will enable them to get jobs in the hospitality industry, are all on work release from the City Jail. They have somehow run afoul of the law, and the staff here bails them out, puts them through an intensive life skills training program, and teaches them how to work at every job in a restaurant.

The chef who started the program wanted to do more than just serve great food, he wanted to give back to the community in a way that serves everyone. The program has a very low recidivism rate, meaning that few of those who complete the program end up back in jail.

At the same time, they have been able to demonstrate real savings to the community in terms of the cost of incarceration and the legal system to prosecute and manage their probation.

The restaurant is not very large and sits on a side street in a location that isn't out of the way, but just isn't on a main thoroughfare.

Probably to get cheaper rent.

But it's relatively easy to get to and I am meeting both Flo and T.K. there since he is coming directly from work and Flo went to City Hall for a committee meeting. As I come in, the young hostess asks my name.

"Jefferson," I respond and look about for the rest of my party, but neither are here yet.

"This way," she responds and takes me to a high table in the middle of the room that probably seats twelve. Apparently we are getting the end seats as we walk to the other end away from the entrance. I take my seat on the end of the table so I'll be able to see them coming in and ask, "Have you been in the program long?"

"About two months," she responds.

"How did you get chosen?"

"I don't know. I was sitting in my cell, waiting to go back before the judge and Miss Toni came by. She knew my name and she said to me, "Sister, you don't belong here. I said, you're right, I don't.

"She asked if I'd ever worked in a restaurant and I said I'd never even eaten in a restaurant other than McDonald's.

"So she told me about the program, said I'd get a deferred adjudication, which at the time I didn't even know what that meant, but she told me. I said I'd be so happy if I didn't have to spend one more night in that cell, so here I am."

"What did you do to get sent to jail?"

"I beat up a white girl who was always making remarks about my weight, and saying I was a hoe and all that BS. I'm not no hoe. And I can't do much about my weight, although I've lost almost fifteen pounds since I came here.

"They teach you all about nutrition. Say you need to know 'bout those things if you're going to cook and serve food to paying customers. So now I eat the right things, eat the right amount of those things and balance out so I'm not keeping the weight on the way I was."

"You look good. I was surprised when you said the thing that started it all was your weight. Keep going and I'll bet you'll be pretty attractive to a lot of guys."

"Oh, I got a boyfriend. He says I'm already looking mighty fine. Tells me not to talk to all those other guys who keep wanting me to go out with them. But until I finish this program and get my own place I'm not going out with anyone."

"Is that what you're working towards? Your own place?"

"Yes, ma'am. I talk with some of the others who finished here. They're all doing good, working here and there. The staff keep in touch with us once we complete and make sure we're doing what we were taught, make sure we're staying out of trouble and away from the bad influences, if you know what I mean.

"So yeah, I'm working for my own place and to get my life going for me, not for all those others who think they can use me."

"Good luck," I wish her as I see Flo come in.

"What do you do, ma'am?"

"I'm a librarian at Central High School."

"Could you recommend a book I should read?" she asks. "I didn't read so good before, but they're giving me lessons and now I want to read, but I don't know what I'd find interesting."

"Tell you what, I'll pick out four or five and drop them off here for you tomorrow. What's your name?"

"Andrae. Just Andrae."

Flo arrives at the table, "Flo Lopez, this is Andrae our host tonight. We've been having an interesting conversation about how she got here and how she's working to get a place of her own. She'll make it, I'm confident of that."

Flo shakes hands with Andrae, "Nice to meet you."

"Your server will be right with you," Andrae says.

"No hurry, we're still waiting on one more," I respond, but she leaves anyway.

"Traffic bad?" I ask Flo.

"From City Hall?" She laughs. "I just walked it."

"Which committee was today?" I knew her assignments at one time as she often asked me to help research things so she could be better informed in the meetings, but she hadn't asked for anything this time.

"Public Works. Going over the department budget for next year. They want to accelerate some of the projects and slow down others for one reason or another.

"In the end it will be about the same amount of money. We can easily transfer the extra in from the reserves.

"They just wanted to know what kind of reactions to expect from residents who will be affected before they make the changes.

"So we gave them the feedback they were looking for, reprioritized a few at our suggestions and that was about it."

"Not controversial," I observe.

"Oh, no. You'd be surprised at who gets all riled up about fixing streets that have broken pavement or drainage issues.

"We don't get storms all that often, but when they hit us the water just runs through the streets and sometimes into people's homes, or back yards.

"Can't let that happen, so drainage actually gets higher priority in many cases than the street repairs and rebuilds."

"Is that why you decided to run for office? To make sure folks' homes weren't flooded and street repairs were made?" I'm wondering why she seems so fulfilled by this aspect of the job.

"When I ran?" she seems surprised by my question. "As you remember, all I talked about then was making government effective at a cost that the people could afford, but it seemed to me and a whole lot of others that parts of what the government did were neither. Street repairs? That was a symptom, not the issue."

"So people heard what they wanted to hear."

I think I see the underlying strategy we used, but I wasn't really focused on it at the time since my job was to get her in front of as many voters as possible. She honed the message.

"Those who wanted government to be responsive to something they needed heard one part and those who just wanted to keep the taxes low heard another part."

"No one gets elected by telling people I don't care if the government serves you well or at all, but I'm gonna raise your taxes every year so I can get mine. But that's exactly what a lot of people seem to do once they get here.

"It's been like a high school class election. It's not what are you going to do for me as class president, it's whether my friend is the one who gets elected, and then I forget all about it."

T.K. arrives, sees us and heads right for the table. "Sorry, I'm later than I thought." He stops long enough for a kiss and then one on the cheek for Flo before sitting down across from her.

"What am I interrupting as usual?"

"We were talking about why Flo ran for Council," I try to bring him into the conversation.

"I thought it was to serve the people?"

"Yeah, that's about it..." Flo responds. "But sometimes it seems the people have their own ideas about what serves their interests."

I hear a weariness I'd not heard before, "What are you referring to?"

"We put the Reverend Lindo on the commission to give him a stake in the outcome and he's still whipping up opposition to our reelection. I found out last night that she's recruited Paulette Simpson to run against me."

"Paulette?" I'm surprised at this revelation. I know Paulette. She's been the den mother of her neighborhood forever. Whatever needed to be done, she was the first volunteer.

An elderly person needed to get to a doctor's appointment, either she would take them herself or find someone who could. Someone didn't have the money for their child to play sports, or play in the band, or raise money for a class trip? Paulette was out raising the money with a bake sale or car wash or one thing or another.

She was able to convince some retail stores in the area to donate money or goods or services to help people out. And she never asked for anything in return.

So she is someone everyone knows, everyone owes her a favor and would most likely vote for her if asked.

"Paulette's never expressed any interest in sitting in meetings all the time -- and that comes with the territory."

"Surprised me too," Flo sounds tired. "...and I'm probably not going to run for re-election if she files. It wouldn't make any sense. She'd beat me easily."

"Hold on..." T.K. interjects. "You've done an outstanding job for your constituents and the city.

"People recognize who you are and what you stand for. Paulette doesn't stand for governance, she stands for helping people. There's a big difference. I can see how you could beat her in an election."

"If the people are thinking about it," Flo responds. "The problem is the Rev Lindo is going to continue to whipsaw all of us incumbents throughout the election.

"He'll beat it into his congregation that we're the enemy and people will have such a negative impression of me… and the rest of the Council members… I just don't know how you overcome that."

"You think if Council approves the recommendations of the commission that he'll continue to work against you?" T.K. asks as if he has a contrary opinion, but I don't know if Flo is picking up on that.

"You know I'm getting threats from people already? We haven't even accepted the report."

"Why did Mayor Blackwell release it before accepting it?" T.K. asks this in such a way that it appears to be something that's been bothering him.

"For that exact reason," Flo responds. "She wanted to gauge the reaction before we took any action. Give us a chance to understand what will happen if we do."

"Politically? Or as a community?" T.K. almost challenges her thoughts. "There's likely a difference."

38 – REGINA BLACKWELL – MAYOR CITY OF FORT CHRISTIAN

"Our regularly scheduled meeting of the city of Fort Christian will now come to order. Madam Secretary, do we have a quorum present?" I begin the meeting, looking out at the overflowing chambers, again.

"Yes, Mayor Blackwell."

"I would like to deviate from our regular agenda to make a statement," I pause to get the attention of those in the chambers who are continuing their conversations over my opening of the meeting.

"I believe that many of you are here to see if Council is going to take up the matter of the commission report this evening. The answer is it is not on the agenda and we will not be taking any comments on it.

"So if that is the sole reason for your attendance tonight, you may wish to return to your families.

"I can't tell you when we will take up that matter, but since the jury is still deliberating in the case of former Patrolman Webster, I felt it would not be appropriate to take any action on the commission's report until Council has an understanding of the outcome of that trial."

Petes raises his hand, what now?

"Council member Cochrane? Did you wish to say something?"

"I do," Petes turns his attention to Tex Anthony, who is sitting in the front row. "As you know, I did not endorse the recommendations of the commission.

"I think it very appropriate that Council take its time with this report. It makes some recommendations that I do not believe are in the best interests of the city of Fort Christian.

"For that reason I would like to encourage all citizens to obtain a copy of the report from the City Secretary. Read it. Make up your own mind and communicate your thoughts not only to your Council member, but also to the Mayor, the district attorney and the Chief of Police.

"While you may think that only the voting members of Council will make the final determination of whether to socially re-engineer our city, that's not the case.

"We will be looking for input from both the DA and the Chief as to the feasibility of such a grand experiment. You need to understand that impact on you, whether the recommendations will make you feel safer at night.

"Whether you want the kind of responsibility this ill-advised departure from what we have known would foster upon you. So please request a copy of the report and tell us what you wish us to do with it. We can simply not accept it, and in my judgment, that would be best for all."

"I would ask the rest of Council to withhold your comments at this time." I decide to shut this discussion down now. "We will return to this probably next meeting. That will be the appropriate time to discuss your thoughts. So back to the agenda for tonight..."

39 – T.K. JEFFERSON

Mustapha and I are conducting a review with the field crews on the latest exploration pad we wish them to construct in a new reservoir area.

"The subsurface data would indicate that we can drill here for a long time. The lateral wells appear to be laden with carbon deposits.

"We expect heavy natural gas as well, which will be good, so we can set up on-site electrical generation we can fire with the flare gas and reduce the venting to the atmosphere.

"It will also reduce our cost of electricity since we are not buying the fuel to generate. That also reduces our break even on this set of wells.

"Even better.

I note Brad in the hallway. Seems he's pacing back and forth. Why doesn't he simply come in if he wants to talk? I'll never understand him. One minute he seems to be lord of the manor and the next, the most insecure person in the building.

Is that what it's like to report directly to the CEO? One minute you're at the right hand of God and the next you're a non-person? I couldn't imagine living a life with that much insecurity.

Mustapha continues his portion of the briefing and I note that Brad is still hanging around. I nod to Mustapha and exit out the back of the conference room.

Brad is talking with one of the administrative assistants. Brad never does that because Leticia would have his balls if he ever even thought of getting it on with someone else. And since all the money flows through her, Brad has no choice.

"Hey Brad. You need something?"

Brad looks up like I've just rescued him from Purgatory.

"Yeah… you're in the middle…"

"No problem. Mustapha has this portion. What do you need?"

Brad nods towards his office, "Follow me."

I do and shortly we are back in his ample office. Brad closes the door behind us. "Need to talk to you."

Brad drops the morning newspaper on his desk and I see the headline. 'Guilty,' in the largest type they could produce. I instantly know what that means.

I nod to the paper, "What was the sentence?"

Brad looks down at the newspaper, "That's part of what I need to talk to you about." He leaves it hanging there, which is never a good thing.

"I thought we'd worked that out," I respond since he's implying either he or Tom is still unhappy.

"Tom's not buying your counter. Thinks your situation is unique and doesn't apply to the others. What you've been doing has no direct benefit for the company. What the others are doing does. Apples and oranges, he said."

At least I know he talked with Tom about it. My bigger concern was that he wouldn't even talk to him and just make me resign. That Brad wouldn't want to go back and voice my concerns.

But he did, apparently.

"Thank you for at least trying…"

"Tom's not pleased… thought you would do what we asked."

I don't respond, trying to understand how he has come to this assumption since he shouldn't know one way or the other.

Then Brad pushes the newspaper in my direction. Let's me read Tex Anthony's lead article about the jury finding Patrolman Webster guilty of murder in the second degree and sentencing him to ten years to life. I hadn't heard any of this.

I read on, where Tex talks about how Mayor Blackwell had deferred discussion of the commission report at the regular Council meeting. I read all about Petes' passionate plea for voters to contact their Council members to voice their concerns.

And then the reference to me as chairman of the commission that had made such controversial recommendations. He specifically identifies me as a Director at Horton Exploration and Production Company.

So Tex apparently felt a need to identify once again who I work for. Is someone paying him to do that, knowing the company won't be pleased?

"I'm not quoted," I point out.

"Not the point. Tex Anthony is still tying you to the company. Did you resign from the commission?"

"No." I can't beat around the bush when Brad is being this direct.

"I thought I was very clear about Tom's expectations."

"And I gave you a counter argument where Tom was acting in an arbitrary manner if he didn't…"

"Tom can damn well act as he pleases and that shouldn't be any of your concern."

"Can you explain why this is such a big deal to Tom?" I ask in a not unreasonable tone of voice.

"The report isn't such a big deal to Tom, although I have to let you know we have some directors who are just livid about it. Calling and emailing Tom multiple times a day. Tom hand-picked most of his directors, so he knows they're not going to do anything stupid, but they are making life unpleasant with their accusations that Tom has lost control of the situation."

"He never had control of the situation. That's an unreasonable expectation," I push back.

"Don't tell a board member that," Brad responds. "Board members think they run the world through their direct influence with CEOs. Always want them to do what they ask. Think that's a way of regaining the power they lost when they left wherever they were to join a board."

"Understand."

"Anyway, Tom greatly values what you do for the company. Doesn't want to lose you, so he would like to offer you a new position."

Quid pro quo, I instantly think to myself. His way of forcing the situation. At least I should feel good that he's not simply firing me for insubordination. Not resigning from the commission when directly asked.

But then I quickly think of the promotional opportunities within the firm and come to the conclusion what he's about to offer is not going to be a promotion.

"What is Tom thinking?"

"Nigeria. You're the absolute best we have at doing the analysis and picking the well sites. We've not been getting the production from the last few well sites as we were earlier. Tom would like you to move to Nigeria, take over the operations there, and get us back on track."

"Take over the operations… does that mean reporting to George Schultz or…"

"George is coming back, so you would be replacing George," Brad clarifies, apparently expecting this question as well. George is the same grade I am, so this is a lateral and not a promotion.

The fact it's taking over a remote oil field, it actually is a demotion.

In Fort Christian I have responsibility for our largest identified reserves and highest production wells. In terms of impact on the company, I'm being sent to Siberia. Important role, but not one that anyone really cares about.

"When will this be effective?" I ask, dreading the answer.

"Immediately. You need to get over there as quickly as possible. I don't know if Sina will be going with you, that's up to you. George has already returned for a medical procedure he couldn't have done there. So the thought is he won't have to return if you can go tomorrow."

I close my eyes, unwilling to engage in the reality that has just shifted ninety degrees to the right. I never thought Tom would do something like this to me.

I've always been at the main office in Fort Christian, working my way up, but always focused on the Permian Basin wells. I can see the logic that I need to be rounded out in order to take on any more responsibility.

But just the way this is being handled… normally Brad and I would have a conversation about taking on a new role at least a year in advance, maybe more. Give me a chance to prepare before arriving in country for good.

Even take a few visitation trips so I could meet the people I would be working with and the government officials with whom I would be working.

The whole process is meant to ensure that everyone can work together. In this instance the Company is violating the approach that has worked so well in every other senior executive change.

This is clearly Tom's way of forcing the situation without it appearing to be so.

"Nigeria is an important assignment, but it's ninety percent operations and only ten percent development. Am I really the most qualified person for this assignment?" I'm reaching for straws here.

"Tom thinks there's untapped potential there. Said that if anyone can find the reserves you're the one."

"I can go, but I'll need to be back and forth for a while to ensure there's a smooth transition on my end. Mustapha is good, but he's not ready…"

"What happens to your team isn't your concern. You have a new job and need to fully engage it immediately. Would suggest you call George on his cell phone and arrange to meet with him. Best way to have a smooth transition. Mitsi has your tickets. You can pick them up on your way out."

I look at the basketball tournament trophy on the table behind Brad's desk, I think about Deshaun…

40 – T.K. JEFFERSON

Sina and I are talking on the phone when my administrative assistant pokes her head into my office door. “Mayor Blackwell on line two.”

“Hold on, I have a call coming in.”

“T.K., this is Regina Blackwell. We haven’t talked since you filed the report. You may be aware that we took no action at the last Council meeting waiting for the verdict before starting on the next phase of discussions.

“So tonight is the next public meeting and we need you to come brief us. Answer questions. We have cleared the agenda, so this is all we are discussing tonight. Can you be at City Hall at 6:30? This will be a long one, and I think it’s imperative that you be there as the spokesperson.”

This is absolutely the last thing I wanted to happen tonight. If I don’t go, the Rev will be the one briefing Council, and all that work is for nothing. If I go, Tex will report on it and Tom will likely be upset. Another difficult meeting with Brad before I go.

“Any chance this can be postponed?”

“No.” Mayor Blackwell is very clear. They won’t hold up the meeting just for me.

“I understand. I’ll be there, but can I talk with you before the meeting, at say 6:15?”

“Come to my office,” and she is gone.

At 6:15 I show up at the Mayor’s tiny office. I’m surprised that it’s actually smaller than mine and she is running a billion-dollar corporation of sorts in the city government.

"Evening, Mayor."

"T.K., what's on your mind? We only have a few minutes." The Mayor is distracted, apparently preparing for what she knows will be a difficult meeting.

"My company is transferring me." I put that out there so she understands that my role in continued advocacy for the recommendations is ending.

The Mayor stops her search for something she apparently wanted for the meeting, looks at me quizzically and then asks, "When?"

"I leave tomorrow. Already have my ticket. I'm sorry."

Regina Blackwell seems to have all her energy sapped as she sits against her desk and considers the turn of events.

"I must admit I didn't see this coming."

"I was just told today, so I had no warning either."

"Today and you have to be there tomorrow? Isn't that unusual?" The Mayor is trying to piece this all together.

"Never seen it happen in my entire career with the company. But that's not the issue. I wanted you to accept my resignation and appoint Dr. Molina as the new chairman to be the spokesperson for the commission. I know the Reverend Lindo should step into that role as vice chairman, but we both know what will happen if he does."

"There is baggage there," the Mayor notes, apparently seeing what I saw. That while bringing him onto the commission reduced the public outcry for action, it has now boxed in her maneuvering room. "You think Dr. Molina would be the strongest advocate?"

"Actually I don't, but she has the right credentials to be credible."

"Who do you think would be the strongest advocate?"

"Based on the discussions it would be Reverend Lindo, but he would push to consider some of the extreme positions that were tempered in the final document.

"And that would just sink it, from what I can tell. The public pushback would make it hard for any of you to step up to that decision."

Regina Blackwell nods, although I'm not sure if she's agreeing with my analysis or nodding in understanding of the change of circumstances.

"T.K., I'm not going to accept your resignation now. I need you to present the findings and discuss certain aspects I intend to drill down into.

"From what I've seen, that will be essential to the Council's understanding of what you are proposing.

"But I have a question, and then I really must finish preparing for the session that is about to start." She stands and begins looking for whatever it was she had been looking for when I arrived.

"Did someone put pressure on Tom Horton?" she asks.

I counter with a question of my own. "Has anyone been putting pressure on you since you released the draft report?"

"The only reason my phone's not ringing right now is because my assistant has intercepted them at her desk."

"Then you can assume Tom has had conversations about the report and not with me."

"He's not discussed it with you?" she asks.

"Not directly."

Mayor Blackwell nods to herself, apparently understanding something she isn't sharing. "I need you to sell this set of recommendations tonight, then. That's our only hope of adoption."

"I've been instructed not to speak publicly about the report." I put this out there so she understands why I'm here. That causes her to stop looking for a moment.

"Why?"

"Fear of negative blowback on the company. The comment was made that the recommendations are too controversial."

Mayor Blackwell looks at me as if she were looking into my heart.

"I'm going to ask something I have no right to ask, T.K. I need you to make the report to Council as chairman of the commission and sell it tonight. That is your civic duty as chairman of the commission.

"I'm asking this because it's our only hope of changing the dynamic of racism and divided community we've been living with forever. I can't wait another hundred years to see that change happen.

"And even if we take this step now, there is no guarantee it will succeed. But I know if we don't, there is no hope."

I have never gone against the wishes of my management, never deliberately done something I was told directly not to do. But I don't live here anymore, so even if I do what she's asking, I'll not see the results.

I hand her the resignation letter and say,

"Thank you for the opportunity you gave me. At least we will have started a conversation."

As I walk out of her office I hear the Mayor call after me, "Please at least stay to listen."

I leave the building and go to my car, but I don't open the door. I see in my mind's eye Deshaun playing in that last scrimmage with the Boy's Club players.

I see him looking through his backpack for his house key. I let him walk into a situation that took his life because I didn't recognize what could happen.

I remember Duke out there with the boys for all the years we played with them several times a week. He is as dedicated to helping them as I am, and now I won't be able to help them, won't be here for them.

Won't be able to help Demetrius or Tony or any of the others coming up.

The clock strikes the half hour. The meeting is about to begin. Do I stay and do what's right, or do I go and hope someone else will step into the void?

I didn't have a chance to talk to Dr. Molina before recommending her, so she's totally unprepared to lead the discussions.

She'll be able to answer questions about what we were thinking, but will she be able to sell it?

Probably not.

And in the vacuum, the Reverend will try to fill the void and that will be the end of the discussion.

I take my phone out of my pocket and dial a familiar number.

"Sina, I'm staying for the meeting. See you in a bit."

As I walk into the Council chambers I see Flo taking her seat. Late as usual, since Mayor Blackwell is already calling the commission members to come up to the table that had been set up for us.

I stride up to the table and take my seat with the other commissioners. Mayor Blackwell nods to me, and I see a look of relief.

"Chairman Jefferson, the members of Council have a copy of the report your commission has filed with the city.

"We have all had a chance to read it and we will have many

questions as the evening goes on, but please tell us why we should accept these recommendations.

"What is the thinking of your commission members that led you to believe this is the set of essential actions we must take in order to change the dynamic of police and community relations?"

I glance around and locate Tex Anthony in the back of the room. Curious, since he's usually up front. I look at the sea of faces who are all looking to understand what the city is doing about its police.

I see Mr. and Mrs. Bush in the fourth row back at the end, talking with a couple I don't recognize.

And then I see Demetrius, sitting behind them. And Tony sitting next to him. Further back Shorty, Will and Randy are sitting together. Standing just inside the door is Duke, in uniform.

I turn back to look at Council, nod to Flo, who is smiling at me.

"Mayor Blackwell and members of Council, thank you for the opportunity to have been of service to the city of Fort Christian in working together with the distinguished commissioners you appointed to this task.

"It has been a privilege for me to exchange ideas and explore approaches that collectively we believe can fundamentally change the very nature of policing and law enforcement in our community.

"The conviction this week of a young officer in the needless death of a citizen of this city is a clear indication and warning to us all that something is fundamentally wrong.

"Some things must change so that the members of our police department ensure the safety of our citizens, and not prove to be a major threat to them.

"It has been said the circumstances of this one event cannot be duplicated. Everyone has taken a look at what happened and steps have been taken to theoretically prevent a second such occurrence.

"That may be the case, but putting a thumb in a dike that has fissures all through it may stem the tide waters for an hour or a day, but such action will not prevent the wall from coming down when forces change even a tiny amount.

"What the commission found as we reviewed the facts and data we gathered and received from others is that the system we have in place is flawed. It is what I refer to as a 'default system.'

"Now what do I mean by that?

"I mean that what we have in place developed over decades. Practices that the first set of officers used were effective for them. But as they were replaced by new officers, those practices were like rituals… handed down from someone else.

"They don't reflect the strengths and weaknesses of the replacement person. They don't reflect the needs of a changed society.

"In order for our police to reflect the needs of our community today, the most important recommendation is that the police officers be assigned to micro-communities -- extended neighborhoods, if you will -- within the city and be required to live in their micro-community.

"The most important recommendation is that our current officers are exactly that -- simply officers of this city government. They are here to represent the law enforcement interests of all citizens, and most importantly to understand the needs of the "extended neighborhood" in which the officer lives, works and hopefully plays.

"We believe law enforcement must become the responsibility of the community first. And then the officers become the local peacekeeping representative, just like you are the legislative representatives of your districts -- your micro-community."

Petes raises his hand, but Mayor Blackwell doesn't recognize him. "Please continue, Chairman Jefferson. We will hold our questions until you have completed your statement."

That's good, I note in passing. The Mayor is at least letting me have a moment to sell the report before it's attacked.

I nod thanks to her, then take a deep breath before changing my life forever.

"In our findings, we have recognized that if officers live where they maintain order, rather than being called police officers, which carries a lot of baggage, that we should call them peace officers because that is their primary function, to maintain the peace.

"And we believe further that the peace officers who live in our extended neighborhoods should also be unarmed."

I pause to organize my thoughts as a murmur begins to move through the crowd. This must be how Atticus Finch felt while delivering opening arguments in *To Kill A Mockingbird,* I think. Then I step away from the table to continue.

"They are the local authority to use the community resources to enforce the laws of the city, county, state and federal governments.

"But the vast majority of the work involved does not require the officer to carry a weapon, we believe.

"When it does, we recommend that there be an armed element of our law enforcement department that responds, limited to officers with at least ten years of peace officer experience.

"They should be the backup for any situation where the use of deadly force is required -- as in situations where someone's life is in jeopardy without it.

"Similar in concept to the Special Weapons and Tactical teams of the department, these officers would be called in as necessary, but not be the front line of contact in most situations."

I take a sip of water as I'm finding my mouth is getting dry.

"We recognize that a peace officer will rely on interpersonal skills to be successful. So we are recommending that the city increase training in sensitivity, cultural norms and behaviors, situation de-escalation, and negotiations.

"We also believe the peace officers should rotate through community and first response organizations, so they have the opportunity to build personal relations with teachers, school children, physicians, medics, legal aid, and volunteer organizations.

"These relationships will enable the peace officers to understand how to plug people into the community resources that are there for any situation a resident encounters.

"It will also provide the peace officer with relationships that currently exist only in an ad hoc way and only when an officer takes the time to build those relationships.

"Our final recommendation is that those officers whom we have labelled armed senior officers, those who have been on the police force for more than ten years and who wish to remain armed, should receive a one-time salary adjustment to reflect the changed nature of their role.

"They will spend a greater percentage of their time in more hazardous situations. Officers should elect that role given the change and should only be eligible when they have obtained and maintain weapons and related skills proficiency."

"In discussions leading up to these recommendations we were asked why they are essential to achieve what the Commission deems the balanced needs of the community.

"We have been told that Fort Christian has a 'western' tradition of rugged individualism dating back to the mid-1800s. That is often used as a justification for why every Texan should have the right to openly carry weapons.

"We are counting on that rugged individualism to make what we propose workable.

"If our citizens want to sit in their homes and places of work, worship and play and have an elite group of people enforce the peace through gunfights in the street, that would be one thing.

"But we believe the opposite is true.

"We believe the people of Fort Christian want to be responsible for themselves. The people want the freedom to live as they wish, to live where they wish, work where they wish, worship where they wish and play where and when they wish.

"We obey the laws that are needed to enable freedom. And law enforcement should not get in the way of that freedom, but should only address the behavior of those who elect not to obey the laws -- the ones who deliberately put others in jeopardy."

"So, while I know you have had calls from those who were not part of our deliberations, have casually skimmed our report and have not considered the facts and data reviewed by the commission members, you are getting a different call from the us.

"That call is to change the default processes in place, adopt a community-first approach to law enforcement, and de-escalate the tension and misunderstanding, and --quite frankly -- the fear that exists today.

"You have the chance to rewrite the nature of the narrative of this city from one of confrontation and coercion to one of reconciliation and togetherness.

"You have the chance to change the perception the world has of Fort Christian and to show that we in fact do embrace a Christian ethos, even though we are an increasingly diverse population."

The murmur has become a stir, and Mayor Blackwell has to utilize her rarely used and mostly ceremonial gavel to restore order. Eventually she motions me to continue.

"As a city, we cannot wait another hundred years to address the changes needed to ensure the freedoms every citizen is entitled to, to ensure every citizen has the right to live a life of freedom from fear, and has the freedom to become all they can possibly want to achieve.

"We need everyone who lives here to succeed, to contribute, to give back to the larger community -- for it is only as a community, working together that we can enable everyone's success."

I push the microphone away and sit back in my chair. I am greeted by dead silence as apparently everyone is waiting to see what happens next.

Then it happens.

The Rev claps, slowly. Then the rest of the commission members except Petes do as well.

Then, slowly, so do most of the rest of those in the chamber.

41 – T.K. JEFFERSON

I'm packing the things in my office I need to take with me to my new home in Lagos, Nigeria when I get the call to come down to Brad's office.

I wondered if I would see him before I left. I now have my answer.

I walk the short distance looking around, knowing I won't see this very often now.

Have I committed corporate suicide? Have I, in the span of a month, killed any hope of promotion? And is my career now permanently sidetracked because of a civic duty I fulfilled?

If that's the price for taking responsibility, then I've willingly paid it.

Brad is looking out his window when I arrive. He's apparently thinking about something, but I don't know what it could be.

"Morning, Brad. Last minute instructions?"

Brad slowly turns around. His look is not one I recognize. He's neither happy nor sad, almost confused. Maybe that's not something I've seen in him before because if he doesn't understand something that doesn't seem to be a problem for him, generally.

He just assumes someone in the room knows the answer and will take care of whatever needs to be done.

But this time he seems to be struggling with something. He points to the newspaper on his desk. The headline reads: 'Jefferson to Police: I'm Coming for Your Guns'. Looks like Tex is trying to sell papers.

"I never read the paper," is my response.

"Tom does," Brad avoids taking responsibility again. "Most of his golfing buddies read the paper. Even some of our major shareholders read the Fort Christian paper so they can track what's being said about us. This is not what Tom wanted them to be reading."

"I assume you've read it."

"I've skimmed it."

"Does it specifically link me with Horton Exploration and Production?"

"Actually it doesn't. Not this time. But Tex has made that linkage clear in the past, so there's no doubt in the minds of people that you're one of ours."

"Since you've obviously had a conversation with Tom about the recommendations, what's his opinion?"

"Tom hasn't said anything about the recommendations. Just that he's getting all kinds of unwelcome feedback."

"Are people saying they're going to divest their holdings in our stock because somehow my recommendations are going to cause people to drive their cars less miles, or buy fewer products that are made with oil or natural gas?"

"I can't answer that." Brad is feeling trapped again. Between what Tom expects him to do and the hypocrisy with which this whole thing is being handled.

"If people are just talking but not doing anything, why should we as a company care?"

"Because Tom thinks that some of the people who are calling him may do something if he doesn't prevent the city from taking up your recommendations."

"Did you hear what you just said?" I push him now because I can sense weakness in his position.

"What?" Brad has no idea.

"You said people, golf buddies, board members, shareholders are expecting Tom to prevent adoption of a city commission's recommendations. Those recommendations have nothing to do with the business of this company. How could Tom prevent their adoption?"

"I'm just the messenger here," Brad says to deflect my question, one he evidently doesn't have the answer to.

"Then let's go have a chat with Tom."

"Now?" Brad can't imagine letting me talk with Tom because it would become obvious that he's not up to handling this matter. And Tom certainly isn't going to want to do anything directly.

"Tom's not here."

"Then call him like he calls you. I know you have his cell number. Where is he? On the seventh tee?"

Brad looks at the clock on his wall behind me. "More likely the fairway on the fifth…"

"Let's have this discussion with the one who's getting the calls. Because you certainly aren't."

"Are you?" Brad tries to use this as a defense.

"I am. Curiously not everyone thinks I'm…" I can't even think of which of the labels people have assigned to me I should start with.

"…crazy?" Brad completes my sentence.

"Because I do," he says. "You had an important role here. Tom likes you personally and that's always important when you work for a family owned and operated company. I think Tom actually respects you more than he does me. But that's not what we're here to talk about."

"What are we here to talk about, Brad?"

"I need the ticket the company bought for you to fly to Nigeria."

My mind freezes for a moment, then screams at me, 'why would he want the ticket back?' and it can only come to one conclusion.

"It's in my office."

"You'll need to bring it down to me on your way out." Brad says this in such a way that I can tell it's probably the hardest thing he's ever had to say.

I nod once, see the trophy sitting on his table and nod to it. "Would you do something for me?"

Brad doesn't answer. I'm sure because he doesn't want to commit to anything at this point.

"Give that to Devin. He earned it."

Brad looks at the trophy but doesn't comment.

I extend my hand. "You're not the bad guy here, but at some point you need to take a stand for what you believe. And unfortunately, none of us who have worked for you have any idea what that is."

Brad doesn't shake hands, so I nod to him again and walk back to my office, now looking around, knowing I'll never be returning here. That makes me sad because I enjoyed what I did, enjoyed the people I worked with.

I learned a lot about people, about the oil business, and had the flexibility to do things that were important to me outside work, like play ball with Deshaun Bush and all the others.

I'll miss this…

42 – REGINA BLACKWELL – MAYOR CITY OF FORT CHRISTIAN

I'm just finishing reading a plan from the community development office on low income housing options when T.K. comes to my door.

"Do you have a minute?"

I glance at the clock and wave him in. "Thought you would be on an airplane somewhere by now."

"The good news is I won't be leaving -- at least not right away. The company changed its plans for me."

"That's an incredibly good thing. Should I call Tom Horton and thank him?"

T.K. shrugs but doesn't answer, which tells me there is more to this story. "Do you still wish me to accept your resignation from the commission?"

"That's why I came by to chat. If you have a minute, I don't want to keep you from other things."

"This is probably the most important conversation I'm going to have today." I'm seeing a glimmer of hope now that I didn't a few minutes ago.

"You did a good job last night, but I'm afraid you didn't seal the deal. Still too many questions about how what you recommend would actually work.

"One of the key questions that keeps coming up is who is capable of leading the department through such a difficult transformation. No one out there has the experience doing that since no one has done it.

"We can't afford to accept the recommendations only to put the wrong person in to lead the change and have it fail. Then we would all be out of jobs here."

I see T.K. react to my comment which leads me to ask,

"Did Tom Horton let you go?"

"Indirectly. I know people at other oil companies. Probably won't take me long to find something. It's just more likely to be in Houston or Midland than here. So I'll still be leaving, I just don't know how long it will take to get hired on."

"I'm so sorry. Is this because of your recommendations? Or was there some other issue?

"I was not made aware of any issue with my job performance." T.K. won't say anything negative directly.

"I'm going to need you to think through how we sell the commission's findings as long as you're available to help," I say. "I'm going to need you to do some research on who could lead this transformation, transition, or change -- whatever you want to call it.

"That's going to be the key to garnering the support on Council that's needed. At the moment you have one yes, one hell no, and three undecideds. You've got to find a way of answering their skepticism.

"And you know the skepticism doesn't stop with the Council members. Tex and Zana have to be touched by you. Someone has to turn them around or this has no chance of passage."

I pause to mentally inventory our next steps.

"Now, from a strategy point of view I don't know how you convince Roxanne and Alvin. They have divided opinions and political realities.

"They both attend the Reverend Lindo's church. But they also were elected by white majority populations. So they have to figure out how to bring along both constituencies if they want to be re-elected and ensure anything we do isn't undone by the next Council."

"And, finally, there's The Rev, who endorsed the recommendations," T.K. points out. "He understands that if he can get this much done, there is a chance that things will get much better for his congregation and the black community.

"He understands that his work won't be over, as someone is going to have to hold the city and department accountable. I can think of no one who will do that better."

"But how do Roxanne and Alvin bring along their white constituents?" I ask. "I mean I'm glad that Reverend Lindo is apparently on board, because that wasn't terribly clear at the meeting last night."

"You're right that the key there will be Tex and Zana," T.K. responds thoughtfully. "Let me go have a conversation with them."

"T.K., I didn't have a chance to say this last night, but you will truly be missed for what you have done for this community."

"I haven't done anything yet, other than make a set of recommendations along with a group of others."

"I'm talking about having faith in your convictions, and doing what you believe, whether that's at the Boy's Club or serving on this commission and masterfully leading a group of diverse but good people to understand that they can change this city if they will just stand with you."

"Not how I would have put it, but I need to have a conversation with Tex and Zana."

43 – ZANA GONZALES – EDITOR FORT CHRISTIAN STANDARD

Tex and I are reviewing options for his next article on the city commission report when T.K. Jefferson wanders in. And I use the term wander precisely, because he clearly doesn't have a good of idea of where he's going or where to find whoever he's come to see, although I expect it's Tex.

Gloria at the front desk points to us and nods in response to a question he asks her. He now walks with determination towards us.

"Should I leave?" Tex asks, seeing who is coming.

I wave him to stay seated. In a moment T.K. knocks on the door to our conference room. "May I disturb you?"

"Come in, Commissioner Jefferson," I respond.

He shakes hands with both of us and then takes a seat.

"Do you have a minute for a quick conversation that may help you and the people of Fort Christian to better understand what I didn't say very well last night?"

"I thought you were thoughtful and articulate. Were you disappointed with your explanation?"

"Deshaun's death profoundly affected me," he begins. "That's why I accepted a role on the commission. I wasn't looking to be chairman, didn't come in with anything more than some notions that we may be looking at the wrong solutions if we only do what we've always done."

"The definition of insanity?" I suggest, seeing where he's trying to go.

"You know that I worked with Deshaun from when he was only about six? Played ball with him at the Boys' Club?"

"I'm aware of what you do for those boys, what you did for Deshaun," I confirm. "You and the others, including Sergeant Marion."

T.K. nods. "If Deshaun had been killed in a military operation defending his country, I could accept that.

"But in this instance, his death served no purpose other than to widen the gulf between groups in our community, and to reignite the anger, frustrations and fear that some have of our police force.

"Some want to cast the whole issue as racial, and the statistics support that perception. But statistics seldom tell the whole story.

"I am convinced that police officers often fear for their lives because they don't know the people they're dealing with.

"One member of the commission had a good idea that the officers should patrol where they live, should be part of the community they are responsible for, and should not be perceived as a coercive force, but rather a moral force."

"That's a pretty big leap from where we are today," Tex points out.

"It is, but in the judgment of the members of the commission…"

"With the exception of Council member Cochrane…" Tex clarifies.

"Council member Cochrane did not endorse the findings of the commission," T.K. acknowledges. "But he was integral to the discussions that led to the recommendations that we made.

"I think, although he will clarify this as the hearings proceed, that all of us including Council member Cochrane believe it takes everyone assuming responsibility for the safety and well-being of the community.

"Just like the schools, where the parents abandon the responsibility for preparing students to learn or give them hope for a future which leads students to resort to gun violence in our schools.

"When citizens abandon the responsibility to obey the laws and ensure their neighbors do as well, then we have situations like what has occurred with Deshaun."

T.K. stops for a moment, apparently reliving some part of what happened that day.

"There are so many points at which a single decision made differently would have resulted in a different outcome. But it's on all of us, not just the police.

"Our expectations of them have pushed us to arm them. We don't need to do that. Remove the weapons from the initial discussions. Seek to defuse hostilities, seek to mediate resolutions.

"Drawn weapons should be limited to the most experienced officers, who have a decade or more of de-escalation experience, who know from experience when they must use force to save lives or incarcerate an armed and dangerous individual or group.

"Only if we create a corps of peace officers will we change the narrative of race relations in Fort Christian."

"Is that what you felt you didn't articulate very well last night?" Tex asks.

"This is personal for me. It has nothing to do with where I work or which church I attend, or whether I live on the south side or the east side.

"This is about the future of this community. The two of you have the power to enable the changes that are needed to fuse a new future, bringing this community together, replace the past approaches that are no longer serving the needs of the community or providing social justice for everyone."

"You know, you're starting to sound like a less angry version of the Reverend Lindo," Tex observes.

"Actually, I've spent so much time with him over the last month that I think that he's starting to sound like an angrier and more eloquent version of me."

T.K. smiles a weak smile, but nevertheless he seems to relax for the first time since he entered the building.

"What is it you want us to do? We just report on what happens in the community. We're not supposed to take sides in this discussion," I point out.

"Sides? Who said anything about sides? I'm not at all about who is on what side of the issue. I'm concerned about the community.

"Doing something that makes this a better place for all of us who live here and not just the chosen few who think they can control things.

"But you do have the power of editorials. You can and must look at all the evidence, determine whether what has happened is acceptable or whether systemic change is warranted.

"I mentioned a few minutes ago that I firmly believe as long as citizens decide that someone else can be responsible for their kids, for their safety, for being informed about the leaders we choose and the choices they make to enable us, we are abrogating our responsibilities to our community.

"Living in Fort Christian isn't a hall pass to heaven. We have to earn that right. We have to be responsible for ourselves, our children most importantly, for our extended families, our neighbors, our neighborhoods, the city and so on. Do you see where I'm going?"

"I do," I acknowledge. "But there's a flaw in your analysis. I've seen all too many great ideas that never see the light of day because no one has any idea how to make that idea possible.

"I can't speak for Tex, but I think you're asking too much of your neighbors, your elected officials and most importantly the people you would have live this new peace officer role.

"Part of what makes the system work is that no one officer has to face jeopardy situations very often. As you point out, most of what they do is routine.

"But you would have a subset of officers go to work nearly every day wondering if they will come home that night because if they are sent out, there is a reasonable probability that someone may shoot at them."

"I disagree," T.K. responds, clearly enjoying this discussion.

"We routinely ask what you've described of our soldiers, only there they are dealing with significantly more deadly weapons and foes.

"And it's not just the regular soldiers. We ask that of those reservists who we have much more frequently sent into conflict situations because we have tried to keep the regular Army smaller than we have in the past."

"You've clearly done your homework…" Tex starts to ask his next question.

"And that's all I'm asking of you. Do the homework. Look at the facts and data the commission reviewed.

"Some of it will require non-disclosure agreements when you get into personnel records, but I'm sure the Mayor would let you review even the most sensitive information to give you the background you need to make an informed decision about that editorial.

"I believe in democracy. I believe that it's the most effective form of ensuring freedom and individual achievement because you create your future -- not some government bureaucrat who looks at your SAT scores and then relegates you to the scrap heap of humanity at age eighteen."

"You seem to think we have some pivotal role here," Tex

observes. "Do you see your role as the gadfly who comes in, sees that the Emperor has no clothes, wakes up the citizenry with a call to arms and then abandons his role in how to get the Emperor re-clothed to someone else?

"Because if that's why you're here, you've just identified the Achilles heel of your whole set of recommendations.

"Chief Andrews couldn't implement those recommendations even if he were twenty years old and looking at his whole career ahead of him. By the way, if he survives to retirement I'll be shocked.

"You expect Regina Blackwell to manage this kind of transition? She's an excellent mayor. Popular because she keeps the taxes down. But she would be the first to tell you that managing large scale change is not what she's about.

"So don't you see? You've attempted to shoulder Sisyphus' stone and move it a long way up the hill, but now you're expecting the Mayor and Council and Chief Andrews to push it up and over the top, when none of them can even see where the top is."

"Yale?" T.K. asks Tex suddenly, "Only someone from Yale would talk about Sisyphus."

"Guilty," Tex acknowledges, like someone whose Hallowe'en costume had been guessed.

"That's a challenge I would pass back to you," T.K. responds. "Do the research. Who has been successful in transformative leadership of a major city police department?

"Identify that person in your editorial. Lead from where you are. Isn't that the definition of leadership?"

44 – FRANCIS "DUKE" MARION

Council is conducting the first public hearing on the commission report, so I better get in there to find out what others are saying before the Mayor calls on me.

As I walk in, I look around at all the faces, mostly black, a few Hispanic, but mostly black. They're the ones pushing this agenda.

That fucking Padre at Second Baptist is stirring the pot. I can deal with him, but what I didn't see coming was T.K. How the fuck did he suddenly get religion and take their side?

I just don't understand that. Doesn't he understand what his suggestions would do to me? And I've been out there all those years with him, helping those kids, helping Deshaun become what he could be.

And for all that I've done to help him, you'd think he would at least come talk to me before suggesting this totally unworkable set of recommendations.

Luckily, Petes has tempered them somewhat. But at the moment he seems to be the only sure vote we have.

Got to get the troops spun up to ensure he gets re-elected or we may find ourselves with no friends on Council.

Then I notice T.K. is here, sitting off to the side. Not with anyone I know, not talking with anyone. He looks like he doesn't have a friend in the world at the moment, and that's exactly where I need to keep him.

I'm surprised he's even here, given the calls I know were made to neutralize him.

The response I got was that he was being reassigned. Hmmm.

Apparently not fast enough.

Walter is speaking. He was on the schedule just before me by design.

"The commission report is pure fantasy that would serve only to unnecessarily put officer lives at risk.

"Disarming any portion of the force would make it less effective because criminals would simply ignore the officer, knowing they can perpetrate their crimes without fear of capture.

The Mayor asks, "What percentage of enforcement actions involve coercion?"

Walter responds matter-of-factly, "One hundred percent, whether it's acknowledged or not, coercion is an essential part of the ability to prevent crime."

The Mayor asks the Chief, "Is that accurate?"

Chief Andrews responds, "I'm not a psychologist and could not offer a factual answer to the question."

The Mayor asks, "Do you have any further comments Mr. Johnston?"

"No, Mayor Blackwell."

The Mayor asks, "Would Sergeant Francis Marion as president of Local Chapter 777 of the Benevolent Order of Police Officers, please come forward with your prescheduled comments?"

I pass Walter to take the same seat before Council. I have the same charts and graphs I used in negotiations available to present as they are the ones I hope will turn the tide of sentiment to the increases I know Petes will champion once we get to that point.

"Mayor Blackwell and members of Council. The local chapter of the Police Benevolent Order wishes to ensure that events like what happened recently cannot recur.

"But we are constrained by the budget that understaffs our department and has continued to reduce resources to us for the past two decades, a time that has seen increases in corresponding incidents of crime in our city,"

I see Mayor Blackwell is not happy with my characterization of conditions but that's what this is all about.

"This first chart shows the decline in staffing over the past twenty years. I would point out that the rate of decline has been most severe during the current administration.

"This has now been shown as a deadly lack of investment by the city. This next chart shows relative pay of our officers and the other major city officers in Texas with the second graph showing our relative position of major U.S. cities.

"What this shows is that Fort Christian pay is in the lowest quartile for both Texas and nationally. We also have need of increases in funding for new technologies that have been adopted by other major law enforcement organizations, in some cases a decade ago or more.

"If several of those technologies had been available to us, there would not have been a need for an officer to respond to the call that ended Deshaun Bush's life.

"The one… well, two areas really, where we agree with the commission is first, the need for more training, and in some instances specialized training we do not currently receive.

"The second is the need for raises for officers. I've just shown the degree to which officers in Fort Christian are underpaid. However, we do not agree with the segmentation approach of armed and unarmed officers.

"We believe that would lead to increases in violence and jeopardy for our citizens.

"Finally, the idea of a forced relocation of officers would seem to be an unnecessary expense to the city. We would also expect that if such a recommendation were approved that such a forced relocation would be subject to negotiations as to which officers would be forcibly relocated and to the nature and amounts of assistance each officer so relocated would receive to hold the officer and his or her family harmless in such a changed policy by the city.

"It would seem to my membership that the blueprint for improvements in police effectiveness are as I've discussed,

- full manning of the department as called for in the original manning tables,

- increases in pay and corresponding benefits so that we may attract experienced officers to fill those vacancies,

- increased training to provide the knowledge and improve skills in areas of police responsibility and finally

- investment in the technologies that will enable our officers to be more effective in what we do,

- while reducing exposure to jeopardy as our current situation more often puts us into."

"One final note, while the commission may have good intentions, what we observe in the data they reviewed and the nature of their recommendations is that individually the members are ill-informed and selectively sought out information and data that would confirm rather than refute their own pet preferences.

"This could have been avoided if the Council had simply appointed at least one member with law enforcement training and experience.

"Bringing expertise into the discussions would have made for more balanced discussion and resulted in a road map that would look very much like that I just outlined. Thank you."

As I return to the back of the Council chambers I hear Mayor Blackwell call, "Reverend LeRoy Lindo."

I turn around and watch the Rev, decked out in a clearly tailored black suit make his way to the desk. He picks up the microphone, apparently desiring to stand to make his presentation.

It's all about theater. He's here to put on a show. The only question is how over the top will he go?

"Mayor Blackwell and members of Council. Thank you for giving me an opportunity to mourn the death of hope in our city. That's why I'm dressed in black this evening.

"This is my mourning suit. I only wear it to funerals, which in the last few years, I have attended more than my share.

"And unfortunately, if all of you decide to ignore your citizens, as the city Councils before you have done for decades or more, as shown in Mr. Marion's charts, and approve the good-old-boy investments Mr. Marion asked for, from hard earned taxpayer dollars, there will be many more funerals I will be attending."

The Rev turns around and looks at those in attendance. I'm sure he thinks he's at his church since I would assume most of the folks here are in his congregation.

I could be wrong, but that's what it looks like to me. The Rev turns around and resumes his comments.

"Mr. Marion hopes that you will suspend your disbelief of the expertise of his members. But you should disbelieve him,

"The crime statistics he referenced, but did not show, validates the lack of expertise in our law enforcement department.

"I would agree they use outdated techniques, not because of technology investments not being made, but because of a rampant and deliberate racism that pervades the department.

"If given the toys he has asked for, we would not see a decline in racism, we would see it ramp up as those tools, as he referred to them as, would be used to invade privacy and increase the number and frequency of racist interactions.

"The thought of this department harassing innocent people of color or Hispanic national origins more than they do today should give pause to every citizen of this city.

"If you created the white supremacist society here that seems to be the end goal, your children would need to pick up the garbage, bus tables in restaurants, provide many services and repair what's broken in your households.

"Are those the jobs you hope your children aspire to? Well, I have news for you, we don't want our children to aspire to those employment opportunities either.

"We want them to be professionals, to enjoy the same standard of living you do, to have the same freedom of choices you have.

"That's what we want our children to aspire to. And for them to reach their aspirations they must be self-confident, to feel capable, to know they have a supporting community that wants to see them succeed.

"Show me one officer on the Fort Christian police force who could be described as supporting the aspirations of young boys of color or Hispanic national origin.

"Show me a path to a future that is color blind. Show me how we all live together in this community, where there is but one Baptist Church, one people and one community.

"I don't know how we get there unless we start somewhere. The recommendations of the commission are only a start.

"Adopting them will be the easy part because in essence the Council will be holding the citizens of Fort Christian accountable in a way no Council has before.

"Instead of taking tax dollars for increasing levels of services to the citizens, the new orientation would be citizens who ensure their own exercise of freedoms through their own acts of living within the laws and taking responsibility to see that their families, friends and neighbors do as well. The expectations of everyone should be the intolerance of lawlessness rather than people who aren't like you."

The Rev pauses for a moment, apparently gathering his thoughts. I can't believe he used my slides against my arguments. Didn't see him doing that or I'd have never put them up there. Need to figure out how we counter his arguments.

"I want to return to Mr. Johnston and Mr. Marion's comments. What they show is that police officers in our community are only concerned for themselves, their hopes, their wants to increase their numbers and arm them with weapons that will ultimately result in more innocent lives lost.

"They are completely out of touch with the reality of the situation. If they want to kill people they should enlist and go fight in wars protecting our country in someone else's.

"That way our citizens can live peaceful lives and not fear when a policeman shows up. Cities are no place for guns of any kind. We had an assault weapons ban that lasted ten years and violent crime diminished during that decade.

"Unfortunately we let that law lapse and the number and severity of mass shootings has only increased, taking the lives of innocent men, women and especially children.

"We simply have to take a different approach to weapons on our streets. And the place to start is with law enforcement. We have to model the behavior we want.

"We have to start today. The commission report is just that. It's not the end, but a beginning to see if we are what we profess.

"Can we be the force for good in our communities or will we continue to erode our liberties by increasingly depending on armed arbiters of justice?

"As a member of the commission that authored this report, I fully support the recommendations and strongly encourage your immediate adoption of them."

Mayor Blackwell stops the Rev from leaving the microphone, "Reverend Lindo. I would like to ask a question."

The Rev picks up the microphone, "Yes, Mayor."

"The recommendations would significantly change how law enforcement would be conducted in Fort Christian."

"Yes, ma'am. These recommendations are the minimum we felt would be necessary to change the trajectory of racism and divisions within the social fabric of this city."

"Did the commission discuss how we should go about implementing your recommendations?"

"We did. There is nothing in this set of recommendations that this Council could not adopt and instruct your personnel department, your training department and your legal department to enact.

"The harder part is communicating to every citizen their new responsibilities.

"In our discussions that should be led by members of Council, conducting meetings in every neighborhood, to explain the new expectations.

"The micro-community peace officers selected for each area should be at the meetings in their area to introduce them and talk about roles and responsibilities.

"I understand the nature of your question. Change management is always the most difficult part of any change. And this is a much more substantial change than we see very often."

The Rev has toned down his rhetoric. I wonder who got to him.

45 – T.K. JEFFERSON

We are probably halfway through the scrimmage.

Devin has joined us and is now a regular member of the adult team. So we have enough players even though Duke hasn't participated since the tournament.

Tony slips in behind Will for a hard-fought lay-up and comes away with an ear-to-ear smile that makes all the work we put in with these kids worthwhile.

Will picks up the ball and we are about to head the other way when I see the black mustang sedan that Duke drives pull up in the parking lot.

I see Duke sitting in the car, watching us. I wait a minute, but he doesn't get out of his car. Finally I start walking towards him, but he starts the car and drives away.

"T.K., we're waiting on you," Shorty calls, but then apparently sees Duke's car driving away and doesn't say more.

We finish the fast and fluid scrimmage about a half-hour later. I line up the boys for their three-point drill. Tony comes up and stands in line first. "Why didn't Sergeant Marion join the scrimmage?"

'Sergeant Marion', why doesn't Tony think of him as Duke? Even though they have played together for years, he's still Sergeant Marion. He isn't seen as a friend. He's not seen as someone who is here for them. He's a representative of the police who harass black boys like him.

"He probably got a call," I say.

Tony takes the shot, sinks it and waits for the ball to come back so he can take another. "Why is everyone mad at you?"

"What do you mean?" I have to ask.

"All the adults. They say you're trying to take guns away from the police."

"Only some of them, those with the least experience," I say.

"Why? What good would that do?"

I have to think how to explain this, "Okay, let's say a policeman approaches you wearing a gun, what do you think?"

"I think I must have done something wrong and I'm gonna have trouble to deal with."

"What if a policeman approaches you without a gun, what do you think?"

"He wants to talk, most likely."

"Okay, Tony, which conversation would you rather have?"

"I'm happy to explain myself to the second man, but the first one? I'm afraid I'm going to jail."

"But we have a presumption of innocence in this country, until proven guilty. If everyone is responsible for obeying the law that should be the presumption.

"But a law officer comes up to you with a gun, you expect you're going to be arrested and it doesn't matter if you're guilty or not. Do you see what I'm trying to change?"

"That won't work, T.K. We gotta lot of drugs and guns here. People selling the drugs are happy to shoot policemen who try to arrest them. If the police can't shoot back? What happens then?"

"That's why I only want part of the police to not have guns. Those who are more experienced, who have been working the routine law enforcement for a number of years will have the option of being armed, or having access to weapons in their cars, to respond to situations that only can be handled by armed teams.

“No lone rangers here. People have to work together to support each other.”

“That might work… but why you? Why are you the one who’s trying to change things?”

“Someone has to step up, just like you do in the games we’re playing. You get the ball, you step up and work the shot until someone from your team, whether it’s you or one of the other guys, has a clear shot.

“I’m just trying to work the ball in so we can have a shot to make things better for you, your friends and family, and everyone who lives here.”

“Is that the real reason Sergeant Marion isn’t playing with us anymore? That he’s upset with you trying to change things for him?”

“I don’t know, Tony. But I don’t think he’s upset with you or any of the guys here. He’s just got a lot of things going on. Other priorities at the moment.

“But luckily for us, Devin’s helping out so we’re still able to give you a run for your money.”

46 – REGINA BLACKWELL – MAYOR, CITY OF FORT CHRISTIAN

Council is meeting in open session to consider a resolution adopting the recommendations of the commission report.

This is where we finally have to make a decision. I still have questions about how to ensure the recommendations can be successful.

Zana wrote her editorial, which supports a conditional adoption. She sent her reporters out to assess the state of the city. Are the people ready for what is recommended, or is it likely to fail?

They came back and told her the city could do what is required, but it will all come down to who leads the effort and how it is implemented.

She even gave a list of names of police professionals from around the country who have implemented large-scale change in their departments.

The problem is that none of them are from Texas. None are from cities similar to Fort Christian. I just don't know if any of their approaches would translate well enough to be successful.

Petes is explaining why the resolution should fail,

"I have provided you an alternative resolution which I would recommend you adopt as soon as we vote down the resolution to adopt the recommendations.

"We have the blueprint for success offered by Sergeant Marion and endorsed by Chief Andrews. I have incorporated all of those elements in the alternative resolution.

"We can rest assured that if we properly support our police

department, the issues that led to the recent tragedy will be addressed to our satisfaction without uprooting families and trying a social experiment that no one can tell us with any confidence will do anything to bring us together as a community as has been claimed.

"We absolutely must support our police if we expect them to support us and keep order in our community."

Flo raises her hand, "It's inappropriate for us to be talking about an alternative resolution until we take action on the resolution that has been moved and seconded, the resolution to accept and adopt the recommendations of the Citizen's Commission on Police Reform.

"I want to stress the name of the commission because I think we as a Council and community have lost sight of why we formed this commission in the first place.

"One of our officers killed an innocent citizen. As a result, this Council voted to establish a commission of citizens, not police professionals, to look at how we reform the police department so innocent citizens feel safe in our city and not threatened by police officers.

"If we do not adopt the recommendations, Council member Cochrane is suggesting that we do what we always do rather than reforming what hasn't worked.

"He is suggesting we do what the police officers want us to do rather than what the citizens want. And doing what the police officers want hasn't made us safer.

"Frankly I was a skeptic of what would come out of this commission, a skeptic that a reform that could offer hope to the people of Fort Christian could survive the scrutiny of facts and data.

"I have been pleasantly surprised and pleased with the recommendations. As a school teacher I see what the lack of parental involvement with their kids has done. I deal with it every day in my classroom.

"I see the parallel in the larger community with the lack of citizen involvement with law enforcement. We are all expected to obey laws. That is the foundation of democracy.

"So law enforcement should be the responsibility of everyone and not something someone does to us.

"I am pleased to be the sponsor of this resolution, to be the Council member who moved its adoption and I now call on my fellow Council members to stand up, do what's right for the city, and put our trust in the people, where it belongs."

Petes has left his mike on, remarks even though not recognized, "In God we trust, the people, well that's another matter."

Roxanne raises her hand, "Council member Williams?" I recognize her.

"We have suffered a tragic loss as a community, and I refer not just to the loss of Deshaun Bush, but a loss of confidence.

"We are no longer confident that those who protect us, will. We are no longer confident that those who we employ to enforce laws see themselves as also subject to those laws.

"It took a jury this past week to reverse a nationwide trend that exonerated police officers from their violent and misguided actions that took innocent lives.

"I don't know if the recommendations of the citizens on the Commission for Police Reform will bring us together as has been suggested, but we have to take a first step away from what isn't working.

"I have received the same calls, emails and people stopping me and wanting to talk about what we need to do as a community as the other members of Council.

"I am pleased we have a commission that made recommendations that have engaged members of our community. They did not simply suggest we do what so many other cities have done in similar circumstances.

“By this resolution we are trying something different. We are blazing a new trail through the wilderness of race relations. We are seeking to find the path to reconciliation that can bring together the two communities of Fort Christian.

“This set of recommendations may take us down that path or it may not. I have no illusions of a simple fix for what has taken centuries to address.

“And that’s the issue before us. Do we address the core problems, the root causes, or do we paper over our differences, and hope that our law enforcement professionals can do what they have not done?

“While not part of this set of recommendations, I want to go on record to say that regardless of what course of action Council authorizes tonight, I am calling for the replacement of Chief Andrews.

“I would prefer that he simply retire. But if he does not, then this Council must replace him as quickly as possible.

“He has shown an inability to adjust to the changes occurring in our city and he has not led the modernization needed to ensure safety, law and order.”

Roxanne remembers she wanted to say more, “Oh, and I seconded this resolution, not to bring it up for discussion, but because I believe it the only reasonable course of action for this council to take, given all that has happened.”

Alvin comes out of his fox hole. “I recognize the efforts of so many to help us understand the nature of the decision we are making.

“My only fear is that we may end up encouraging the very behavior we are seeking to suppress. I agree with everything that has been recommended, except removing weapons from officers with less than ten years of experience.

"This reminds me of what we do with our soldiers. We put a gun in the hands of kids, mostly, and send them into places where people are shooting at them.

"We sacrifice our young for the economic interests of big corporations.

"Here we are suggesting the opposite, but with the same effect. We are disarming our youngest officers, sacrificing them, if you will, so a bunch of liberals can say they did something different.

"We talk incessantly about guns falling into the hands of kids who sell drugs and shoot each other up, either with drugs or guns. We have to take guns away from them and not the police.

"We have to keep guns out of the hands of kids who go into schools and shoot up their classmates. I don't see how this set of recommendations does that."

Flo comes right back at him, "Council member Hill, as you know I greatly respect you and what you have done, creating a business and employing folks who live here. I am aware that you lost your son in the never-ending wars in the Middle East.

"I can't imagine the pain you have felt. I can't imagine the sacrifice your son made for his country.

"But ask yourself, would your son want to live in a society that lives by the gun as we did so long ago?

"Or would he say that ensuring the ability for you and his family to live in peace is the reason he went to war?

"I knew your son. He was one of my students, not so long ago. He was a bright and articulate person, who I'm sure you were rightfully proud of. I was proud to have been his teacher.

"I specifically remember one conversation we had. He was trying to understand why a police officer had stopped him on the street coming home after a school game.

"Why had they singled him out? He couldn't understand it because he hadn't done anything different, hadn't been involved in anything that would have given anyone a reason to question him, and yet he was stopped, removed from his car and told to assume the position, which he didn't even know what that was.

"That led the officer to strike him with a night stick and forcefully push him into the position the officer wanted him to assume. Do you remember that?

"I assume he came home and told you what happened. What the commission has recommended can address that kind of behavior by our police department.

"Nothing else that has been proposed will do anything other than make that kind of behavior more likely to occur.

"So I hope, for your son's sake, that you will reconsider your vote and give us a strong statement by Council."

Alvin sits through Flo's comments with a stone-faced expression.

Time for a decision. So two votes for and probably two against. It's all up to me, as it should be. What do I want to say?

"I have listened to the commissioners who formulated this set of recommendations. I want to thank them for not only their service to the community, but for taking a hard look at what is possible and what may be needed.

"I want to thank all who came forward and shared their thoughts with us during our public hearings.

"I want to thank all who sent notes or called Council members to share their thoughts. And I want to thank the many dedicated city employees who have shared their insights, who have researched questions both commissioners and Council members had.

"This look into what many believe is wrong with our city has been invasive and thorough, to use a phrase one commission member,

Doctor Maria Molina used in her response to our questions.

"Elected officials who neglect to listen to their citizens do so at their peril. That was the reason the commission was a citizen's commission and not an elite group of law enforcement practitioners or consultants or professors.

"That was an alternative approach the Council decided was not what we needed in this instance.

"We did not want to be back deciding what to do about another needless death at the hands of a police officer in three years or five years.

"Our professionals tried to tell us that collateral deaths happen in law enforcement. That may be true, but they will not happen again in Fort Christian, and that is true.

"Not because law enforcement will see that it doesn't happen, but because the people of Fort Christian will see that it doesn't happen.

"There are many advocates for change, some as radical as Reverend Lindo's wholesale change of everyone and everything.

"Ultimately that may be what's required, but today I don't agree. The other extreme is to hire more officers and arm them with the latest and greatest whatever they need or want.

"Ultimately that may be what's required, but today I don't agree. What we have before us is an historic opportunity.

"The history of this opportunity will be written not by the vote tonight, it will only be an enabler of our future, whether yes or no.

"The history of this opportunity will be written by what the people of Fort Christian do after tonight. And that is both unknowable and the cause for my caution.

"I want to say we should move boldly forward into a new future, but I'm torn that we may not have the right leadership to ensure the recommendations will deliver a city that is the vision.

"For that reason, I agree with Council member Williams, that regardless of the outcome of this vote, it's time for new leadership in the department.

"So where am I on this issue? As a life-long resident of this city, and the longest serving member of Council, I fundamentally believe in the courage and wisdom of all of the people of Fort Christian when they work together. I have witnessed it time and again.

"My vote may require a challenge unlike any other put before our citizens, but I am confident we will find a way to make the plan work.

"And for that reason I believe this is our time to listen and let the people lead us."

I look at Alvin and Petes on my right and Roxanne and Flo on my left.

"Is there any more discussion?"

No one responds. "Then would the Board Secretary call the roll?"

"Council Member Cochrane," she asks.

"No."

"Council Member Lopez."

"Yes."

"Council Member Hill."

"I am dedicating this vote to the memory of my son, Alexander Hill, yes."

Flo turned him. Unbelievable. I am so relieved.

"Council Member Williams?"

"Yes."

"Mayor Blackwell."

"Yes," I happily respond, but also realize the challenge to make this work.

"The resolution is adopted with four in favor and one opposed."

"I want to thank Council for having the courage of your convictions and giving us an opportunity. This meeting is adjourned."

I gavel the meeting to a close.

48 - T.K. JEFFERSON

Of course Sina won the argument about whether I would take the job as Chief of Police.

But even she paused when she saw how much less money we would have to live on. The oil industry pays well in comparison to public service.

Petes Cochrane made a big deal out of my lack of law enforcement credentials or experience at the Council meeting where I was confirmed for my new job. But the resolution carried anyway.

So today is my first day on the new job. I'm filling out the paperwork to get on the payroll when there is a knock on my door. I look up and see Reverend Lindo standing there.

"You're not wearing your mourning suit," I point out.

The Rev looks down to see what he is wearing. A tan suit with a blue thread through it. "This is my celebration suit."

"I hope you can continue to wear it, my friend," I stand up to shake his hand. "I wanted to thank you for helping get the city to this point where the dialog can change."

The Rev responds, "I believe the city has a much better chance of making this work with you in this role. I told you that early on, if you remember.

"Any other Chief would have been clinging to what he or she knew. You're passionate about making it work and I know you will find a way."

"I hear the union is going to be putting all their efforts into replacing the Mayor and most Council members so they can flip things back. If that's the case, this may be a short-lived effort."

"I won't be helping them, and in fact I'm already raising funds for reelection campaigns. There is one exception to that, but about all I'm going to be able to do is hopefully offset what the union will be putting into Petes' campaign."

"You're changing sides," I note.

The Rev responds, "I tell everyone I judge people by what they do, not what they say.

"That's why I'm particularly glad you are the one in this office rather than someone who talks a good story but hasn't done anything to demonstrate leadership."

49 – FRANCIS 'DUKE' MARION

I walk down to the Chief's office not knowing what kind of reception I'm going to get.

I've known T.K. a long time, but he's surprised the hell out of me for coming up with those recommendations and surprised me again by somehow getting chosen to be the new Chief.

Never could have seen that one coming. I approach his office door, see him sitting at the Chief's desk and all of a sudden this is real.

Up until now it all seemed like some joke or something. Nothing changes this much. That's part of what I like about being an officer, things are relatively predictable.

Once in a while things get out of hand, but we all come together and have each other's back.

He apparently hasn't heard my approach, so I knock. T.K. looks up and the first glance is he seems happy to see me, but then a cloud passes over his expression.

Apparently he's expecting something from me other than a congratulations. "You shouldn't be here," I inform him.

T.K. rises and comes around the desk to meet me half-way. "If you'd not sent Richie Webster out on patrol alone that night I wouldn't be."

I step into his office and close the door, so what I have to say won't be overheard. When I return my gaze to him T.K. has a curious look.

"We miss you at the Boy's Club. Everyone wants to know when you're coming back."

"Wasn't sure you'd want me back," I admit, surprised this is one of his first comments to me, given the change in relationship.

"I can't imagine you not coming back. We're part of a team that's been together a long time."

"We have," I have to admit.

"Now we have to figure out how to be a different sort of team. One that's going to have a much bigger impact than one player at a time."

"I've been more concerned about keeping my job as president of the union than listening to what the people have been saying to us," I admit.

"After the Council vote I resigned as president. The members all think it was because I didn't prevent the changes. In reality I'm here to let you know I want to help you make them work.

"I'll run interference with the union and Walter, make sure they know we have to do our jobs as they are defined for us, keep the bad guys off the street.

"And if you can be the front guy getting the people to welcome us rather than dread our arrival, we just might be able to change things for the better."

T.K. responds, "You miss Deshaun as much as I do."

I nod. "I've also turned in my weapon. I don't want to be backup. Someone's got to show this can work and I guess that might as well be me."

T.K. gives me a hug. I slowly hug him in return.

50 – T.K. JEFFERSON

Six Months Later.

Duke drives the cruiser down Seventh Street while I'm talking through the car speaker on my cell with Sergeant Walters, who is the desk sergeant tonight. "How many did you book in?" I ask.

"Eighteen and six were taken to Memorial to treat wounds."

"Knife or gunshot?" I ask, trying to visualize the fight between rival gangs that required the SWAT team to break up.

"Knife, but we have a trunk full of weapons we took off them which were mostly guns. Not sure why they didn't use them, but the guys who went out were sure glad they didn't."

Walters fills in the details he knows I'm looking for.

"Make sure dispatch tells everyone out on patrol to keep an eye out for secondary skirmishes. I doubt anyone is going to be happy so many of their friends are in the lockup. Were any of the wounds life threatening?"

"Don't know," Sergeant Walters responds reflectively. "I understand Dr. Molina is on tonight so she might be able to give you a better idea."

"I'll give her a call in a bit, thanks. You're doing a good job, Walters. I appreciate the insights you bring to so many difficult situations. Talk to you later."

"Sounds like it was serious if there were that many of them involved," Duke notes. "Only six with wounds, makes it sound like we may have gotten there early enough to keep it from going over the top."

"I still don't like having to send in the SWAT team. We should be past that by now. Should have them talking first."

"How do you know they didn't?" Duke challenges my assumption. "I know you're impatient to see results but it took more than a hundred years to get here. You can't overcome that history in a month or even six."

"Sorry, Duke. You're right. Some things you just have to keep banging away at. The gangs are probably the most visible, although I had hopes they might be the first to understand what we're trying to do."

"You've spent too much time with the kids at the Boys Club. They're not typical of the gangs. They're operating on a whole different level. They have hope. These guys just have each other."

"I don't see it that way," I respond. "Kids are coerced into the gangs. They carve out the loners who no one hangs with. They intimidate them but constantly remind them that if they were to join the gang, no one would get over on them."

Since I've been spending more time with officers on patrols, I've periodically spent more time with Duke in addition to the time we've been at the Boy's Club.

Consequently he seems to have gotten to know me better, although I'm not sure I can say the same.

"How are things going with Cindy?"

"She moved on," Duke informs me quietly.

"What happened?"

"She decided I was never going to marry her." Duke hesitates before continuing. "She said she loved me and knew I loved her, but that wasn't enough. She wanted the warm body to cuddle with every night, not once a month, which is kind of what it had become.

"So she made me an apple pie, handed it to me and sent me on my way. That was the last time I saw her."

"I'm sorry. Guess I ask impossible things of you, but don't ask about you anywhere near enough."

Duke glances at me, "You think that's part of your job?"

"Absolutely. I spent a lot of time just talking with the people at my old job. Learned about their families, their hopes and dreams, what was important to them."

"You certainly didn't take the time to do that before you changed the lives of nearly every one of us."

I sit quietly, realizing that Duke is right. I didn't start with the people in the department because I started with the people who were being harmed by it.

But he continues, driving slowly past the sleeping buildings.

"Most of the guys I talk with… they really want this to work. They're starting to feel a part of the community where they patrol, and like to be able to recognize people and have them want to come up and talk. I'm seeing things change in a way I didn't think would happen."

"You're not just trying to make me feel better, are you?"

"Unit fifty-three, please respond… report of an altercation at 2713 San Jacinto. In the parking lot. Eight to ten involved. Unit twenty-nine, please provide backup."

"Dispatch, this is unit fifty-three, we are about… seven minutes out."

"Dispatch, this is unit twenty-nine, we are… twelve minutes out."

Duke speeds up but does not turn on his light or siren. We sit quietly as he follows the directions shown on the map on the screen between us.

"Twenty-seven-thirteen…" There's something about that address

I'm trying to remember. But it doesn't come to me until I see the lights in the parking lot of the Second Baptist Church. Rev Lindo's church.

Neutral territory for the gangs in the city.

And then I see the kids, for that's what they are. Not much older than Tony, or any of the others at the Boy's Club.

We pull up and we're out of the car together. Two policemen approaching the fight. Slowly, just coming to talk.

"Evening, guys," I begin. "What seems to be the problem?"

The fighters move apart. I see the blood on the cheek of the black high school aged boy. Bare knuckles.

I see the other is Hispanic. His knuckles are bleeding as well, although he has a swollen eye. Nearly shut. Hard to tell which one is getting the best of the situation.

"No problem," the black boy responds. "We just got a difference of opinion here."

"As to who she should go out with?" I ask. "What's your names?"

The black boy stands up straight, "Zander."

The Hispanic boy responds, "Antonio."

"Aren't you him?" Zander looks at me more closely.

"Him?"

"You're T.K. Jefferson." He looks at Duke. "Are you Sergeant Marion?"

Duke nods.

"My brother is Zeke Stone. He plays with you guys couple times a week. He's gotten so good I can't play him no more."

"Why don't you come play?" Duke asks, "Guarantee we'll help

you catch up."

"So what's this all about?" I ask.

Antonio points to the other and announces, "He slept with my sister. I gotta defend her honor. That's just how it is."

"Does she love him?"

"She's only fifteen," Antonio responds, "She don't know nothing about love…"

"She came on to me," Zander responds. "We did it in her bedroom. I mean what else can I say?"

"Antonio," I look at him, "What do you want Zander to do? Marry her? Stay away from her?"

"Stay away. She needs a life without a kid at fifteen. You know? She can be someone. Not just an uneducated mother to a bunch of cross-breed kids no one will want to claim."

Zander bristles but stays quiet.

"Do you love her?" I ask Zander.

"I do… well, I think I do. She's the first girl I've done it with."

"How old are you?" Duke asks.

"Fifteen, but I got a part time job after school."

"She may love your dick, but she won't love your bank account." Antonio responds.

I put my arm around Zander. "You ought to go home and think about what you want your life to be like, make the decisions that will take you there, not back into a relationship that will just make life hard."

I pull Antonio towards me and put my hand on his shoulder.

"Your sister should be proud of you for defending her honor. If you can talk to her sometime about deciding what she wants her life to be like, you'll be doing her a big favor." I let that sink in for a moment.

"You guys cool?"

I get head nods from both and they walk away in opposite directions, each with their respective posse.

Duke starts back towards the car and I catch up to him. "Nicely done. But will it make any difference?"

"We can only do what we can do."

I look up to see a newish black Dodge Charger with its windows down, slowly passing our vehicle.

A light reflects off a gun inside, and I push Duke away just as I hear the pop, pop, pop of shots fired.

Pop, pop, pop again. The driver guns the engine and the car speeds away just as I feel the searing pain in my right side that spins me around and I'm suddenly flat on my back looking up. "Duke? You okay?"

Silence.

"Duke?"

I hear a car pull up. Doors open and the sounds of running towards us.

"This is unit twenty-seven, two officers down, repeat, two officers down. Parking lot of the Second Baptist Church…"

51 – ZANA GONZALES – EDITOR, FORT CHRISTIAN STANDARD

Tex doesn't agree with the changes I've made to his editorial draft. We are sitting in the glass conference room at the paper where all discussions like this one have occurred.

"They caught the shooters, so I'm not seeing why you want to push this on the community."

"We saw, for the first time, that community members stepped forward and turned in drug dealers who've been living amongst them for decades," I respond. "And peace officers were able to take them into custody without the use of weapons…"

"Unless you consider the bodycam a weapon…"

"Well, the peace officer just had to say that if the dealer shot an officer it was like signing their own death warrant because it would all be recorded and ready to play to a jury.

"For the first time the people were responsible for the arrest. The peace officer was just their representative on site."

"I get what you're saying, that moral authority runs from the people through the peace officers to keep the order and enforce the laws.

"Judges and juries get to see and hear what happened, not just take testimony. And that erases the doubt and makes it easier for the prosecutor to make a case.

"So theoretically, crime should drop dramatically. But have we crossed over into a Big Brother society? Are we relying on technology to remove the ambiguity that is life from any controversy?

"Are we stepping across the line into a society that only judges us by what we do, and not so much by what we intend?"

"Welcome to the future," I kid him.

"But isn't that better than the dual community divided by race even more than by economic achievement? The other Fort Christian world Reverend Lindo brought to our attention, even though we always knew it was there?

"Our editorial on adoption of the recommendations of the commission was conditional support. The condition was that the community would need to support the changes and assume responsibility for themselves and their neighborhood.

"It took the shootings of T.K. and Duke for the community to finally understand what that condition meant. And they stood up, turned in the drug dealers and faced down the intimidation that resulted."

"But there are new dealers in town," Tex points out. "We didn't put them all in jail, they just moved into another neighborhood, a different street. They're being a little more discreet, but they're still peddling their wares for all who want them. So what have we really accomplished?"

"I think we served notice, not just to the drug dealers, but to the gangs and burglars and petty thieves that Fort Christian isn't going to play by their rules any longer.

"We've served notice to those who practice spousal abuse that your neighbors aren't going to continue with a blind eye. You're going to be confronted, you're going to be held accountable.

"There's a new sheriff in town and it's not T.K. Jefferson at police headquarters, it's your neighbors and friends who care about you as much as they care about the community in which they live."

"For me the test will be the schools," Tex muses aloud. "We've seen parents turn over responsibility for the education of their kids to the schools for decades.

"And it's not just their education that's been abdicated. The number of free and reduced-price breakfasts and lunches the schools serve show that it's responsibility for feeding their kids as well.

"For their social and emotional health. The number of school shootings by students. The number of weapons taken from them.

"The schools were never intended to play the roles they are playing today.

"The schools are doing as well as can be expected, but still… parents make all the difference when they engage their kids, communicate values and morals and ethics -- to say nothing of care and love for them.

"I know this all sounds vague, but those are the bedrocks of a community, not just the success platform the kid needs to be a high achiever in any realm."

"You sound like you're still the pessimist," I note.

"Some of the people may get what we are trying to do, but I don't think we are getting the right people and we certainly aren't getting all of the people," Tex drives home his analysis.

"In my mind, the question is how do you get all of the people? The shootings were a catalyst, no doubt. A clarion call, if you will.

"The resulting behaviors we've seen are encouraging, but I just don't know how you get to where we need to be from here."

"Then say that in your editorial," I instruct him, which I hate to do, but make an exception in this case,

"Put the challenge out there for the people of Fort Christian. Point out that the people aren't living their values, they aren't communicating their values and they aren't ensuring that the future will reflect their values unless they are engaging the future generations morally, ethically and with love.

"The people have to have the courage to stand up."

52 – REGINA BLACKWELL – MAYOR, CITY OF FORT CHRISTIAN

Election Night Six Months Later.

T.K. enters my campaign headquarters. He still walks slightly bent over from his wound.

"A second term?" he asks.

I nod. "All the negative stories that came out those first six months nearly swamped us, but then everything began to change after you and Sergeant Marion were shot.

"That seemed to be the wake-up call. People saw what you were doing. Saw that they had to take responsibility because you couldn't do it alone.

"Zana and Tex did that editorial, calling everyone out. And then they did positive stories about how much the atmosphere of the city was improving. That was the catalyst."

Flo, who has been watching the results come in, comes over and stands next to me, "Leadership. T.K. being out with officers, responding to calls with them. Showing them how he wants them to interact with people. It's made a huge difference."

"Enough of a difference you changed your mind about re-election." T.K. notes.

Sina joins us, "Looks like Paulette Simpson will be joining City Council this term."

"She defeated Petes Cochrane?" T.K. asks "That means he will probably become counsel to the police officer union. Duke mentioned that possibility to me a while ago."

"Still not seeing much of a change in the school," Flo reminds us. "We still got a long way to go to become the community we all want.

"So don't stand there congratulating yourselves.

"Have the courage to live your convictions, and get back to work for the people of Fort Christian."

THE END

About the Author

dhtreichler is a futurist, technologist and strategist who toured the global garden spots as a defense contractor executive for fifteen years. His assignments covered intelligence, training and battlefield systems integrating state of the art technology to keep Americans safe. His novels grew out of a need to deeply understand how our world is changing, developing scenarios and then populating them with people who must confront how increasingly sophisticated technology is transforming our lives and how men and women establish relationships in a mediated world.

Keep up with all of dhtreichler's latest work and essays at www.dhtreichler.com and www.GlobalVinoSnob.com.

Also by dhtreichler

TRUTH

A Cat's Redemption

CHOICES

HOPE

Emergence

Barely Human

The Ghost in the Machine: a novel

World Without Work

The Great American Cat Novel

My Life as a Frog

Life After

The Tragic Flaw

Lucifer

The End Game

Succession

I Believe in You

Rik's

The Illustrated Bearmas Reader – Ralph's Ordeals

The First Bearmas

Made in the USA
Middletown, DE
08 March 2020

85830690R00222